The Iether Consummation Volume 1: Awakening

D. Art & Kay
McKinney

Our heartfelt thanks to our beta readers, whose investment of time and thoughtful feedback enabled us to shape this book into its best form

ISBN-13: 979-8-3304-8704-2

The world of Iether

Chapter 1

Hinna crouched behind the crumbling wall of what might have once been a house, listening to the soldier grumble.

"Now where did that wench get off to!"

His comrade grunted. "She has to be close around here somewhere."

The Gavenian army had captured her, and about a hundred others, while raiding along the border. En route back to the Gavenian kingdom, they had stopped for the night in a large, ruined city. She was not sure what city it had been, but based on its size and location, it could have been the capital of the erstwhile mighty human empire. Her training as a records keeper afforded her a great deal of knowledge about her enemies, but it offered no protection in her present predicament.

Under normal circumstances, she would have flown away, but it was late at night, and without the sun's power, her own was non-existent. She regretted having to run away from the rest of the prisoners, but she refused to be used as an object of pleasure by the filthy humans. Perhaps it was her own youthful ignorance that made her think she stood a chance of escape, or maybe her pride had determined that she would rather die than be defiled by the likes of them.

As the soldiers drew near her hiding place, she lost her nerve and bolted from the shadows to dart down a rubble-strewn street. She could hear the soldiers shouting at her angrily, and only by throwing herself into another partially collapsed building did she avoid being perforated by the barrage of iether bolts fired in her direction. She scrambled to her feet and looked hurriedly for an exit, but the only way out was a hole in the floor, where it had fallen into what was likely a basement.

With the sounds of her pursuers rapidly approaching, she dove into the opening and landed sprawling onto a pile of rubble. She pulled herself up painfully; she had obviously injured her right ankle in the fall. She did not care about the pain, but it meant her hope of survival was greatly diminished.

One of the soldiers called down the hole after her. "C'mon, you little scamp, you're going to suffer for making us climb down there!"

The other soldier spoke almost reflexively. "Isn't she going to suffer anyway?"

"Shut up, you idiot! If we don't at least provide the captain with a body, it will be coming out of our pay."

Hinna did not want to hear any more of the disgusting conversation, and hurriedly hobbled down an old corridor that dissuaded her of any notions of this place's being a basement. She turned a corner, and her heart sank. It was a dead end where the ceiling had collapsed.

As the soldiers moved toward her, she could hear them calling out lewd things they would do to her when they caught her. They carried torches, so it was probably easy for them to follow her footprints through the filth of this forsaken place. She was dependent on her night vision, which was not particularly helpful at the moment. She felt her way along the wall, moving to the caved-in portion of the tunnel, where the faintest amount of moonlight shone through a small opening in the ceiling. There was no way she could climb out, even if she had not been injured. She knelt and searched the floor for anything to throw at her aggressors. If she could get them to kill her, then she would not have to fear the serial raping that they continued to threaten her with.

Light from their torches came around the corner before the soldiers did. In the added illumination, she could see a hole in the wall, and beyond, something metal glinted faintly. She lunged through the hole and crawled toward the object.

She rose slowly, wincing at the pain in her ankle as she studied what appeared to be a dust-covered blade staff. Grateful for a real weapon, she reached out toward it, but froze as though she had accidentally reached for a venomous snake. A human knelt on the opposite side of the blade staff. His face was not visible, as his head was lowered. He was wearing the tattered remains of a thick cloak that was heavy with dust. He remained absolutely motionless, and she sighed with relief as it dawned on her that it was nothing more than a statue. She grasped the blade staff by its shaft and began to lift it.

"May I help you?"

Hinna jerked sharply and fell backwards with a fearful scream, dropping the blade staff, which clanged loudly on the floor. Her pursuers responded to the noise, and like angry hornets came bustling through the hole in the wall, torchlight filling the room.

Hinna stared in terror as the presumed statue stood, allowing the filthy cloak to fall from his shoulders and hit the floor in a puff of dust. He wore strange clothes, which hung loosely about his lean, muscular body. Vivid green eyes were set in a narrow face, his subdued features framed by short, thick, blond hair.

One of the soldiers called to him heartily. "You there. Thanks for finding our varmint for us!"

The strange man analyzed them briefly and waved his hand dismissively. "The isper belongs to me."

"Finders keepers, eh? Well, do her quick, and we need the body to be mostly recognizable when you're done." The second soldier looked disappointed, but both of them stepped out through the opening and stopped somewhere down the corridor to wait.

The stranger gazed slowly around the room, his expression calm but sober, as if he were slightly sad. After a minute of contemplation, he turned toward her. She gasped involuntarily and snatched the blade staff off the floor, scrambling crab-like until her back was against the wall. "Stay back! I am warning you!" she yelled as menacingly as she could manage, waving the blade staff that she was holding with both hands like a battle-axe.

He walked calmly toward her and knelt at precisely the staff's length away from her. He smiled with a strange warmness in his surprisingly bright green eyes, a kind of gentleness that she would never have suspected a human could possess. He reached out and touched the tip of the blade staff with two fingers. The blade began to emit a warm blue light that rapidly ran from the tip of the blade and down the shaft.

Hinna dropped it instinctively. The stranger seized the blade, and in a single, smooth motion, flipped it so that he held the shaft in one hand. Her breath caught in her throat, and she turned her head away so that she would not see the killing blow coming. The blade came down with a loud, rasping sound, but she felt nothing.

She opened her eyes. The glowing staff was sticking out of the solid flagstone next to her, like some kind of short light post. The stranger took a seat on her other side and leaned back against the wall, shutting his eyes as if to relax. Despite the fact that sudden death no longer appeared to be a concern, she felt more nervous than before, being pinned between the blue staff and the oddly dressed human. He spoke softly, his eyes still closed. "And what is your name, isper?"

She flinched involuntarily at the question but answered without hesitation. "I . . . I . . . I am Hinna," she stammered, flustered by the seemingly impossible turn of events.

There was a moment of silence before he spoke again. "Hinna, what can you tell me about the human empire?"

She blinked; it seemed odd that a human would ask her about human history, but again she obliged him. "The human empire was disbanded more than a century ago, following a bloody civil war. This location here, I believe, is the remnants of what used to be the capital."

He sighed sadly as he muttered, "What have you done, Miralla? Why am I here?" Hinna remained silent, but could not help wondering how long this fellow had lived here in these ruins. The stranger spoke again. "Hinna, why are you a prisoner, and who are your captors?"

Hinna glowered at him angrily. Not that it did any good, since his eyes were still closed. "I was forced to be a prisoner when those despicable humans raided my town, and they are just one of the five human kingdoms that are the enemies of my people!"

He seemed to ignore the hatred with which she spoke as he moved on to another question. "What can you tell me of the kobay?"

His questions were strangely generic. "The kobay are unified as a tribal commune, where each tribe has equal say. They normally leave the humans and the isper alone, though there has recently been trouble brewing with increased human incursions into kobay lands." She took a breath, and then continued on a hunch. "The seerrine have withdrawn deep into the western mountains, and no one else is really sure what their status is currently."

A smile flitted across his face as she gave the answer to his next question before he could ask it. There was again a moment of silence before he spoke. "And what of the darkness?"

Hinna stared at him blankly. "D-darkness? Do you mean . . . nighttime?"

He opened his eyes and frowned, and Hinna felt for all the world like she had just failed an important exam at the college where she had trained. He looked at her thoughtfully and clarified his statement without so much of a hint of disappointment in his tone. "The darkness that seeks our destruction. The shades and fellbeasts. The enemy that lurks in the background, seeking to destroy the Creator through his creation."

She shook her head. "Well, I have heard that story before. But it's just a fable, isn't it? Something to scare children into staying in their beds?"

Their conversation was interrupted by one of the soldiers calling down the corridor. "Hurry it up, will ya? We ain't got all night!"

Hinna stared at the floor, a little dejected. "If you don't do something to me, they will." He stood up, and she cringed, still looking at the ground initially, but as he spoke, she glanced up at him with uncertainty.

His voice bore a serene confidence. "Hinna, I am Nirim, second guardian of the empire, and I assure you they will do nothing to you."

He walked toward the hole in the wall, drawing the blade staff free from the stone. He stepped through and disappeared down the underground passageway.

At first, all she heard was the soldiers cursing at Nirim, but then there was a blinding flash of light, and what could have passed for a slight tremor in the ground. This was followed by a brief period of silence before she heard footsteps. She braced for the worst as she saw torchlight growing brighter as the footsteps approached. However, much to her relief, it was Nirim who ducked back through the hole, now carrying a torch. He set the torch against the wall and began to look around the room.

Hinna asked hesitantly, "Are they . . . ?"

Nirim interjected, "Gone? Yes, they will likely be running until they pass out from exhaustion."

Hinna looked away from him angrily. "You should have killed the worthless scum." She turned back to him in time to see that he had arched one eyebrow. She tried to soften her voice, but only made it sound gruff. "I mean, the fewer humans the better, right?"

He only crossed his arms, and her face grew red as she realized that her words had not delineated her savior from her captors. She dropped her eyes back to the ground and muttered, "You should have killed them." He shook his head but said nothing as he walked slowly around the room, intently inspecting the walls and floor.

Hinna looked glumly at her swollen ankle; she probably would not be walking on it for days. She watched Nirim for several minutes before she inquired curiously, "What are you doing?"

"I am searching for some clue as to why I am here. Miralla would not have left me without any guidance."

Hinna was not sure what that meant, and asked the first question that came to mind. "So why are you here?"

Nirim stopped inspecting the wall long enough to give her a concerned look that caused her to drop her gaze. Hinna tried a different question in hopes of rapidly forgetting her own idiocy. "Ahem, right. Who is Miralla?"

Nirim answered, this time without pausing his

investigation of the room. "Miralla was the imperial seer, a direct descendant of the great mystic himself. She was the one who tricked me into coming down here, but her purposes for doing so remain a mystery."

Hinna shook her head. "Imperial seer? The empire has been gone for a long time, and I don't remember there being any record of a seer."

He spoke absentmindedly as he went about searching the stand where his staff had been. "Yes, it has probably been well more than one hundred years ago that she locked me out of time in this place. I should have known she was planning something devious, but how could I resist her?"

Hinna's eyes widened. "You're over one hundred years old?"

There was no hint of humor or teasing in his voice. "No, I am twenty years old. Have you never heard of the time lock?"

"I guess not." A few moments passed before Hinna asked cautiously, "Was she your wife?"

"I am not sure why you are asking that, but no, she was my older cousin." He grimaced. "Unless, of course, that kind of relationship is normal to you?" Hinna shook her head vigorously to indicate that was not the case. Nirim sighed with relief. "Good. At least some things are unchanged."

He stopped abruptly, as though something he had said had reminded him of a crucial detail he was overlooking. He stood up and stretched out his left hand, but then paused, turning to her and asking, "Tell me, what do you know of the iether?"

Hinna thought briefly before speaking with a sense of authority. "Well, let's see. The seerrine are all born with blue iether runes on their arms, able to do a wide array of things with their power, but they can't use it for fighting. Only a few of the kobay have the red iether, but those that do are incredible warriors. Of course, all the isper are blessed with the glorious gold iether, but it only works well on bright, cloudless days. But iether-deprived humans are the worst, killing everything that moves with their ietherized weapons."

His eyes narrowed at her, but he refrained from saying anything. Instead, he turned his attention to the room around them. Blue light began to shine through the long-sleeved robe that he wore, and Hinna gasped and blurted out, "Y-you're a mongrel!?"

The room quickly filled with blue iether motes, which accumulated on a particular flagstone on the floor. He knelt and blew the dust from the stone.

From where she sat, Hinna could tell that the stone looked as though it had been coated with some kind of plaster. Nirim smashed the plaster with the butt of the blade staff and wiped away the pieces. He stared for a moment, and then laughed dryly. Hinna strained to see, but from where she was, she could not make it out.

"What is it?"

Nirim chuckled again before he said with all seriousness, "Mostly insulting."

Chapter 2

Nirim gazed at the delicate etching, cut in the flagstone by Miralla's iether, that had been hidden beneath the plaster. He read it silently.

My dear cousin,

Please excuse my less-than-honest means for getting you into this place, but I have foreseen the fall of our beloved empire, and the role you will play in bringing our deliverance from the darkness. You are the only one who can muster the other guardians, you are the only one who can prevent the destruction that is coming, and, of course, you are also the most gullible of the four guardians. Find Spite, as he will know what has transpired in your absence, regardless of however long you remain out of time. Space does not permit me to say more, so I have provided Spite with the necessary information.

For the purposes of the Creator,
Miralla

He laughed lightly. He could almost hear Miralla's lilting voice speaking those very words with the liveliness that made her so endearing.

"What is it?"

Nirim could not suppress his last chuckle as he looked toward the young isper woman who had spoken. She was dirty, haggard-looking, and her clothes beaten and torn nearly to rags. Yet her multihued hair spoke of her unified heritage, running from a deep red near her scalp to a pleasant ocean blue at the tips, which matched the color of her eyes perfectly. Even in his time, the isper had largely kept to themselves, so her unusual beauty made her seem a precious jewel in the dusty, murky confines of the room that must have been his prison for over a century.

He responded without a hint of his thoughts escaping. "Mostly insulting." He glanced down at the engravings on the floor, and then back toward her, reflecting on her less-than-thoughtful descriptions of him, and of humans in general. "Has anyone ever told you that you have a particularly, uh, shall we say . . . strong . . . way of describing things about others?"

Confusion flitted ever so briefly across her face, but then she smiled broadly. "No, no one has, but thank you for saying so!"

He put his hand to his temple as though dealing with a headache, which, in a sense, he was.

Hinna's tone shifted as she asked quietly, "Are you going to rescue the rest of my people from those evil humans?"

Nirim stared at the hole in the wall as he rose. "I would like to, but scaring a couple soldiers is far easier than defeating a whole battalion." She nodded soberly and leaned back against the wall with a sigh. Nirim walked over to the adjacent corner and picked up a small, overturned clay pot. He was surprised to see that the inside looked clean.

Hinna must have guessed his purpose and cautioned, "Don't try to drink any water you find in the city. It's all tainted."

"Tainted?"

"Yes, the whole central portion of the human lands is diseased with poisonous waters and miasmic clouds. The only reason the Gavenians would dare pass through here is that it's neutral territory, and no sane isper would follow them into this horrid place."

He wondered what had happened that the empire's most fertile plain had been transformed into a cesspool. He hoped that she was merely exaggerating, but he knew the hope was almost certainly vain. Putting his hand flat against the wall, he noted that while it was not wet, it was slightly damp. Hinna was watching him with great interest. Nirim held out his right hand, and Hinna failed to suppress the audible squeak that indicated her surprise as red iether began to glow along his arm.

He clenched his hand into a fist and drew his arm back slowly. Water flowed from the rock and streamed through the air briefly before falling into the small jar that he held upright in his left hand. He dropped his right arm to his side, and the red iether faded. He took a sip of the water to Hinna's concerned outcry.

"Don't drink that! It could be poison!"

He stared at her long enough that she started to fidget uncomfortably before he answered. "The red iether purifies the water. Otherwise I would not be so bold as to drink it first."

He held it out to her, but she crossed her arms with an irritated frown. "First? You mean I would have been your poison checker if you had doubts?" Nirim shrugged and turned as though he were going to walk away with the water, but her voice rang out quickly. "Wait! I do want some!"

He handed her the jar, took a seat next to her,

and spoke his thoughts while she gulped the water as though it were her last opportunity to drink anything. "So the world I knew has vanished while I was stuck in time, and the only person who can reliably tell me why I was subjected to such a strange fate is likely far beyond the western mountains."

Hinna sighed with relief as she finished the water in the pot. She responded to his extroverted dialogue with what he was beginning to recognize as her normal lack of tact, though her tone was compassionate. "I thought my day was going badly. Yours sounds much worse." She paused reflectively for a moment before changing the subject. "Why can you use two forms of iether? I understand that your dastardly heritage contributes to one form, but I can't think of why you would be able to use two."

Nirim gave her a stern look, but the clear, innocent expression on her face told him that she neither meant to be unkind, nor recognized his disapproval. He decided now was not the time to instruct her in proper manners, and returned to gazing across the room. "I am part seerrine and part mystic, but not enough of either one to be of much use. I can barely get away with the simple parlor tricks you have seen, let alone do anything so magnificent as my ancestors."

Hinna repeated his statement out loud, as though it would evaporate from her mind if she did not. "Seerrine and mystic." She looked at her ankle thoughtfully. "Can you heal my ankle then? I mean, with your iether?"

He shook his head. "No, the rune of second sight has no such function, and the rune of flux has similar limitations."

Hinna's eyes widened. "How very useless!"

In spite of himself, the corners of his mouth curled into a slight smile as he quipped, "Why, thank you, Hinna. I feel so much better hearing it from you."

She leaned back and returned his smile with a frightening degree of geniality. "You are welcome."

Did she speak so bluntly to her own people? The few isper he had interacted with in the empire seem to be more socially competent than the one sitting next to him. Perhaps this was a change in their society since his time, or perhaps Hinna was strange even among her kin. Not that it would matter. He would leave her to find her own way home as soon as they got out of the now diseased plains. He felt a slight tinge of guilt at plotting on leaving an injured young woman to fend for herself in hostile territory, but it was only ever so slight.

He turned to ask whether she could tell him the status of the trackkus, but his question stopped abruptly as he realized that she had fallen asleep during his mental sojourn. It was mildly ironic how much they had in common circumstantially. They both were in a place that was nothing like what they had grown up knowing. Neither of them knew where their family members were, nor if any remained. And certainly not least, neither one of them was prepared to deal with those grim realities.

Nirim was not technically a soldier; he had no battlefield experience, nor was he hardened to the butchery that commonly passed for warfare. He was a guardian, one of a few individuals preemptively trained to stand against the darkness, should it show itself. He knew most of its forms, and he was familiar with its treacherous ways. He carried the iether-imbued astral blade staff that ensured his combat prowess regardless of the mild nature of his own runes. However, at the moment, none of that mattered. Apparently the empire was no more, and the darkness had receded into the periphery.

It was this latter fact that concerned him the most. It was likely a falsehood, as the most dangerous enemy is the enemy no one believes exists. He found it a little odd that an isper historian would not be familiar with the darkness. Of course, their being played as pawns of the darkness for nearly a millennium before it was purged from their lands might have something to do with it. Any proud people would not be keen on holding that memory close to heart, and the isper were certainly proud of their own people.

Nirim wondered what might have become of the rest of the imperial family. He was in the direct line of the prime empress, but because of the precedent she had set, neither he nor his recent ancestors had been eligible to hold the empire's highest title. If there had been civil strife so severe that it destroyed the empire, he doubted that many of the imperial line could be left, if any. A chill went down his spine at the thought, and he determined to keep his familial status as secret as possible.

He slowly drifted off into a guarded rest that was akin to sleep, but shallow enough that he would not be caught unawares should something occur. On this particular night, his skills were wasted.

***

Hinna woke with a start and looked frantically around the room, trying to remember where she was and how she got there. She caught sight of the silent form of Nirim, who sat resting peacefully off to her side. The torch had expired, but morning light was coming in from the corridor beyond the chamber's small exit. Her ankle felt sore and stiff, but at least it was not throbbing any longer. Actually, her ankle was not the only thing stiff; every muscle felt uncomfortable from having slept sitting upright leaning against a stone wall.

Hinna struggled to a standing position but took

only one step before she plunged forward. To her surprise, she stopped an arm's length from smacking into the stone floor face first. She jumped when Nirim spoke. "Careful there. I don't think you are ready to put your full weight on it."

She turned sharply to see that he had caught her from falling. He helped her stand on one leg as she asked incredulously, "Weren't you sleeping?"

Nirim shrugged nonchalantly. "Only a little."

Hinna moved her gaze toward the corridor, commenting, "It must be morning already." Nirim nodded his agreement and swept her off her feet into his arms. She struggled in protest. "Put me down!" she ordered. "I will not be carried by a human!"

He ignored her as he ducked through the hole in the wall and surveyed the corridor. He ignored her as he determined that the near exit was far too high to jump and proceeded down the other direction.

"Why are you ignoring me, you brute!" Hinna hissed, for fear that patrolling Gavenian soldiers might hear her.

He waited to reply until he had made the turn in the corridor and walked smoothly into the dark interior. "Because you seem to be unaware that it would take you half a day to get out of here if you had to hobble through." Hinna pouted slightly, which only appeared to amuse him based on his smile, but she stopped struggling.

Nirim passed the collapsed floor that she had fallen through and continued on into the pitch blackness without hesitation. She voiced her concern about the eerie journey. "Shouldn't you light a torch or something before you trip and drop me?"

"I don't need any more light than this to see where I am going."

Hinna muttered, mostly to herself, "Well, maybe

I need a little more light than this to be comfortable."

Nirim stopped for a moment, then continued with the blade staff on his back emitting a warm blue glow that made the long stone passageway partially visible, and substantially less spooky. They had traveled for about half an hour before Hinna whispered, "Thank you." She did not like humans, and she certainly did not want to admit that this one had done her any favors, but his strange propensity to be considerate toward a ragged isper prisoner was touching, primarily because she was that prisoner, but she wanted to believe that it would be touching regardless of her own condition.

They turned at an intersecting corridor and ascended a flight of stairs that brought them to the insides of a long-abandoned wine cellar. He crossed the large, low-ceiling room and entered a narrow alcove, where there was another staircase not visible from the room. She looked at him curiously. "Have you been here before?"

"Many times, though it barely looks recognizable now."

They continued through a ruined building and emerged into a relatively flat, open area overgrown with weedy plants and dead trees. Nirim gently set her down and walked slowly to the nearest tree. He snapped off a suitable branch and whittled it smooth with his blade staff as he walked back to where she leaned against the doorway. He motioned at the ground. "Please sit." She puzzled as to what the connection was between the stick and sitting, but she eased herself to the ground.

Nirim sliced a strip of cloth from his long overcoat and knelt beside her. Using several of the smaller sticks he had cut from the branch, he braced her ankle and tied the cloth snugly around it. Hinna winced, but refrained from complaining. She looked dubiously at the makeshift splint. "Well, thank you, but you certainly are not a physician of any kind."

He gave her a strange expression, which she assumed meant something similar to a reluctant acceptance of reality. "Apparently not." He handed her the large stick. "Here, use this to walk."

She accepted it, and he helped her stand back on her feet. She took several tentative steps with the aid of her new walking stick, feeling all too self-conscious as he watched her silently. Hinna turned around and asked, "So where are we going?"

Nirim smirked, but he spoke with his usual calm tone. "'We' are going to the southern edge of this blighted valley. Then 'you' are going back to the isper lands, and 'I' am going to the western mountains."

She frowned, thinking it was a little sad. She would not have much time to learn firsthand about the past if she were to part ways with the only human to have seen it. She would need to be creative. "And just how are you supposed to get to the western mountains without my help?"

He responded without a moment's hesitation. "By walking. Likely faster than with it, I suspect." She opened her mouth to object, but he continued, not giving her a chance to voice her thoughts. "Now let's go before the reality of this place sets in."

Chapter 3

Nirim turned away from her to look out over the ruined courtyard, and to conceal the smile that came spontaneously to his face at her silly, pouty expression. The courtyard of the imperial residence, a place where just yesterday for him there were laughter, children playing, extended family talking about the latest news. Yet now it was empty, long abandoned, even dead in some senses. A crushing weight was cast upon his shoulders, as he began to feel the loss of every friend and family member he had known.

He took a deep breath and started walking purposefully toward a partially standing mixture of broken walls and rubble that had once been the Tower of Vain, so named for the greatest head of the order of knowledge from the empire's brighter past. Hinna hobbled after him as fast as she could, calling, "Wait up! Where are you going? There doesn't appear to be an exit in that direction."

He waited for her to catch up to him before he commented, "You are correct. There is no exit in this direction."

She shook her head, brow furrowing in concern. "You must be very dense."

He ignored her, telling himself that he would only have to put up with her for the better part of another day. He crouched and entered the doorway of the ruined tower. He glanced back to see Hinna peering fearfully after him. He called back reassuringly, "Just wait there. I will be back in a moment."

He stepped carefully through the collapsed interior to stop at the back of a large, circular central room. He swept stone fragments from a trapdoor that sat recessed into the floor and descended the ladder below into a storage area under the stone floor. The objects around him were greatly decayed. He gazed sadly at what had been a pile of linens, now a cohesive lump of dirt. The blade staff served an uncommon function as he used it to cut cobwebs while he made his way toward the far side of the small room.

Kneeling in front of a locked metal chest, he smiled as he blew the dust off of the little engraved plate that read *Istallia*. "Forgive me, empress," he muttered as he put his palm to the keyhole of the chest's lock. Red iether pulsed down his arm, and the tumbler in the lock clicked as the iether forced it into the unlocked position. He raised the lid and lifted out some tied bundles.

As Nirim emerged from the ruined tower, he was surprised to see that Hinna seemed worried. She sat on a large fallen chunk of wall, anxiously awaiting his return. Her face lit up when she saw him, and she sighed with relief. "What took you so long?"

He rolled his eyes and muttered, "Sorry."

She did not seem to recognize his tone as anything other than sincerity because she replied, "Oh, well, I guess it's okay this time."

He handed her two tied bundles of fabric. She studied them for a moment before returning her gaze to him in curiosity. "What are they?"

Nirim's voice carried the faintest sound of sorrow. "Summer traveling clothes for a woman of your build."

She jerked upright. "And just how do you know

what my build is?"

Choosing the refuge of silence, he merely walked behind a crumbling wall segment that was still standing. Nirim heard her call out defiantly in his direction, "You had better not peek at me, despicable human!" He was not concerned with her suspicions. In fact, the thought had not crossed his mind; rather, he was grappling with his own emotional response to memories that were but a few years old for him.

The four cousins had sneaked out of the imperial grounds and spent the night camping in the woods. The then empress-to-be, Ista, as they called her in their close circle, had worn those clothes on that occasion. When they were discovered, the imperial steward was furious, and had had the clothes locked away in the storage space of Vain's Tower. It was laughable to think that such an act would prevent his cousin from running amok for more than a couple of days, but it had made the steward feel better regardless.

He stared out over the gray and black ruins that sprawled out before him, where once the imperial district of the capital had stood. Hinna had not exaggerated; there was nothing green as far as the eye could see, even from the slightly raised plateau that had once been the location of the imperial residence.

Hinna spoke from where she waited a few paces away. He had not noticed her arrival, as apparently being injured did not necessitate her being noisy. "A-are you okay?"

Keeping his eyes forward, he answered, unfortunately forgetting her deficit in comprehending sarcasm. "Never better."

Despite her inability to discern the meaning of his tone, she clearly recognized that his statement conflicted with his mood. Her soft voice reached him again. "Are you sure?"

Nirim rose to his feet instead of answering. "We need to leave this place. Are you ready?"

Hinna hesitated for a moment. "I am, but . . . ."

He watched a hint of worry play across her face. Ista's clothes fit her perfectly, and for a moment, the striking resemblance between them forced him to turn away again as he took a calming breath. He did not ask her to continue her unspoken concern as he began to walk down toward the south edge of the city. She hobbled behind him silently, using the stick he had cut for her as a crutch.

Nirim was grateful that there was no sign of the Gavenian army, and he assumed that they had broken camp first thing in the morning and moved on. He glanced at a torpid pool of water that appeared to be tinged yellow. The air also smelled acrid, as though it too were corrupted. Other than the occasional clump of brown grass or stringy weeds, there were no living plants. There were, however, plenty of dead trees and dried-up bushes.

It was a long walk out of the city, as they had to break several times for Hinna's sake, but they did manage to make it out of the once-urban rubble pile by midday. Nirim stopped outside of the city and turned to her. "I don't suppose you know if the trackkus is still functioning?"

She gave him a blank look. "Trackkus?"

He shrugged. "That answers my question well enough."

As they continued down the road, Hinna seemed to be overladen with curiosity. "What's a trackkus?"

Nirim saw nothing wrong with telling her. "The trackkus is a large metal carriage that runs along a metal-clad stone dike, propelled by blue iether."

Her voice was filled with amazement. "That's an incredible idea. How does that even work?"

"Not sure, actually. I am not an imperial rune graver, so I could not tell you the details of its mechanisms. All I know is that there is no faster way to travel over land, but if you have never heard of it, then they probably aren't operating any longer." She looked disappointed but did not bother him with any more questions about it.

After walking for several minutes more, she asked, "So what are we looking for in the western mountains?"

He corrected her in a less than subtle manner. "I will be looking for a seerrine I knew from my time."

She seemed to ponder this for a second before voicing his own unspoken fears. "Will this seerrine still be alive? I know they can live a long time, but still, isn't that pushing the limits of even their lifespans?"

Nirim masked his concern as he responded. "He was tough, even for a seerrine. I am sure he is still alive."

Actually, he only hoped Spite was still alive, and furthermore, he hoped that it would not take him a decade to find him in the uncharted western expanse. He decided to change the subject. "Hinna, what is your role among the isper?"

"I keep records. I help maintain and chronicle the histories of our people." Her words had a clear measure of personal pride.

"So you are a librarian?"

She appeared upset, speaking hotly. "What! No! I am hardly so domestic as that. How could you ever confuse me with such a low-status individual? Clearly your education on such matters is greatly lacking." He found it amusing that she was so sensitive about the matter, but for the sake of avoiding more of her laughable rebuking looks, he refrained from expressing his mirth out loud.

"So where do you work then?"

"Most of the time I work in one of the codex repositories, where we store, organize, and maintain the codices. Occasionally I deliver a requested codex to a scholar in some remote place, which was what I was doing when the Gavenian raiding party showed up."

Nirim decided not to challenge her definition of librarians. "So your family was not caught in the attack?"

She shook her head. "Not at all. My family is safe within the central sphere."

He looked at her questioningly. "Central sphere?"

She pinned him down with another one of her dour expressions. "Surely you are not that ignorant? The central sphere is the inner part of the isper territory that is well fortified. It keeps scum like humans out."

He merely shrugged off her insult. "I don't think such a division existed in my time."

She stared at him wide-eyed. "You mean anyone used to be allowed to come into the interior of the homeland? That's . . . that's just unthinkable! Like some dark and terrible secret hidden to protect the innocence of the population."

He wanted to make some sarcastic comment about how horrible that must be, but he knew that his wit would be utterly wasted on her. Instead, he merely stated the obvious. "Times change, I guess." He felt a measure of regret that they did not, in fact, share much in common in terms of circumstances. Not that it mattered.

As they reached the rim of the valley, he could see woods and pasture lands sprawling out before them in a series of rolling hills. He glanced back at the wide, open, blackened depression that contained what looked like a mason guild's dump, what with all the crumbling stone buildings surrounding the central mound they had come from earlier that day. A patchy, faint, yellow haze hung perpetually over the valley, and the whole thing seemed surreal. He faced back toward the more familiar spread of farms and villages to prevent the sinking feeling that threatened to overwhelm him from getting any worse.

He turned to Hinna and gestured broadly toward the southeast. "Your homeland awaits you, Hinna. Do be careful on the road." He started walking, but stopped when she addressed him with surprising earnestness.

"Thank you, Nirim, for everything. I don't think I would have made it back there without you."

"You're welcome," he replied, and continued toward the very red setting sun. He had gone only a handful of paces before he heard her call his name hesitantly from behind him, sounding a little anxious. He stopped again and moved to face her.

Like most people, Nirim had a list of mistakes that he would occasionally bring to mind and wish for all he was that he had never made them. His act of turning around completely was promptly added to that list.

Hinna stood before him, eyes bashfully considering the ground, her hands clasped in front of her to reduce her nervous fidgeting. Red light from the sunset made her flawless complexion practically glow. Her multihued hair flowed softly around her face and over her shoulders. In that moment, he knew he had never seen something so beautiful in all his life. He was captivated, breathless, left wondering if he could be imagining the whole scene.

She raised her eyes toward him and tilted her head to one side. There was no mistaking that she was waiting for an answer. Nirim racked his brain for any memory of her asking a question, but he came up blank. Maybe he had not heard her; he could not deny that he had been more than a little distracted. When he spoke, it was supposed to be a question. "Yes?" His voice was embarrassingly unsteady, and he was not sure it sounded like a question at all.

Indeed, Hinna was certain it was a statement, as she clapped her hands together in glee. "Oh, thank you so much! I promise I won't be any trouble at all."

Nirim tried to smile at her as he turned back toward his direction of travel. What could she possibly mean by that? His heart sank with a sickening feeling that told him he had just made a terrible mistake, one that would likely haunt him for a lifetime.

As though confirming his temporary lapse into the sort of idiocy he had long deluded himself into thinking he possessed immunity against, Hinna materialized at his side, grinning like a happy child on her birthday. Nirim put one hand to his temple as he accepted his punishment for being an idiot, while speaking with a slightly pained tone. "And how long do you intend to travel with me?"

She looked thoughtful for a moment before responding happily. "Until I chronicle all the historical information that your small brain holds. I know humans have a highly limited capacity for knowledge, but we isper can hold vast amounts of information with high fidelity in our minds."

Nirim muttered with resignation, "I was afraid of that."

She waved her hand apologetically. "Oh, please, don't worry about it. It's not your fault that your race has deficient mental capacities."

He was kicking himself mentally, as he had been looking forward to being free of such incidental verbal abuse. He was tempted to tell her he had merely been joking, but he was not callous enough to stomp on her clearly unremitting delight in being able to travel with a small-brained but storied person such as himself.

Furthermore, he could not quite dismiss the relief he felt that he would not be traveling alone, though, logically, he had no reason to feel relief. His limping, insensitive companion was more likely to cause him trouble than aid him in adapting to a present time that was far out of his own context.

Chapter 4

Hinna was not particularly impressed by the human village from which they had purchased supplies. The people were rude, and they stared at her as though she were a freak of nature. They had also been reluctant to accept Nirim's imperial coinage—that is, until they realized it was made out of gold. On several occasions, Nirim had quelled disconcerting looks by simply stating, "The isper belongs to me." Hinna found his statement to be curiously annoying, but patently vague. She was too embarrassed to ask what he meant by it.

Thinking on these things reminded her that she still needed to inquire about the traveling clothes that he had gotten her. It had not escaped her notice that regardless of their antiquated style, her clothes were substantially nicer than what she saw the village women wearing. The difference was far from subtle, and it was more than just in the refined fit. The fabric itself was of a quality that she had never personally possessed, even among her own people.

She glanced at Nirim as they walked westward in the early evening light; he appeared to be lost in thought. "Nirim?"

"Yes?"

She tried to sound as casual as possible. "Whose clothes am I wearing?"

Nirim spoke absently, as though her question did

not warrant a return to reality by his wandering mind. "Oh, those belonged to my cousin."

"Miralla's?"

It made no sense for him to look surprised that she remembered his cousin's name; had he not been listening when she had explained the fact of her mental superiority?

Nirim spoke softly, as though he suspected the previous owner would overhear their conversation. "No, that outfit belonged to Ista. She was also Miralla's cousin."

That hardly told Hinna what she wanted to know. "What was she?"

Nirim smiled fondly as they continued their steady pace. "She was a dear friend."

Hinna sighed with exasperation. "Come on, Nirim, that doesn't tell me why she had such nice clothes."

He spoke somberly as he seemed to return to his internal reflection. "Don't worry, Hinna. It doesn't matter anymore, nor will anyone come looking for them."

Hinna was bothered that he was being so evasive, but she needed to remain on good terms with him if she was to get from him the history of the human empire from his time and before. If she collected enough information, she would be able to publish her own volume on the topic, and likely gain universal acclaim as the only person able to write authoritatively about it, since most of the human records were destroyed, lost, or simply unavailable since the fall of the empire. Materials produced by the empire were viewed with suspicion, and anything deemed too impractical, like histories, had been burned during the humans' civil war.

Of course, she could not tell him that becoming a famous cross-cultural historian was her primary motivation for following him around. Based on the long, blank look that he had given her when she asked if she could continue traveling with him to learn more about human history, she surmised he was not overly interested in her motivations. She wondered if he had always been so moody and vacant-minded. To be honest, though, that latter part was probably just a feature of his race, so she could not really consider it his fault.

Lost in her own musings, she only realized Nirim had come to a sudden stop after she smacked into his back. "What's the holdup?" she complained as she peered around him.

Two groups of about a dozen humans each stood opposing each other. They appeared to be soldiers from the two different kingdoms. An overturned merchant cart lay in the middle of the road, with neither its contents nor its driver anywhere to be seen. A tall, burly man wearing armor with the insignia of a large wild cat spoke gruffly. "And how do I know you didn't pillage this merchant's stuff? Seems convenient that you just happened to find it this way, don't you think?" The man waved a long, ietherized weapon of some kind at the other group.

From the opposing side, an ordinary-looking older man, bearing an emblem of a flame surrounding a sword on his clothing, spoke in a steely tone. "Just because Yorasin's finest are unable to protect the border roads from bandits does not mean you need to blame us."

The burly man snarled, "You stupid Imperians are always swiping stuff! I ought to put a few holes in you just to be . . . ."

He trailed off as he, and the rest of the humans, turned to face the newcomers. Hinna began to feel especially uncomfortable, as the human soldiers reminded her of the recent terror wrought upon her. The burly man spoke with disdain as the others stared suspiciously at the two of them. "And who are you to eavesdrop on official government business! If you confess to your banditry and return the stolen goods, I might just go easy on you."

The older Imperian seemed to be more interested in something else. "What's with the isper?"

Hinna flinched and whispered to Nirim. "We should run while we have the chance."

Paying her no heed, Nirim spoke calmly, and with an air of authority she had not heard him use around her. "We are not bandits, but simply travelers going from one place to another. As to the isper, she belongs to me." The burly man laughed with what Hinna considered to be an ugly, snorting sort of sound, while the Imperian merely frowned at them with a disapproving look.

The Yorasin commander spoke sharply as he raised his spear-like weapon to point in Nirim's direction. "State your name and allegiance, or die as an anonymous criminal!" Still Nirim seemed unphased by the fact that two dozen soldiers from two different kingdoms were breathing death threats at them.

Hinna's body was on the alert, and she was ready to bolt for cover. Now that it was day with plenty of sunlight, she would be long gone before the humans even had time to fire. She hesitated, however, as this would leave her newfound fountain of knowledge defenseless. Much to her dismay, Nirim spoke softly, in a low enough tone that only she could hear him. "Don't move, Hinna."

What kind of idiotic plan was that? But despite her own common sense, she stood as still as the current circumstances would allow.

Nirim thrust the blade staff into the ground in front of him and brought his hands out low to his sides.

He seemed strangely tense, but his voice was nothing more than the calm tone that was his mainstay. "I am Nirimialin Esternon, and my allegiance is solely to the imperial throne."

Hinna thought that both of the apparent leaders of the represented kingdoms looked like they might pass out from shock, and a hushed murmur rippled through their adjoining soldiers. She felt confused. Was his name Nirim, or was it Nirimialin? Why would he have two first names? Humans were just plain illogical sometimes.

The Imperian man recovered first and spoke coldly. "Is that supposed to be some kind of insult against our forefathers?" He raised the sleek gray metal device strapped to his wrist, and it began to glow with blue iether.

The burly fellow shook his head in an obviously demeaning fashion, though his words seemed sincere enough. "Well, I guess that means you're far too crazy to be a bandit. Now scram while I deal with this problem." He gestured at the Imperian soldiers rudely as he turned back toward their commander.

Hinna remained motionless, but whispered loudly to Nirim, "Let's go while we still can."

Nirim did not move. "We are not alone out here." She looked quickly at his left arm and saw a faint blue glow that was nearly invisible in the bright sunlight. His voice came again. "Remember, whatever happens, don't move."

Hinna was at the limit of her nerves. They were facing overwhelming odds, there was something else lurking out there, and he wanted her to just stand there in the open with nothing but his bullheadedness between her and certain death? "You're going to get me killed, aren't you." He said nothing, but she could have sworn that he smiled at her comment. Regardless of her urge to run like her life depended on it, she did as he had said.

The two groups had returned to insulting and threatening one another vigorously when an ear-piercing tone sent the soldiers writhing to the ground with their hands over their ears. It seemed not to affect her or Nirim. Half a dozen seerrine burst from the tree line, wielding dual long daggers, their iether runes aglow with blue iether. Hinna was surprised to see that they wore full armor, which clashed with her perception of them as moderately tribal.

The tone died away as another seerrine emerged from the woods and called tauntingly to the soldiers, "Come on! You weak-willed, bipedal bottom feeders aren't even worth the time it takes to end your short lives." The seerrine appeared rather young to be leading a group of bandits. Her long, blue-silver hair was tied back into a generous single braid. Her metallic bronze eyes matched the subdued earth-red tones of her scales. She peered sharply at Nirim and Hinna. "And what are you doing still standing? Oh, but don't worry. I can't miss from here."

She brought a small pipe with holes in it to her lips and blew hard. The same tone they heard before sent the soldiers back into writhing spasms, but from Hinna's position, behind and to one side of Nirim, the tone sounded muted, as if the air was too thick to transmit the sound at full volume. The seerrine slowly lowered the simple flute from her mouth, glaring at them with a mixture of anger, frustration, and suspicion. "Fine. We will have to do things the old-fashioned way, since we can't have any witnesses." She turned to two of her comrades on her left. "Dispose of the human, but leave his isper slave alone."

The two seerrine soldiers smiled gleefully and headed toward them. Hinna swallowed nervously, but reminded herself that she was not the target of their aggression. Strangely, this did little to assuage the uneasiness she felt. The seerrine were stronger and faster than humans, and so in a physical confrontation, Nirim did not stand a chance.

Apparently Nirim was not knowledgeable enough to recognize this fact, as he chose instead to sternly warn the approaching seerrine. “If you flee now, I can assure you that you will not be harmed, but if you persist, I cannot guarantee your safety.” The seerrine hesitated, as the stranger’s voice was far more serious than a normal bluff. They glanced toward their leader to see if this threat warranted a change in plans.

The female seerrine looked at the incapacitated soldiers who twitched feebly on the ground, and then back at Nirim. “What makes you so confident, servant of the long-dead empire? Why should we fear you? You aren’t even armed with one of those iether-spitting weapons your kind seem to be infatuated with. I call your bluff, human.” She gestured toward Nirim with the sweep of her arm, and the two seerrine warriors resumed their approach.

Hinna was about to suggest that a hasty retreat was in order when Nirim snapped both of his arms up and away from his sides. The blade staff, sticking vertically out of the ground in front of him, erupted into a narrow column of blue iether fire, and the two of them became surrounded by a perfectly circular wall of blue flame that instantly charred the ground beneath it.

Hinna flinched involuntarily and remained frozen out of sheer terror of being burned by the whirling inferno. Nirim stood undisturbed, watching the scene before them. The seerrine soldiers fell over one another as they turned tail and slithered away as fast as possible. Their leader looked surprised, and a strange expression crossed her face. She quickly called a retreat, and the rest of the seerrine bolted at her command. The leader paused at the edge of the trees and glanced back, taking a long look at them before disappearing as her comrades had done.

Nirim waited a minute longer before he dropped his arms, and the iether flame rapidly dissipated, though the ground continued to smoke slightly. Nirim retrieved the blade staff and turned to face Hinna, looking a little concerned. "Are you all right?"

Hinna checked herself to make sure she had not lost a limb or something from the blue fire, and then looked at him, pondering out loud, "And here I thought you were defenseless in a real fight."

He gave her one of his strange, serious expressions. "Almost, but not quite." She nodded her affirmation, and he turned back around, shaking his head. The whole situation was very odd, but she was glad that she had not lost her inside source for human history.

By the time they walked up to where the human soldiers were lying, they were slowly picking themselves up off the ground. The burly Yorasin captain grumbled loudly from where he sat. "Seerrine bandits this far east? Who ever heard of such a thing?"

The Imperian commander muttered coldly as he helped one of his men back on his feet. "Imagine that. Seerrine successfully sneaking through Yorasin patrol territory." He looked a little embarrassed when he realized that Nirim and Hinna were standing within earshot. He bowed politely to them.

"Thank you, stranger, for your assistance. My apologies for misjudging you earlier." He paused, glancing at Hinna with a slightly worried expression on his face.

Nirim answered the unspoken question flatly. "She's not."

Hinna blinked and studied the two men. She wanted to know what he meant, but she was afforded no opportunity, as the older man continued, “Good, good. Is there anything I can do to repay you? Please do not hesitate to ask.”

I don’t suppose you can provide me with a current map and some information?”

The Imperian captain seemed pleased. “Yes, of course. Come with us to Sivanic.” Seeing their questioning expressions, he gestured northward as he explained. “It’s a border town just northwest of here, about half a day’s travel.”

Nirim shrugged noncommittally. “Very well. Let’s go to Sivanic.”

The large Yorasin commander spoke grimly. “Careful who you keep company with, stranger. It could be very bad for your health.”

“Thank you. I will be cautious.”

As they followed the Imperian patrol down a dusty side path, Hinna listened intently to the history-laced conversation. The captain introduced himself. “I am Baldric, captain of the perimeter guard for this area.” He cleared his throat as he transitioned a little stiffly to what was on his mind. “Nirimia- . . .”

Nirim cut him off. “Just call me Nirim, please.”

Baldric sighed with relief. “Good, that’s far easier. Now, as I was about to say, you need to be careful whom you mention the empire to. It remains a point of contention for many even now.”

Nirim asked innocently, “And does it for you?”

Baldric laughed as he shook his head. “Of course not.”

He glanced at Nirim and appeared to be taken back that Nirim was not joking. “Uh, don’t you know that?”

Nirim looked thoughtfully at a tree in the distance for several moments before he turned to Baldric and stated carefully, “Let’s just say that my understanding of history is out of date, so you may have to be specific about some of the more recent changes."

Baldric eyed him a little nervously. "Well, you seem well spoken for someone without an education, but I don't mind indulging you in a bit of history. When the empire was disbanded and the imperial capital sacked and burned, those who remained faithful to the imperial throne fled northwest and founded the kingdom of Imperia. We are the smallest of the five human kingdoms, and also probably the most hated. Resentment toward the empire remains strong, even more than a century after its dissolution."

Hinna interrupted. "So what happened that the empire was disbanded?"

Baldric eyed her curiously, but Nirim explained, "Hinna is a historian interested in human history. Just don't ask her opinion on human-related matters." Baldric blinked, and then both he and Nirim erupted into laughter.

Hinna was at a loss concerning the cause of their humor, but before she could interject her displeasure at being left out of such a good joke, Baldric answered her question. "Many details have been lost, but essentially the imperial throne came up empty after a long line of powerful rulers. A power struggle exploded into a civil war, with different groups fighting to support their favored choice. Ultimately, after years of conflict and a great deal of destruction, the empire ended up being parceled among the warring factions that had been vying for the throne. In the end, it doesn't really make much sense."

Nirim nodded. "Makes me wonder if some important information is missing."

Hinna piped up unbidden. "I don't know. It sounds like normal hu—"

Nirim cut her off by interrupting with a random

question. “Hinna, if you were empress, how would you handle the line of succession?”

Hinna blinked, losing her train of thought as she contemplated this notion. After a moment, she began with a carefully crafted, mildly existential explanation that used water falling off a leaf as its principal metaphor in communicating her opinion on the successional flow and imperialism. After about ten minutes, she could tell that she had reached the mental capacity of the humans, as their eyes were glazing over. She sighed internally but wrapped up her answer quickly. She did not quite catch what Nirim muttered in response, but it sounded like some kind of apology.

Chapter 5

"Hail, Animus!"

A familiar voice called down from the rampart of Gerialin, the fortress town that the seerrine had built to restrict the movement of humans into the western mountains. It was an impressive settlement whose wall ran the whole width of the mountain pass, capped by a tower that soared several stories into the air. But the entire thing seemed a little wasted, as the humans were too preoccupied with killing one another to know much more than that the city existed, let alone what it was for, or even where it was located.

Animus yelled back up at the wall angrily. "Don't call me that, Astroligin!"

The large metal gate swung open, and she led her warriors into the courtyard that served as a staging area. She dismissed them with a wave of her hand as she turned to face her longtime friend, who had descended the ramp from the wall and stopped directly in front of her. She crossed her arms and frowned at him. "How many times must I remind you that I would prefer you not call me by that name? It's reserved for the savage humans so that they don't choke on their own tongues while trying to pronounce my real name."

Astroligin laughed. "As if I had forgotten your preferences! Rather, I have no regard for them."

She rolled her eyes at him. While he was older than her by a good twenty years, he rarely acted like it. His earthy-green scales and tawny metallic hair made her jealous from a tactical standpoint, as he would blend into his surroundings easily. Her own brighter colors were not well-suited for the kind of sneaking she had been assigned.

Astroligin cocked his head to one side, looking a little bemused. "So I take it your venture was not a success?"

She winced and stared at the ground before gesturing toward her quarters. "Let's talk in private, shall we?"

He chuckled with a completely unnecessary degree of glee as he said chipperly, "Oh, this is going to be good." She shot him an angry look before she proceeded up a nearby ramp.

Her home in Gerialin was a modest two-room house built on top of a larger complex that included the dining hall, a library, several public spaces, and a number of one-room quarters for visitors and dignitaries. She was stationed in this forsaken place for two reasons. The first was personal, on behalf of her father, and the second was professional, on behalf of her people. Normally she was successful in her military operations, but this past week had been a veritable nightmare of one setback after another.

By the time they reached the relatively secluded sitting room in her quarters, she had severe reservations about divulging any detailed information about her travels to Astroligin. It was not that she did not trust him, but rather that he had a terrible habit of saying the most provocative things on a whim, and she had no desire to damage her living space so soon after being out on the road for a month.

The other seerrine looked thoughtfully at the

sparsely furnished room before turning to her and spreading his arms out in a greatly exaggerated gesture. "Now, tell me what terrible fate has befallen you, my friend. You never found the one you were looking for? Perhaps human bandits inflicted losses on your soldiers? Or maybe you found nothing at all?"

Animus realized that he was far too jovial for their conversation to end politely, but a month away had caused her to miss his banter, so she ignored the sure signs that she should not share details of her recent failure with him. "If I had found nothing, I might be in a better mood, and you clearly overestimate the abilities of humans, bandit or otherwise."

She sighed with regret and turned her gaze toward the wall. "I think I found the human that our elders seemed to be looking for." She shook her head. "And it could be the same human my father raved about for years."

Astroligin sounded a little confused. "That seems like excellent news. All you have to do is confirm the man's identity with your father, and you have single-handedly solved two of the biggest challenges ever given to western-born seerrine!"

"Need I remind you that last time I talked with my father, he thought he was a chicken?"

"Oh, right, how could I forget."

He stressed the final word a tad too strongly for her taste, even if she could not be certain whether he had meant it intentionally.

She returned to the original topic. "Do you see the human here with me now?"

He stroked his chin, looking pensive. "Unless it is exceptionally small, or unless you left the poor beggar outside the wall unconscious, then I can only conclude that you must have eaten the human whole!"

Animus stared him down with a penetrating gaze

until he looked at the floor and muttered, "Sorry. You were saying?"

"We traveled toward the interior of the human lands, but before we could get there, some men jumped a human merchant carrying meat. Apparently the undisciplined oafs were tired of rations and decided that the merchant was expendable. Fortunately, I got to them before they killed him, but I had to render him unconscious. Of course, it was only a moment later that not one, but two human patrols showed up. We hid in the woods, but I had to leave the merchant under a bush. These patrols must have been from opposing factions because they were about to get violent. Then this human and his pet isper show up and interrupt them. They accused the newcomer of being the cause of the trouble, for some strange reason."

Astroligin nodded his concurrence. "Yes, pesky humans. They can barely hold a rational thought, let alone operate peaceably."

"Anyway, I wasn't about to let them kill the poor isper, so I intervened."

"Naturally."

Animus took a deep breath and then let it out as she resumed. "So I incapacitated the human patrols, but it was like the other human was shielded by something. I couldn't touch him. I was already in a bad mood; how was I supposed to know that he was iether-bound? I mean, humans are giant rats. They're everywhere out there, and you have to work at it not to squash one of the disgusting buggers. How could I have even known who he was?"

Astroligin raised his hand in a calming manner. "Animus, I do believe you are leaving out a crucial piece of information from your tale of woe. Why didn't you ask him to come with you to Gerialin?"

She grimaced dejectedly at the floor. "Because I

tried to have him killed."

"You did WHAT?!"

Animus shrugged as though she could shed the guilt for her rash actions. "Well, he challenged me. It made me angry that a puny human would call me out like that, so I called his bluff—only it wasn't a bluff."

Astroligin peered at her curiously as he asked, "And how can you be so sure that he is the human of interest that you were seeking?"

She looked at him with a level gaze. "Because he carried an iether-imbued astral weapon like my father's, and because he used its power. He must be an iether wielder."

Astroligin arched one eyebrow skeptically. "A human?"

"Yes, and what's more, he had a seerrine name."

Her friend recoiled slightly as he said with a sense of exaggerated wonder, "Wow, you really did mess up."

She gave him a sarcastic look. "Why, thank you for that word of encouragement, you bastion of comfort." She turned angrily toward the wall and threw her hands up despairingly. "Now what am I supposed to do about this mess I have created? How can I possibly make right this wrong?"

Her friend re-positioned himself by the only window in the sitting room and stared out of it as though seeking inspiration. He straightened sharply, as if a thought had occurred to him. Animus watched him a little nervously. "Yes? What is it?"

Astroligin whirled to face her, wearing a mischievous grin. "You will have to make restitution for your transgressions."

She did not like the sound of this. "What could I possibly give a human to atone for trying to have him killed? Money? A dagger? Food?"

His voice remained flat, but there was a twinkle in his eye. "You could always offer yourself as a potential mate."

Had Astroligin been any slower, he might have been injured, but as it was, he had his iether flowing a split second before Animus's concussive burst of sound blew him through the thin plaster wall and sent him cartwheeling across the courtyard before he stopped by smacking into the wall near the gate. He rose quickly and dusted himself off. The rune of resilience had prevented him from coming to harm, and he made his way back toward her quarters, nodding calmly at the half-dozen soldiers who watched with stunned expressions on their faces.

Animus crossed her arms as she waited for him to return. "That wasn't funny at all, Astroligin."

He looked where the window had been, at the hole in the wall that more than slightly resembled his form. "Apparently not. But I was only half-joking, you know. Just because we seerrine are highly civilized in our intimate relationships does not mean that humans are. They'll take partners from anyone who remotely resembles them."

She raised her hand sharply, and she thought she saw him flinch involuntarily. "That's enough! I need not know anything more about it, and should that filth come anywhere close to me, he will suffer my wrath."

He snorted. "And I suppose this might endanger his life for a second time? Wouldn't that merely be digging a deeper hole?"

Animus glared at him momentarily before she sighed and flopped down on a low couch, carefully tucking her tail under her to keep it off the floor. His question was not worth answering, so she simply stared in frustration at the new full-length window in the wall.

After a few minutes of quiet, Astroligin asked,

"So what are you going to do?"

Animus shook her head. "I have no idea, but I don't have to submit my report for a week, so I should have sufficient time to state things as delicately as possible."

He mused out loud for what she presumed was her benefit. "Well, you are the one who was entrusted with this critical mission. You should be able to come up with something reasonable. Though there's not really enough time to go and retrieve this fellow, I suppose."

"The mission was making contact, not retrieval, and since I made contact, the mission was technically successful. Retrieval will likely follow if the elders decide that it is warranted. Now, go bother someone else for a while so I can compose this blasted report." He shrugged and left her quarters, abandoning Animus to her troubled thoughts. What could she write to the elders concerning her confrontation with the human?

Hot springs made a large portion of their land a proverbial paradise, but ever since they had begun to rapidly chill, there had been little agreement about what should be done to halt the problem, or even if they could. What was worse, everything they knew suggested that their home would be a frozen wasteland without those hot springs.

A careful review by the knowledge keepers had revealed that there was, in times past, a handful of humans with incredible iether powers, powers that surpassed even their own Ankenkinds. The elders had concluded that they must seek the help of one of these ietherized humans, if they still existed, motivated in part by the fact that the current Ankenkind was a young child, and several decades away from coming into his full power. Her mission had been simple: find the human capital, and determine if there were any humans left that could potentially rekindle the hot springs and spare them from a fate worse than death. That fate, of course, being migration into the human lands.

Long ago, the seerrine had been isolated tribes, but many had reinhabited their ancestral lands after studying under the great knowledge keeper Vain, and brought with them the teaching about the Creator. For the most part, her people had listened, and learned, and returned to the Creator. Shortly after, and not coincidently, this restoration had led to a unification of the tribes and the establishment of a collective of elders. Under this new system the seerrine had thrived, and developed a civilization that nearly rivaled that of the isper in elegance.

The humans stagnated, often erupting into wars among themselves. The seerrine had pulled as far away from them as they comfortably could. But now, they might have to leave the mountains altogether, and she doubted that the humans would just make room for them. Likely it would be a bloody battle for potential crop land, and with humans having the edge in terms of war experience and weaponized iether, the winner would not be a foregone conclusion.

She pondered the possibility that she had inadvertently doomed generations of her people to horrific warfare over barely hospitable lands because of her rash actions. The thought left her mouth dry and her hands shaky. And how odd the human had been, compared to most of their worthless rabble, so calm amid what most would consider a life-or-death situation. He certainly seemed to outclass the others in terms of iether power.

She had only seen one other iether-imbued weapon before, and it was hardly as impressive as the one this human held. Most seerrine could generate blue iether motes at will, but to draw pure blue iether fire was a rare feat. And what was she to make of his having a seerrine name? The feeling was akin to having a domesticated animal named after a close family member. Equally disconcerting was the human's pet isper. Could such a person really be the key to their survival?

That thought suddenly gave her a brilliant idea. All she needed to do was exaggerate this human's negative qualities, and her own rash actions would pale beside his. She sighed with relief. At least it would alleviate her guilt before her own people, and if this fellow was the one they sought, his character would likely not come under consideration anyway. She might still have to make amends with the human at some point, but the most immediate situation could be resolved easily without anyone calling her capacities into question.

She rose and made her way to the writing desk in the adjacent room. She picked up a quill and began to write in flowery terms about the success of her mission, and the terrible character of the vile human she found that matched her objectives. She could not help but chuckle audibly at how the tables had turned on the silently arrogant human who had bested her twice in the span of a few minutes.

By the time she finished, it was growing late. Not feeling particularly hungry, Animus chose to retire early. Considering the emotional turmoil of the day, this turned out to be a bad choice. Her sleep was fitful at best, racked by horrible dreams of finding the human at the gate, demanding reparations for her foolish actions. Jerking awake, she shook her head, as if to throw the memory of the dream from her mind. She looked around her room suspiciously, as though she might somehow spot him lurking in the corner. Her seerrine eyes could easily tell from the light creeping in under the door that dawn had barely started. She considered trying to get some more rest, but she feared a relapse of the worst nightmare she had ever experienced.

Instead, she rose from her bed and prepared for the day. Surely now, starting today, things would be much better than in the past weeks. She picked up the report that lay folded and sealed on her desk. She would deliver her report to the city's communicant, who shared an iether link with another seerrine in their capital city, and the elders would likely send back an answer by the end of the week.

Animus was feeling rather pleased with herself as she left her quarters and handed the letter off to be transmitted and then burned, as was their practice for sensitive communications. She had turned toward the dining hall when a clamor at the wall drew her attention. The soldiers on duty were shouting excitedly and waving her toward them, and at such an early hour in the morning, too. She made her way toward the top of the wall, hoping that this would not greatly delay breakfast.

Chapter 6

Nirim sat in a small room inside the Imperian outpost that was nestled within the wall of the border town. Baldric had offered them a place to stay so that they could set out fresh the following morning. Nirim utilized the early morning light, pouring over the map that Baldric had given him. Human settlements were distributed around a large central space where the imperial capital lay. A deep pang of sorrow swept over him as he noticed the label read "poisoned wastes." Starting with the northern compass point and moving right, the human kingdoms were Gaven, Lastonya, Dien, Yorasin, and Imperia.

Additionally, the lands of the kobay actually had numerous cities designated, a far cry from the single stable kobay city that existed a century before. Further, the map seemed to indicate that most of the isper lands were enclosed by some kind of wall. He looked at the small black circle that Baldric had drawn on the map to mark the location of the only known seerrine city.

Nirim had barely been able to persuade Baldric not to report the seerrine as bandits. The last thing he needed was a military force showing up and igniting a war while he was trying to find his friend. It would take several days to reach the city, assuming they did not run into any kind of opposition, though it seemed that if he were going to run aground, it was not going to be with the seerrine.

In his time, the seerrine had settled into organized villages in the foothills of the western mountains, with open trade between their kind and his. His friend Spite had told him of how the seerrine had generally turned back to the Creator, thanks to the empire's most renowned head of the order of knowledge, a seerrine called Vain. Indeed, Spite had initially come to the empire as a diplomat for his people's new government, and was later recruited as a guardian. He and Spite shared in the possession of relatively impotent blue iether runes. Spite's rune, the rune of joy, was without function in any context that Nirim had seen.

He leaned back in his chair and closed his eyes. For him, it was only a week ago that they had last talked together. He wondered if he would recognize his friend when he saw him. Nirim sighed, a long, slow sigh, fighting back the physical pain of thinking of his friends as gone. To him, it was as though they had been swallowed up in a catastrophe, with no grave to their names. No place he could mourn, and no people with whom he could join in shared sorrow for their loss. They simply were no more; not even their children or grandchildren remained in any way he could know. It was frighteningly devoid of any closure.

He opened his eyes again to see Hinna standing in the doorway, watching the floor and waiting for him. Instead of saying something that would make her feel awkward, he asked, "Are you ready to head out now?"

She jerked up suddenly, as though surprised that he was aware of her presence. "Y-y-yes, I am."

Nirim nodded, folded up the map, and gathered his things. "Good. It will take us nearly a week to reach the only known seerrine settlement."

He glanced at her, noting that she still stood

unmoving in the doorway, looking a little more serious than normal. He decided she needed a distraction before she started to worry. "You know, there used to be more than a dozen seerrine settlements on this side of the western mountains."

Her face lit up instantly. "Really? What were they like?"

He smiled when he saw her eagerness for some other tidbit of historical information. He talked of the seerrine and their diplomatic relationship with the empire, of their odd customs, and of his friend Spite, who was also a guardian, and the same person he intended to find among the seerrine.

They stopped at the central office to say their farewells to Baldric. When he saw them, he rose from his desk and approached them, speaking warmly. "Ah, good morning to you both." He held out a folded slip of paper. "Here, take this with you. It's a formal pass that will let you past any of our patrols, should they hassle you."

Nirim took it and tucked it into his belt. "Thank you, Baldric. You have been a reliable help."

Baldric grinned. "No, my friend, thank you! I might not be standing here were it not for your aid. One of these days you're going to have to show me how you bypassed that seerrine's crippling attack."

"Let's just say sound travels poorly through thicker air."

Baldric merely shook his head. "Still the secretive one. Well, regardless, I wish you a safe journey."

They turned and made their way out of the city. Hinna glanced at him as they walked and commented, "These human cities are always so dirty. Why is that?"

Nirim looked around, but he did not see any signs of undue filth. "What do you mean?"

"Are you blind? I mean, look at all the dirt!"

He observed the packed earthen byway they were traveling on toward the walled city's main gate. Surely she wasn't objecting to the presence of soil itself? "You mean, like, the dirt road?"

She nodded firmly. "Of course, silly! What else would I be talking about?"

They continued in silence, as he had no response to what he considered an absurd question. As they turned onto the westward road outside the city, she stated, "You have no idea why your cities are dirty, do you?" It was the kind of question that presumed its own answer.

"Precisely," he said in a sarcastic tone, and then berated himself mentally, as her expression reminded him that his sarcasm was completely lost on her. This trip could be the longest week of his life if all their conversations ended this poorly.

***

Days later, they were camped out in a sheltered spot in the western mountains. The area was arid and cool, with little in the way of trees. Sticks from some particularly spiny bushy plants served as fuel for their small fire, and large flat rocks as seats. The mountains had risen quickly out of the preceding woodland, which had died away at their foothills. Nirim decided that if the seerrine had chosen this kind of environment over the one in the human lands, they might be crazier than he had first suspected.

Hinna sat as close to the fire as safely possible, with her traveling cloak wrapped tightly around her. She had voiced her opinion on the cold several times, and it was negative enough that Nirim was secretly hoping she might decide to up and quit the notion of following him around. The whole trip, she had peppered him with questions about a wide array of seemingly insignificant topics related to the human empire, and he was starting to doubt her academic prowess. What did it matter what the imperial family ate as compared to commoners, or what colors the linens in the better hostels were? And with everything she asked about, some bizarre discussion would follow that often ended in demeaning statements about humans.

The oddest aspect of it all was the fact that she did not seem to make the connection that he was one of those "horrible and vile creatures" himself. Of course, he was part seerrine, but that aspect of his heritage went back generations, far enough that it was impossible to know what proportion of seerrine he was. He was essentially a normal human, with a blue iether rune as the only sure indicator that he had had a seerrine ancestor at some point. He had tried several more times to explain to her that she was annoyingly tactless, but these attempts proved no more successful than his first. With some effort, he pushed it from his mind, lest it drive him crazy with frustration.

"Nirim, are you okay?" Hinna asked gently.

He looked up from his absentminded contemplation of the fire. He realized that his face was probably telling tales about his thoughts. "Yes. Why do you ask?"

She watched the dancing flames, her face slightly pinched, as though she were nervous. "Well, you just seem a little distracted, that's all." After a brief pause, she lifted her eyes to meet his. "Is it because what you knew is now gone? Like losing everything overnight?"

Nirim refrained from rolling his eyes at her ability to state the obvious and said wryly, "Yes, thank you for reminding me." She smiled pleasantly, and he quickly added, "However, it would be best if you didn't make a habit of it."

She nodded. "Oh, okay."

She looked like she wanted to ask him something else, but after several moments of silence, Nirim decided that perhaps he had misunderstood her body language. He stretched and laid down on his bedroll, pulling his cloak about him as he spoke wearily. "Let's get some rest now, and plan on heading out early tomorrow." He caught a glimpse of her head bobbing before he closed his eyes and willed himself to fall asleep instantly.

He had learned the hard way that if he did not fall asleep quickly, Hinna would invariably come up with some random question that would prevent him from getting any rest for hours. Tonight felt a little different. He was not sure if it was the cold that distracted her, or the fact that they would be dealing with the seerrine on the morrow.

The latter possibility seemed unlikely. As far as he could tell, the isper and the seerrine respected one another. In his time, the other three races had flocked to the human empire to see its grandeur, and to learn how to rise to such a level themselves. Now that the empire was a memory, even to his own people, humans were apparently viewed, however incorrectly, as barely civilized. He was a little concerned that the kobay held similar opinions. For now, though, he was going to have to convince the seerrine of his respectability.

He groaned internally, as he could only imagine how much help Hinna would be with that. He wondered if he might be able to sneak away and establish rapport with the seerrine before Hinna woke up and started jabbering. As he faded into the sweet blackness of sleep, he concluded that such a plan would fail because she was an incredibly light sleeper.

***

At first light, they continued on to the pass that led to the city. As Nirim had suspected, Hinna was up before him, shivering as she waited for him to be ready to leave. They had hurriedly eaten some dried bread and cured meat as a passable breakfast, but both Hinna and his stomach complained about the insufficiency of such rations. As was his normal operating procedure, he ignored both of them silently.

As they climbed the steep incline that led up into the pass, Nirim stopped and stared at the impressive structure at its height. A massive stone wall spanned the entire pass. It rose precipitously to what he considered to be a gratuitous height. If the ramparts were any indicator, the wall must be incredibly thick. Even if he had an army at his back, the wall looked impenetrable as far as conventional warfare went. Hinna blurted out her typical analysis-free description of the circumstances. “Wow. That is a really big wall.”

Nirim stifled his useless sarcastic response and continued toward the looming edifice. There was no place to avoid being spotted in the pass either, so before long, seerrine soldiers let out the alarm that strangers were approaching. He and Hinna stopped near enough to the wall that they could see the soldiers’ faces, but far enough away that they were not staring straight up the unnatural cliff of the wall’s vertical surface.

One of the guards practically spat down at him, “What do you want, human? Your kind are not permitted here!”

Hinna looked at him curiously, as though she were watching a play being acted out. Of course, as an isper she was not a problem for the seerrine, so he was going to have to do all the work. Nirim cleared his throat and called out with as much confidence as he could supply at that volume. "I am here to speak with the seerrine diplomat Spi . . . er . . . Isperiliuma Angusterolla!"

Startled-looking sentries moved and talked amongst themselves. Before any answer could be delivered, a new face appeared among the soldiers. Hinna straightened with surprise. "Isn't that the seerrine we saw earlier?"

Before Nirim could state his confirmation of Hinna's assertion, the silver-haired seerrine belted down at them a rather angry accusation. "What are you doing here again!"

Even from where he stood, Nirim could tell her face was red. She must have been furious about something, but he could not imagine what might have induced such rage.

Hinna blinked in confusion. "Again?"

Nirim shrugged silently, no more knowledgeable than she, and turned back to the watching group of seerrine just in time to see another one join them. This one seemed far more diplomatic, as he practically physically calmed the angry one, and then spoke in a pleasant tone. "Wait there, human, and I will be out to speak with you in a moment." Nirim bowed politely to indicate his acquiescence.

They waited for longer than he would have anticipated, and he could not help but wonder why he could still hear shouting occasionally from the other side of the wall. Hinna looked at him with a surprising degree of concern. "What will we do if they won't let you in?"

Nirim was starting to feel uncomfortable about the tenacity with which Hinna had taken her mentality of following him everywhere. "I guess I will just have to try to find another pass through the mountains."

A small door that was part of the larger gate opened, and two seerrine emerged from within the fortress. The male seerrine who was acting as spokesman was calm and pleasantly mannered. The female one, with whom he had faced off before, was clearly upset, or perhaps terribly nervous. Neither of those emotions seemed appropriate considering the circumstances, but he intended to pretend like it was not noticeable.

The male seerrine nodded politely. "I am Astroligin, and I do apologize that I don't have a humanly pronounceable name. My friend here is Animus, whom I understand that you have already met." She winced visibly, and seemed incapable of looking Nirim in the eye.

Nirim sighed with relief. Finally here was a stranger he could communicate rationally with. "I am Nirim, and this is my—"

Animus muttered, too loudly to ignore, "Ugh, you filthy varmint . . ."

Astroligin raised his hand smoothly, causing her to cut off mid-sentence. "Now, Animus, we have a traveler here. It's not appropriate to complain about the rodent problem now." The seerrine turned back toward him. "You were saying?"

Nirim stared at him. The seerrine could not possibly think that he was so dumb as to believe that Animus was talking about rodents, could he? And for that matter, why was Hinna studying her surroundings anxiously, as though there were any such creatures around? Nirim's feeling of relief was burned away by the harsh realization that he was going to have to endure such treatment for as long as he was in the seerrine lands.

He restarted his introduction flatly. "I am Nirim, and this is Hinna."

Astroligin smiled politely and spoke mostly at Hinna. "What a pleasure to make your acquaintance.

Now what can we do for you?"

Nirim struggled to retain control at the seerrine's now obviously excessive politeness, but he managed to state calmly, "I am here to see Isperiliuma Angusterolla. Do you know of him?"

Animus's expression changed to one of incredulity, even a little touched by fear. Astroligin's eyes widened, but he took it in stride, answering with a tone of disappointment. "Well, I am familiar with him, but not only is he not taking visitors at present, but we also cannot let a human into this city, as it is a violation of our laws."

Hinna spoke far too cheerfully. "Actually, Nirim has seerrine blood, so he doesn't exactly count as a human."

Nirim took a deep breath before remarking half-heartedly, "Thank you for sharing that, Hinna."

Naturally, she took this the wrong way and smiled at him. "You're welcome!"

Nirim looked back at Astroligin to note that the seerrine's faint smile suggested that sarcasm was not a lost art on everyone. Animus crossed her arms and stared at him intently. "And what if we don't believe you?"

Nirim rolled up his sleeve and held out his arm so that they could see his iether marks. The marks filled with dim blue iether as he drew a sufficient quantity to verify their authenticity.

Astroligin watched his arm for a moment before lifting his eyes back to Nirim's face. "I see. Technically you aren't just human, so we will let you into the city, but technically you are human, so we will not permit you to go beyond. I will send a message to the one you seek, and if he is willing, he can meet you here."

Nirim dropped his arm to his side, which caused Animus to flinch and drop her gaze. He bowed politely to them both. "Thank you for your understanding."

Astroligin smiled oddly, and signaling to the guards on the rampart, disappeared into the city. Animus looked up suddenly, as though realizing too late that the other seerrine had left, and she darted after him quickly.

Nirim leaned toward Hinna and cautiously asked, “Did something about that conversation seem a little strange to you?”

She nodded emphatically, but her reply reminded him why he did not confide in her. “I’ll say! I don’t know if I want to stay in a city that has rodents in it!”

Nirim muttered a single, drawn-out word as he made his way to the door. “Right.”

Chapter 7

Nirim perched uncomfortably on a strange seat at a small table in a room on the upper level of the fortress complex. It was clearly not designed to accommodate two-legged individuals such as himself. He presumed the place to be someone's living quarters, but neither of their hosts had shared such information with them. They ate breakfast together, talking just enough small talk to maintain a sense of conversation without slowing the rate of food consumption. Or at least, some of them did. Animus remained silent, watching him suspiciously, as though he were some savage animal that would leap on her violently if unmonitored.

Between Animus's clear animosity toward him and his own curiosity about the obvious and oddly shaped hole in the wall, he hardly knew what to think or expect. He intentionally refrained from mentioning either, as he did not want to incite the seerrine over a cultural blunder.

Nirim tried to clear his mind as they finished breakfast and Astroligin turned to him, saying, "Before I send your message, do you have any questions for us?"

Nirim shook his head, but of course, Hinna was always full of questions, so she blurted out, "Why is there a hole in the wall that looks like a person?"

Astroligin smirked and said, "Oh, that has to do

with, well, a debt owed."

Nirim instantly felt uneasy about the way the conversation had turned. It became rapidly obvious that he was not the only one, as Animus rose with such force that her chair went crashing across the room. She glared at Nirim with an unnerving degree of what appeared to be hatred. "I would rather die!"

Her level of rage was such that he feared that she might demonstrate such a fact promptly, but after a moment, she did nothing more than leave the room, slamming the door behind her. Hinna turned to look at him disapprovingly. "What did you say?"

He blinked several times before he spoke, bewildered by this bizarre chain of events. "Me? I do believe that you were the one asking the question."

Hinna shook her head. "No, Nirim, it was definitely you that she is angry with." Nirim racked his brain for some kind of sensible answer to the situation, but he came up with nothing.

Astroligin rescued him from the dilemma. "Hinna? Could you go retrieve Animus from the courtyard? She really does need to be part of this conversation. Just tell her that the situation requires her good behavior."

Hinna nodded. "I will." She rose and started for the door, but before leaving, she turned and looked at Nirim. "You should behave, too, Nirim."

He sighed with resignation and quipped, "Oh, you know me." She of course nodded her confirmation of his presumed acquiescence and disappeared out the door.

Nirim merely shook his head, but Astroligin's words cut through his confusion sharply. "You do realize that she is tone-deaf?"

He peered at the seerrine curiously as he repeated the relevant word. "Tone-deaf?"

"Yes. She clearly can't tell any difference in your vocal tones, so she is dependent on your expression and body language to know what the intent of your words is." The seerrine paused momentarily as he looked toward the ceiling, musing out loud. "Actually, it is incredibly odd, since the isper are normally free from any kind of physical defect." He met Nirim's gaze. "Your mannerisms and expressions are highly reserved, so she has trouble identifying your intent."

Nirim leaned back thoughtfully. "Well, that explains one of her many problems."

The seerrine arched one eyebrow in curiosity, but Nirim waved away the notion with his hand as he changed the subject. "Never mind that, but I would be interested in knowing why Animus is so nervous around me."

"Ah, you see, our people are facing a serious threat, and she was sent out in hopes of finding one of the great iether-imbued humans to aid us in our plight. Unfortunately, the circumstances have resulted in her offending that very human, so she must make reparations for her errors. The complicating factor is that the only thing she really has to offer is herself, and it is this particular thing that makes her overly nervous. Frankly, I think she is overthinking the matter. Humans are not that—"

"What! That sounds insane. Surely she doesn't owe anybody anything more than an apology. Who is this fellow? I will see if I can talk some sense into . . . ."

Later on, Nirim would laugh at it fondly, but in the moment, he failed to connect Animus's perspective on the situation with the likeliest source of her discomfort. However, Astroligin's expression of surprise suddenly made sense. Nirim cut off his line of thought as he realized with a strong jolt of shock that he was the human in question. Nirim sank low in his chair as he ran his hands through his hair, thoughts racing around his mind as to how he could explain to the young female seerrine that no repayments were necessary, or even wanted.

Astroligin scrutinized him intently a moment longer before remarking, "You are quite odd for a human, or at least not at all as I had imagined humans to be. Where do you come from?"

Nirim was unsure that this oddness was a positive thing, and for that matter, he suspected that it was not so much about his being odd, as it was about the seerrine's understanding of humans being grossly off-center. He spoke calmly, but with gravity. "Were I to travel for a year without ceasing, I would not be a single step closer to home. I am from the old empire."

Astroligin wrinkled his brow in confusion. "Well, that is a rather strange way to put things, but I am sorry that your home is gone." Nirim only nodded; it was not worth trying to communicate the reality of his situation.

Hinna returned, looking a little dejected. Before they could ask, she said, "Animus wouldn't listen to me. She said humans are horrible, and that she didn't want to be in the same room with one any longer."

Nirim stood up and walked toward the door. "I'd better handle this."

Astroligin's eyes widened, and he opened his mouth to object, but Nirim waved away his objection. "Don't worry about it. Now I won't feel comfortable around her until this misunderstanding is dealt with."

The door closed behind Nirim as he disappeared from sight. Astroligin rose quickly and made his way to the hole in the wall. Hinna asked curiously, "What are you doing?"

He glanced at her with a mischievous grin on his face. "I am going to watch the show, of course." He exited the room, with an uncertain Hinna following close behind.

***

Animus glowered at the empty courtyard's flagstones. The isper had tried to persuade her to return to her quarters and resume conversation with the human. She had even brought up the importance of her compliance for the seerrine's sake. Animus did feel a little guilty that she was prioritizing herself over the greater good of her people. Part of her wanted to rationalize that the situation was not as horrific as she imagined it. She had thought humans were supposed to be unkempt, or so the rumors had always said. Up close the human did not appear to be filthy, nor did he smell bad. Furthermore, he was politely reserved and quiet, almost endearingly so.

She shook her head sharply, muttering, "No, no, no!" None of those things altered the fact he traveled with a strangely compliant isper concubine-slave, or the fact that humans by nature lacked dignity and honor. She shuddered as images flashed through her mind of the creature reaching toward her with an evil glint in his eyes.

A soft noise made her turn. To her horror, she no longer had to imagine the human reaching for her, as he stood barely a few paces away, arm outstretched. In an instant, blue iether raced down her arm and she brought her hands together, sharply amplifying the smack into a powerfully concussive shockwave that could rip flesh off bone.

***

Nirim descended the ramp to the courtyard

below. He spotted her, looking away from him, seemingly lost in thought. He approached her slowly and, stopping a good twenty paces from her, tried to get her attention gently by speaking in a low, calm voice. "Can we talk for a minute?"

He waited, but there was no response from her. He stepped closer and tried again. "Animus, I believe there has been a misunderstanding." Was she muttering to herself?

He stepped again, closer than he would have preferred, but he did not want to startle her if she were already jumpy. Unconsciously, he made the mistake of reaching toward her, as if to tap her on the shoulder. "I think we . . . ."

Animus whirled to face him, her expression fierce and scowling, and he knew instantly that he was in mortal danger. Only his training as a guardian, which afforded him sufficient reflexive command of his own iether, saved him from severe bodily harm.

As Animus clapped her hands together, Nirim brought his right arm up in front of him, his red iether rune brilliantly glowing from under his sleeve. The air around him suddenly became thicker than syrup, and the violent burst of sound dissipated into the nearly non-conductive medium.

For a tense moment, the two of them stood there, eyes locked, one angry, one concerned. Then Animus sighed and dropped her arm to her side, her iether fading away as she spoke with a sullen resignation. "You win again, I see. I guess I have no choice."

Nirim raised his hands and waved them frantically to stop whatever she might do next. "Hold on a moment! There has been a big misunderstanding here. I-I don't need any kind of repayment. You don't owe me anything at all—especially not that!"

Animus studied him cautiously, and it was clear

that she was relieved, but her anger did not appear to be entirely gone. This was confirmed by her tone. "Especially? And why is that? Am I not as appealing as the isper?"

Intimidating silence hung between them as Nirim rapidly tried to make sense out of the situation. Why was she upset now? Furthermore, what did Hinna have to do with anything?

With a start, he realized that Animus's supposed debt was not the only ongoing misunderstanding. He groaned internally. It was, of course, partially his fault for referring to Hinna as "belonging to him," in the hopes that such a vague statement would protect her from the wrong kind of attention. He tried to resolve Animus's clear confusion. "No! Oh, no, nothing like that. Hinna isn't my . . . I mean, we aren't . . . you know, she is just traveling with me of her own choice."

It was remarkably surprising to him that he had no good way of defining his relationship with Hinna. She was not his comrade, or his companion, or friend, or really anything. He was her source of human history, or so she said, but from his perspective she was his source of . . . pain? He wanted to laugh at the thought. Yet under the current circumstances, not only would that be in bad taste, but he also believed it should not be funny, because it was frighteningly accurate.

Animus seemed to calm down from angry to annoyed. She crossed her arms and spoke sternly. "Well?"

"What?"

"Aren't you going to answer my question?"

Nirim scarcely kept his mouth from falling agape, as he wondered if there were any sane people left in the world. He wanted to think there were, but his experiences had been suggesting a more disappointing answer. "No," he said flatly, turning back towards the living space where he could see Hinna and Astroligin watching from the odd window.

He shook his head as he returned, fervently hoping that the rather embarrassing exchange between him and Animus had not carried that far. He heard Animus call after him in a more curious tone, "And why not?"

He ignored her. Why should it matter to her what he thought? He refused to allow his brain to even ponder the question. There were more important things on his mind. Especially how long he would be stuck with these demeaning seerrine before he could talk with someone who seemed likely to be the only other normal person in the world, his good friend Spite.

***

They gathered around the table in the living space, but while Animus was far more at ease than before, he felt especially uncomfortable. He tried to ignore the feeling, telling himself it would be gone soon. Astroligin's opening question was hardly comforting to his confidence. "I saw that you also possess red iether. Are you part kobay as well?"

Nirim shook his head. "No. My human ancestry includes a group called the mystics, who are humans capable of wielding red iether to a small degree."

The seerrine stroked his chin thoughtfully. "You are very powerful indeed."

Nirim glanced at Hinna and Animus to see them nodding in agreement. They would have to be deaf to have missed his mention of the insignificance of his abilities, but there was no reason to correct their unified misconception. Nirim brought the conversation back to why he was even there. "So how long should it take before I hear back from my friend?"

Astroligin looked apologetic as he unconsciously brushed imagined dust from his shirt. “Ah, yes, about that. Animus, why don’t you tell him about your father?”

Nirim turned to her in surprise. “You’re Spite’s daughter?”

Animus straightened in her seat and puffed up her chest with pride. “Yes, I am the only child of the great Angusterolla family line.” She let out her breath in a long sigh and looked toward the wall as she spoke, her voice a little strained. “But my father hasn’t been himself since my mother died, and really, he hasn’t been anybody.” She responded to the confused looks on Nirim's and Hinna’s faces, speaking solemnly. “It has been some time since he has thought or behaved normally. To give an example, the last time I visited my father, he was under the delusion that he was a radish.”

Nirim winced visibly at the thought of his dear friend gone mad, and at the sudden collapse of his sincere hope of finding another sane person to converse with. Hinna asked innocently, “But how do you know he believed he was a radish?”

Nirim had no idea how to prevent what he knew was coming, and Animus answered unsuspectingly. “Because he buried himself in the ground up to his neck and put leaves on his head, and he remained that way for two days until his neighbors took pity on him and dug him out.”

Hinna responded with a painful seriousness. “But how do you know he was a radish? I mean, he could have been a turnip, or maybe even a carrot.”

Both seerrine could not hide their mortification at Hinna’s insensitivity. Nirim spoke flatly, looking directly at Astroligin. “Many problems, like I said, but I don’t suppose I could see him regardless of his condition?”

Astroligin looked at him curiously. "We might be able to make that happen, but I must ask, why are you so eager to see him?"

Nirim hesitated for a second before deciding that it would do no harm for them to know. "He has a message for me, given to him by a mutual friend many years ago."

Hinna piped up unexpectedly. "You mean your cousin Miralla?"

He refrained from giving her a rebuking look and settled for a simple nod. He promptly forgot all about it when Animus blurted out, "Oh, that thing."

Chapter 8

Nirim could scarcely restrain his excitement. "What thing?"

Animus shrugged, looking a little embarrassed. "Well, it's nothing really, but my father taught me a poem when I was very young that he called Miralla's song, so I thought it sounded like it was related."

Astroligin smiled. "Excellent. You can sing it for him and see if it is what he's looking for."

Animus flushed slightly, and she said with controlled defiance, "I am not singing in front of a human."

Nirim raised his hand diplomatically and spoke calmly, despite how ridiculous he thought she was being. "Don't sing. Just say the lines, and that will be fine."

This seemed to pacify her, and she thought for a moment before she began to recite. "It goes, 'To the second of yesterday I speak, to the first now in this time I say, the second stands before you today' . . . something . . . something . . . 'pray'? Or maybe it was 'play'?"

"Y-you—forgot it?"

She glared at him indignantly, holding her head up with pride. "Of course I didn't. I simply can't recall it at the moment."

Nirim stared down at the table to conceal his rising frustration at being so close and yet so far from whatever uncertain puzzle Miralla had rigged for him so long before. Nevertheless, he retained his calm tone. "And what is the difference between the two?"

To his surprise, Astroligin came to Animus's defense. "Animus struggles with being unable to recall information that is structured and paired with music. No one is certain why, but it seems to be tied to her iether rune. At some point, she will remember the rest of the song, but you will have to be patient."

Nirim eyed him with some skepticism. Was he joking? It sounded like an outrageous excuse. But both seerrine looked back at him with somber expressions that told him that, regrettably, they were entirely serious. Nirim sighed with exasperation and muttered a tad too loudly, "Great!"

Hinna snapped her eyes toward him and rebuked him. "Nirim, how can you say such a thing? It must be terrible to have such a mental debility!" Nirim could not hide his smile at the expression crossing Animus's face at hearing herself called mentally debilitated.

Hinna continued to lecture him about the importance of being sensitive to others, which, not surprisingly, made him want to laugh out loud, considering her complete lack of any such skill. Astroligin muttered, "Lots and lots of problems," and Nirim merely nodded.

After a few more moments, Animus interrupted Hinna. "But what does it mean?" Everyone looked at her blankly, so she repeated her question with its referent. "What does the song mean?"

Nirim thought through the rhyme she had recounted. "Well, let's see. It is a coded series of couplets designed to tell me what I should be doing. I am, or was, the second guardian, and so the first thing the song says is that I am now the first guardian."

Astroligin seemed intrigued by the notion. "And what does the second part say?"

Nirim failed to think before he started speaking this time. "The second part says that the second guardian is . . . ."

He trailed off as he sat up straight and slowly brought his gaze from Astroligin to Animus. Nirim did not like where this was going. It had to be some kind of nightmare that he would awaken from at any moment. Or maybe the Creator was punishing him for something, though this felt too bizarre for that possibility.

Animus prodded him to complete his sentence. "And the second guardian is?"

Rather than answer, he raised his left arm, and blue iether flowed brightly through his rune. There was a flicker of light, and the room filled with blue iether motes. The specks began to condense around Animus. She looked at them nervously but remained still. "What are you doing?"

Nirim spoke with a small measure of sarcasm. "Confirming my, uh, suspicions." He did not bother waiting for all the iether motes to gather, but simply dropped his arm, and they slowly faded away. "To answer your question directly, Animus, you are the second guardian."

Her eyes grew wide, and she looked more than a little worried, as Hinna and Astroligin watched the two of them carefully. Animus turned her nose upward haughtily as she said, "As if I wanted anything to do with humans and their problems!"

Nirim sighed with relief in spite of himself; it was enough trouble dealing with a sociopathic isper without adding a selectively amnesiac seerrine to his little band. He told her nonchalantly, "Well, I certainly won't force you to travel with me."

"I will!"

Her instantaneous change of attitude made him wonder if she could be the same person he had met at the gate earlier that morning. Not to mention he wanted to ask Astroligin to stop grinning like an idiot.

Hinna's voice was laden with concern. "We don't have to take her with us, do we?"

Nirim had the same question, but instead he said, "If she wants to come with us, she is welcome. Besides, we have nowhere to go until she remembers the rest of Miralla's song."

Hinna seemed a little unhappy, but said nothing more. This struck Nirim as odd; was not she the one who moments before was telling him to be nice to Animus? He looked back at Animus, who appeared to be beaming with excitement, and asked, "I don't suppose you have your father's bow?"

She nodded. "Yes, it's in my room." She gestured to the next room over. He was about to offer a sarcastic mark about something actually working out when she added, "Though, of course, I don't know how to use it."

Of course she didn't know how to use it, Nirim thought. That would make his life far too easy. There needed to be a major problem, or the world as he knew it would necessarily implode. He rose from his seat and walked toward the door. Hinna called after him, "Where are you going, Nirim?"

"For a long, solitary walk. I will be back for supper." Nirim did not particularly care that he would be missing lunch. He needed to get away from the madness.

He passed a seerrine, who eyed him suspiciously, as he descended the ramp to the courtyard below. Seeing that he was not permitted to enter the seerrine territory, and that he did not want to have to ignore the hundred or so leering looks that the seerrine around the city would give him, he made his way back down the pass into the rocky crags of the western mountains on the human side of the city. He thought it mildly humorous how eager the guards were to let him out of the city, but it was probably just his perspective that made it funny.

Nirim was at a loss. He doubted that Animus would remember anything more of Miralla's cryptic message, and he had no desire to be holed up in the stuffy seerrine fortress city. For that matter, his own thoughts and emotions were a tempest that refused to be stilled. He felt a very real sorrow that the only person who could recognize him was no longer present mentally. And he was confused concerning what role a human-despising seerrine could possibly have as a member of a human-created group designed to protect humans from an ancient evil that was clearly forgotten. Did the seerrine even remember the darkness at all?

That thought reminded him that Astroligin had spoken of a great threat to the seerrine that involved him as the solution. If the seerrine were concerned with raw iether power in terms of solving their problem, they most certainly had the wrong person. Nirim had a very narrow problem-solving skill set, and if it did not involve hordes of shades, it was likely outside his expertise.

Nirim sat on a large boulder and stared out at the arid, rocky landscape that stretched before him. In a sense, the landscape was barren, but in reality, there were hundreds of thousands of rocks of various sizes, scattered along with numerous scraggly plants, and a few animals could be seen here and there. Not unlike the current state of his mind, he thought ruefully. In a sense it was blank, but so many small things raced through his thoughts that despite the overall calm, his mind fairly overflowed with a multitude of thoughts, ideas, and most of all, questions.

Nirim tried to imagine waking up from this strange dream to find himself in his room in the imperial residence. He would eat breakfast at his leisure, then go for a walk in the courtyard orchard that had been planted a generation before his time. At lunch, he would meet up with his cousins, and they would plot their adventures for some future time when they could all get away. He would then gather with his fellow guardians for training and discussion of the latest rumors concerning the darkness and its activities. It was a life of adventure, of genuine family ties, a life where nearly everyone understood him, and communication was natural at all levels.

With a wistful sigh, he realized that part of his problem was being homesick for a home he would never see again; indeed, one that no longer existed. It was only the insanity of the far-flung journey Miralla had sent him on that prevented his own. He wondered what he would do after it was over. Being of noble birth, he lacked most of the skills necessary to earn a common living. He could live off the land, he supposed; as a guardian, he certainly knew how. The idea struck him as strange at first, but by the time he headed back toward the seerrine city for supper, he felt confident that when this was all over, whatever Miralla had involved him in, he would be quite content to live the remainder of his life as a hermit so that he could avoid the craziness that was this current world.

Actually, he was tempted to start right away, but he knew that Miralla was depending on him for some unseen task, and the last thing he wanted to do was live with the guilt that he had failed his cousin's last request, even if he was starting to question her motivations. Somehow he did not have to work at it to imagine her laughing as she watched him bumble from one awkward situation to the next.

***

Hinna stared at the door Nirim had just exited. She felt sad for him. He always seemed a little upset. She wondered if he worried too much about his past.

Animus interrupted her musings. "Hinna, how is it that both my father and Nirim were friends with this Miralla human? I mean, my father taught me that song as a child, and I am nearly fifty years of age. He can't possibly be that old, can he?"

Hinna bobbed her head. "Oh, yes. Well, that is actually easy to explain. Nirim is from a century in the past." She noted that the seerrine were watching her with a great deal of skepticism, so she reiterated. "No, really, he was stuck out of time by Miralla using iether, so now he is like a foreigner without a home, since the city that used to be the empire's capital is now a poisoned wasteland."

Animus put her hand to her mouth. "That's terrible."

Astroligin still looked a little skeptical. "He seems awfully sound for that to be the case. How long ago was it that he ended up in this time?"

Hinna started silently counting on her fingers. "Let's see, it has been . . . eight . . . now?"

Astroligin mused, "Well, I suppose such a catastrophic turn of fate could be overcome by a stable soul in that many years."

Hinna corrected him. "Oh, no. Days, not years."

The two seerrine blinked at each other in surprise, and Animus whispered in a low and concerned voice, "Should we have let him wander off on his own?"

"Probably not."

Hinna was at a loss. "What is the problem?"

Astroligin grimaced but explained hesitantly. "Well, humans are rather weak creatures, and sometimes when they suffer great loss, they do rash things, like throw themselves off a cliff, or intentionally fall on a sword."

Hinna practically leapt out of her chair. "What! He can't do that! I need him."

Astroligin chuckled. "Now, now, don't you think that's a bit of an exaggeration?" He stopped chuckling as Animus rose, too, slower but with equal gravity.

"I need him, too. Come on, Hinna, let's stop that stupid human from hurting himself!"

A seerrine messenger appeared in the doorway at that moment, and promptly leapt to the side as Animus and Hinna bolted past him. He watched them go with apprehension before he turned to Astroligin. "Sir, a message from the elders."

"And what is their verdict on the human?"

The messenger responded stiffly. "They wish to have the disgusting and vile human captured and delivered to the capital at once, so that they may determine his suitability for dealing with our problem."

Astroligin chuckled again. "Very well. Should he survive the protective forces of his female traveling companions, I am sure we can have him there by the end of the week." The messenger stared at him, mouth agape, obviously uncertain as to how he should proceed. Astroligin snapped at him, "Don't just stand there! Tell the elders we will deliver him with all due haste." The messenger nodded swiftly and disappeared through the door.

CHAPTER 9

Nirim was contemplating exactly what his solitary, single-roomed hermitage would look like when he stopped near the entrance to the long pass that would take him to the seerrine fortified city. Something was off. His sense of his surroundings told him that trouble was lurking nearby. He shifted the weight of the blade staff that remained slung across his back so that it could be in his hands in a matter of seconds. He caught rapid movement out of the corner of his eye, but he was not fast enough, nor entirely inclined, to respond with lethal force.

His feet were ripped out from under him, and he was thrown to the ground and held in place. “Hey! What are you doing!” he complained as Animus's coils wrapped unnecessarily tightly around him, pinning his arms to his side while she towered over his lowly position.

“Don’t even think about it, Nirim!”

He groaned out loud as he gasped with exasperation, “Don’t tell me you’re bringing that up again!”

Another face appeared in his vision as Hinna leaned over to look down at him. “Nirim, are you all right? Are you hurt?”

Nirim shook his head violently in the negative, and Hinna’s expression became even more frantic, but rather disconcertingly, the more he spoke, the more relieved she looked. "Of course I am not all right! I am being crushed to death by a seerrine who can't let go of the past." Animus slacked her coils and withdrew them from his person, and he inhaled a deep and grateful breath.

He scrambled to his feet and had started to dust himself off furiously when Animus asked in a worried voice, "Nirim, shouldn't we be saying that to you? What are you even talking about?"

He blinked a few times, staring at the two of them, and then, shaking his head, muttered, "Never mind. Now, why did you feel it necessary to attack me?"

Animus tipped her head to one side curiously, and Hinna explained. "We were not attacking you. We were trying to keep you from hurting yourself!"

He glanced back and forth between them for a moment, but decided he should not pursue further understanding. "Uh, thank you for your concern, but I am not in the habit of inflicting harm upon anyone, least of all myself."

He softened his tone when he realized they both looked a little put off by his comments. He gestured toward the mountains. "Come on, let's go back and get something to eat." They nodded and proceeded with him into the entrance. The location of the city was nearly ideal. The pass was the only documented way through these mountains for a great distance in either direction, and it was bounded by sheer rock faces that rose far overhead.

They had barely gotten into the pass when Nirim stopped quickly. His sensation that not all was well remained undiminished by his overly zealous companions. "What is it? What's wrong?" Animus asked, glancing around suspiciously.

Nirim faced back the way they had just come.

"Something's coming." He pulled the blade staff from behind his back and spread out his stance. He studied the rock walls. He held up his left arm, and warm blue iether light pulsed along his rune.

The rune of second sight had originally been thought to be impotent. It was rare enough that not even Spite could recall having seen one before. Its lack of power was no surprise, since iether marks were waning in the imperial family by his generation, to the point that the next generation was not expected to have any marks at all. However, in time, he had learned exactly how the rune worked and what it could do.

They had all thought the rune was powerless based on the fact that one could not see what one could not predict. The rune could not anticipate anything its user could not, and therefore it merely served as an assumption checker. Working one assumption at a time on a task where there were numerous possibilities meant it had no practical value.

Nirim had learned about its other nature, the ability to accurately quantify and calculate nearly any value. It was this function that had brought him to the attention of the guardians, and then had resulted in his becoming the second guardian. The classification was not one of power or role, but of authority. He had served the guardians as tactician, because he was the only member who could easily comprehend a situation quantitatively.

He spoke plainly for the sake of his companions. "An army is coming. Five thousand troops—one thousand archers, one thousand heavy infantry, and three thousand light infantry. There are also three large ietherized siege engines."

Hinna gasped, and Animus sounded panicked. "Army! We don't have the forces to deal with something like that here. They will sweep the city clean!"

At that same moment, the lead regiment came into view, marching toward them at a steady pace. As he saw the symbol on the banner, Nirim quipped to Animus, "I see that the friends you made among the Yorasins have come for a visit."

"If someone hadn't interfered, they wouldn't have seen us."

Hinna tugged at the back of his cloak with urgency. "Come on! Let's run. They are practically on top of us!"

Animus nodded and grabbed Hinna's hand. "You're right. We have to get out of here."

Nirim stayed still. Animus hissed angrily, "What are you doing! I can't fight that many humans. Are you crazy, or stupid?"

"I have business in this place, and I am not going to let them sack a seerrine city just because they are short on people to bully." He reached out with his left hand and touched the tip of his blade staff, and a blue iether glow raced down its length.

The commanding officer stopped his battalion a hundred paces away from where Nirim stood, unflinching, just inside the mouth of the pass. The commander eyed him warily as he called out, "Stranger, we come with orders from the king of Yorasin to clear out a nest of seerrine bandits from this heap of rock. Either move out of the way, or be counted with the enemy."

Nirim replied loudly, calmly, and resolutely. "There are no seerrine bandits here, and the seerrine that do inhabit this place are under my protection."

The commander frowned as he yelled back a little hotly, "I see you have thrown your lot in with the snake scum, but who are you that you defy the great king of Yorasin?"

Nirim debated saying nothing, but he was not

about to be dismissed passively by some petty army commander who would not know a great king if one hit him in the face. "I am Nirimialin Esternon, of the third imperial line, a guardian of the first degree, the bearer of the Flame, and the last person in this world that you want to cross."

A disconcerted ripple passed through the commander's battalion, but the man himself remained unconvinced. "Empty titles for a landless, army-less rat. Prepare to meet your Creator, fool!"

Nirim was not particularly encouraged by the comments of his companions. He heard Animus mutter in disgust, "Humans are so stupid."

Hinna voiced her affirmation of this seemingly universal sentiment. "I agree. They really are imbeciles."

He hoped that they were, by some illogicality, excluding him from such a category, because from where he stood, there was no way to tell exactly whom it was they were referring to. He pushed the annoyances to the back of his mind, and focused on the army that was now being given the command to advance toward him and cut him down.

He brought the blade staff low, with its blade nearly touching the ground. He might regret what he was about to do in the long run, but frankly, he was not going to let one more person get away with calling him a varmint today. Nirim brought the full power of the blade staff to bear, and the ground trembled slightly at the invisible rush of uncondensed iether. Nirim whipped the blade staff up sharply into a full circular arc. An impressive display of brilliant blue iether slashed so quickly that it remained unclear to anyone, other than Nirim, what was happening. The advancing troops faltered for a second, and the commander flinched visibly before he started cursing at his men for their hesitance.

Animus's voice dripped with disdain. "Nirim! How did you miss an entire army?" Hinna cowered fearfully as the menacing forces continued forward. Nirim simply smiled slightly, watching as the soldiers recovered from their moment of surprise that their enemy was a human iether wielder.

Animus shouted at him, as though she thought the increased volume was necessary to motivate him to action. "What are you trying to do, stare them to death? We need to get out of here before they start throwing iether at us!" Nirim continued to ignore her and raised his blade staff vertically, then let it slide freely through his fist to smack into the dusty rock floor of the pass with a surprisingly loud crack.

For a moment, nothing happened, and Animus had just seized Nirim's shoulder as if to forcibly drag him away, when there was a deafening rending sound, and the ground vibrated. The soldiers stopped their advance and began pointing frantically at the walls of the pass. Hinna grew pale and wide-eyed. "W-w-what did you do, Nirim?"

Nirim said nothing as he watched the effects of the calculated cut he had made through the walls of the pass. The soldiers and their commander fled like scared animals, nearly trampling the battalion that had come up behind them. The top half of both sides of the canyon walls slid free and fell into the pass at the same time, like two enormous wedges sliding smoothly into place, creating a solid rock wall that rose to about half the height of the pass. The loud rumbling noise and the tremors in the ground ceased as the slabs of rock settled.

After allowing his companions a moment to recover, Nirim turned around to look at them. Animus huffed and spoke wryly. "Don't you think completely blocking off the pass was a little excessive?"

Hinna looked more curious. "Are we stuck in the

seerrine lands now?"

Nirim smirked. "Fortunately not. Now, I believe we were on our way to dinner." He walked toward the city, waving off Animus's next question.

"And what exactly do you mean, 'fortunately'?"

***

Nirim sat at the small table inside what he now knew to be part of Animus's personal quarters. He poked at his food, a strange assortment of fish, boiled grain, and pieces of fruit, all mixed together with some kind of sour glaze. The flavor was as crazy as its source. At first, he thought that being permitted to eat in her quarters was a sign of the seerrine's favor towards him. However, he now knew it was so that he would not disturb the seerrine soldiers in the dining halls.

"So, essentially, your elders want to talk with me about solving some problem you're having with hot springs?"

Animus nodded, but Astroligin was more candid. "It's more likely that they will talk at you rather than with you. Furthermore, I can't predict how they will view your action of closing up the pass."

"I don't suppose you could just tell them that the pass spontaneously closed up of its own accord?"

Animus interrupted sharply. "Why would we do that? You are the hero of Gerialin!"

Astroligin understood, however, and stated what Nirim was thinking. "The elders may not see things that way, but instead, they might consider it an unfriendly act."

Hinna added in her typical, cheerfully unhelpful manner, "Well, it was rather unfriendly to drop a mountain's worth of rock in the direct path of an army, I suppose." She appeared oblivious of the three slightly concerned looks directed toward her.

Hinna's face brightened with excitement, and she turned to Nirim with great enthusiasm. "You didn't tell me you were actually part of the imperial family!" Animus and Astroligin looked at him with equal surprise.

Nirim realized that he had not taken all parties present into consideration when he had tried to establish a level of authority with the Yorasin commander. Then again, the seerrine probably cared little what his supposed status was, since they held humans to be hardly above forest creatures. "What does it matter that I am a member of a ruling family whose domain no longer exists?"

Animus asked with noticeably rising excitement, "Are you . . . errr . . . were you the next in line for the imperial throne?"

"No. I was from the lowest line of succession, and the formal customs for imperial succession required that the successor be a woman."

Astroligin stroked his chin as he wondered out loud, "That seems surprisingly refined. I never would have thought it of people as savage as humans."

Nirim smiled but spoke sarcastically. "Amazing, isn't it?"

Animus gave him a withering look, but Hinna spoke openly. "It is, but Nirim, if you weren't the imperial successor apparent, was it Miralla?"

"No, Miralla was from the second line of succession. It was Istallia who was the designated heir to the imperial throne."

Animus leaned back and folded her arms. "Why is it that you all have seerrine-like names?"

Nirim's tone grew warm with reminiscence as he replied. "It is a tradition to honor the great empress, who herself was part seerrine."

He looked thoughtfully at their faces but stopped when he got to Hinna's, whose expression was one of intent contemplation. He did not have to ask, since she raised her wide eyes toward his and blurted out, "You gave me the empress's clothes?!"

Nirim was trying to decide if her statement warranted a response when Animus burst in with her own shock. "You did what! Isn't that a severe breech of your simpleton cultural norms! You can't just give away such a—"

Astroligin interrupted her with some mixture of astonishment and amusement. "Animus, are you . . . ?"

She returned his interruption by profusely denying his unspoken accusation. "No, of course not. Don't be ridiculous!"

Nirim remained silent and focused on eating the remainder of his meal. Why was it so important to them? He had not given Hinna the formal imperial raiment or anything like that. Furthermore, why would it matter to Animus? She acted almost like she was jealous, but that made less sense than anything else.

Chapter 10

Nirim stood at the city gate that exited into the seerrine lands, flanked by Animus, Hinna, Astroligin, and thirty seerrine "honor guards," or so they had been called. He felt it likely that the only reason that he was not traveling bound hand and foot was because Animus held the responsibility for his safe deposit in the capital.

Animus smiled broadly at him. "Well, Nirim, this is a monumental day! You are the first human to see the other side of this city in centuries."

Nirim thought that sounded impressive, but he admitted to himself that he would rather have her remember the rest of Miralla's cryptic message than give him a firsthand tour of her people's lands.

While he was trying to pretend that he cared, Hinna was profusely ecstatic. "Can you believe it! I will actually get to see the magnificent landscape of the seerrine lands personally! It's a dream come true, like being able to visit paradise!"

Nirim did not want to cut her feet out from under her, but neither did he want her to be too disappointed. Not knowing how many more of her irrational comparisons he could tolerate, he interjected as politely as possible, "Hinna, you do know that the seerrine live in a swamp, right?"

To his surprise, she nodded emphatically. "Yes, but it's the most wonderful swamp in the world!"

He sighed, muttering, “If you say so.”

The gatekeeper opened the way, and they proceeded through into a pass similar to the one on the other side. It sloped down and took a sharp bend near another view of the rocky landscape. They made their way down the pass and rounded the corner, turning repeatedly through a series of switchbacks. Nirim chuckled.

Animus looked at him curiously. “What’s so funny?”

“Oh, it’s nothing really, just that it seemed rather ironic that the pass into the seerrine lands is snake-like.”

He found her confused look disconcerting, and he turned to Hinna for refuge, only to see that her expression was equally puzzled.

Astroligin was blunt. “I don’t think I understand.”

Nirim merely continued walking as he said, half to himself, “It doesn’t matter.”

At the last turn, Animus stopped him by grabbing his shoulder. She held out a long strip of thick cloth toward him and smiled slightly. “Humor me.”

Nirim thought that his previous attempt to humor her was failure enough, but against his better judgment, he picked up the cloth and tied it over his eyes. Hinna complained, “I don’t think this is necessary, Animus. It’s not that spectacular, is it?”

“Maybe not for you, but he has no idea what to expect.”

Nirim was led around the corner, and he could tell that the pass opened up, as he felt a gentle breeze on his face. The air was remarkably fresh, and he could smell the fragrance of some blooming flowering plant. After a few moments more, Animus stopped and faced him in a particular direction. “All right, you can take it off now.”

He removed the blindfold and looked out over the expanse that spread out before him. Animus had positioned him at the edge of a cliff that afforded an uncluttered view of a vast portion of a lush, green land. As far as he could tell, nearly all of it was exceedingly carefully curated. Everywhere his gaze rested, there were orchards, arbors, gardens, and probably other types of structured plantings that did not fall into human categories. There were no large roads, but instead, paralleled artificial waterways seemed to serve the function of major thoroughfares. Unlike the arid rocky terrain they had left behind, the entirety of the seerrine lands, at least those visible to him, was a proverbial tropical paradise. Just from where he stood on the mountainside, he could see dozens of cities, hundreds of towns, and an impressive centrally located spire that he presumed to be a landmark of the capital.

"And?" Animus's voice was nearly bursting with excitement.

Nirim met her gaze, smiling politely. "I do admit that it is breathtaking." She grinned happily at him, but her behavior was starting to make him feel uneasy. She was treating him more like a sibling than an acquaintance, and he was maintaining a secret hope that she would change her mind about being a guardian.

They took a long, steadily sloping pathway down from the cliff. Not visible from the vista above them, a series of outposts ran in both directions along the mountain range. As they approached the nearest one, they were met by a number of soldiers, confirming his suspicion that getting into their land required more than simply getting through the pass. Astroligin spoke with the soldiers, who eyed him warily as he and Hinna stood with his honor guard.

While they waited, Nirim leaned over and asked, "So, Hinna, how is it that the isper are welcomed here, and yet you aren't very familiar with this place?"

Hinna shrugged. "We isper rarely ever leave our homeland. There are few things of interest on the outside, so most have not traveled beyond their homes. To make matters worse, the few that live on the fringe between our lands and those of others are often under duress by the humans, so what I know of the seerrine lands is third-hand information at best."

"So you don't leave your homeland, because you don't leave your homeland?"

"Precisely."

He wanted to tell her that her statement was about as precise as a drunken fisherman, but thought the better of it and turned to Animus. "So what is Astroligin's position?"

She laughed. "You humans are so silly, with your preconceived notions of status based on position. We have a different system that humans could not begin to understand."

Nirim sighed in resignation. "Fine. So what does he do?"

Animus glanced back at Astroligin for some hint of progress as she answered. "He is the overseer of Gerialin and its garrison."

Nirim rolled his eyes. "Yep, completely incomprehensible to my primitive mind."

Hinna's unnecessarily happy voice only contributed to Nirim's annoyance as she said, "She did warn you that you wouldn't understand it."

Animus shook her head in disbelief. "You know, you could just leave the isper here? There is no reason for her to follow you to the capital."

Hinna paled and turned to Nirim with a ridiculously unnecessary pleading expression, whimpering, "Y-you wouldn't abandon me like that, would you, Nirim?"

He really wanted to snidely quip that the thought had never crossed his mind. He wanted to, but he knew it would be lost on her. Instead, he merely stated, "Of course not. Just as I would not abandon Animus, or Astroligin, or any traveling companion."

Hinna glanced sullenly at Animus, annoyance tainting her voice. "You didn't have to mention her." Nirim hoped that her frustration was based entirely on Animus's suggestion that she be left behind.

He was not given the opportunity to dwell upon it, as Astroligin returned just then, looking rather satisfied with himself. He announced to them all, "The guards stationed here wanted a formal missive indicating that the human was requested by the elders, but since that would delay us probably more than a day, I was able to convince them to allow our passage as long as you wear this, at least until we get to the capital. Oh, and you will need to give your weapon to someone less threatening."

Astroligin held up a heavy set of fused shackles. Nirim coughed loudly and said with some disdain, "Just fabulous!"

Hinna leaned towards him. "I don't know, Nirim. They look uncomfortable."

He supposed that screaming in frustration would not endear him to the angry-looking seerrine soldiers. He handed Hinna his blade staff and held his arms out. "You realize that treating your esteemed guest like a prisoner is bad taste, right?"

Astroligin clamped the shackles over his wrists and turned the key, locking them in place. One of the soldiers took the key from him and disappeared into the outpost. Nirim watched him go with some measure of curiosity. "Do tell me that there is another key?" he queried lightly.

Astroligin looked a bit embarrassed. "Well, no,

but he will meet us at the capital and relieve you of the shackles once the elders give their approval."

Nirim debated about stating his extreme displeasure with the situation, but it would not matter at the end of the day. No mechanical lock existed that could restrain him, so he felt like it was not worth fussing about.

They passed the outpost and entered an enormous garden complex filled with a wide array of plant life, as well as fountains and various oddities. The gardens led to a large, enclosed waterway, the walls of which were constructed of a polished white stone, and the high, gracefully arching roof was mostly made of clear glass, or what he assumed was glass. Inside the building, elongate watercraft of differing sizes and kinds were held up away from the water channels by simple but elegant mechanical winches.

He watched as a boat was lowered into the water by the winches, and then boarded by about two dozen seerrine passengers. When the craft was released, it was whisked away by the water at a speed easily twice that of a galloping horse. Across the first water channel was a second with a large, gently sloping net for scooping fast-moving boats out of the water. Unsurprisingly, the water flowed in the opposite direction in the far channel.

Astroligin muttered that he would secure them a place in line and left. Animus led them to a series of long benches that ran along the wall, and they took a seat. Their honor guards hung back, not wanting to keep too close of a company with the lowly human. Nirim thought the verdant scape quite beautiful, and he wondered how the seerrine maintained such high water velocities in their artificial water channels, but something more pressing was on his mind.

He turned to Animus, who sat on his right. "Animus, do you know anything about the darkness?"

She glanced at him and then looked back at seerrine bustling through the transit station. "Of course I know about the darkness. Do you think I could be my father's daughter and not know about it?"

"Right, sorry. I forgot about that connection for a moment."

Animus continued unbidden. "And of course, all seerrine know of the day of the second dawn."

"Day of the second dawn? And what is that?"

"That is the day that the glorious white light swept through our land in a single flash, destroying any remnant of the darkness. Even today, our land is free of the shades and fellbeasts that seemed to permeate its haunts before."

Nirim laughed out loud and leaned back against the wall. Hinna, who sat on his left, watched them, her curiosity piqued. Animus frowned at him angrily. "Laughing at treasured moments in seerrine history is a good way to find yourself at the bottom of the waterway."

Nirim shook his head and spoke softly, almost reverently. "There was a time in human history when the darkness rose to destroy us. It came so close that nearly everyone had given up any hope. But the Creator provided a single individual to rescue us from complete annihilation, one young woman with nearly limitless white iether power."

Hinna was hanging on his every word. "Who was she?" she asked breathlessly.

Nirim smiled faintly. "She became the great empress, my ancestor."

Animus looked skeptical. "Are you sure you have those details correct? It seems inconceivable that a human could possibly possess sufficient skill with white iether or a rune powerful enough to accomplish such an act."

With perhaps a little too much force, Nirim said sarcastically, "Some of us don't have a ridiculously selective amnesia."

To his surprise, she rose sharply from her seat and glared at him. "And some of us are completely insensitive dolts! If Miralla was such a great seer, she would have transmitted her message to someone who could recall it!" She turned, not waiting for a response, and headed toward Astroligin.

Nirim turned toward Hinna. "I guess she is kind of sensitive about her—"

He stopped mid-sentence when he saw Hinna's expression, somewhere between angry and sad.

She also rose and rebuked him. "You are really mean sometimes, Nirim. You need to be more sensitive to other people's feelings." She then left and joined Astroligin and Animus. Nirim sat by himself, wondering what exactly had just happened. He sighed as he reconsidered the last few moments. Technically he was not by himself; there was him and his completely unnecessary nagging feeling of guilt.

Astroligin came over to where he sat and said, "Looks like we are next. Because of the number of people we are traveling with, we will need two separate water skimmers."

"Wouldn't 'boats' be easier to say?"

Astroligin chuckled. "Not really."

They made their way to the boarding platform that jutted over the swiftly flowing water. Nirim sheepishly evaded the unpleasant glares that Hinna and Animus were aiming in his direction from where they stood at the front of the group boarding the first skimmer. Astroligin noted innocently enough, "That's odd. I would have thought they would want to ride with us."

Nirim tried to sound as neutral as possible. "Yes,

very odd indeed." Astroligin glanced at him curiously, but said nothing more.

Chapter 11

Animus sat in the forward water skimmer as the craft raced along the waterway. The water skimmer had a central aisle wide enough for two seerrine to pass each other, and two parallel rows of seats that faced inward along either side. Though she sat across from Hinna, she was lost in thought as she watched the scenery whip by.

Nirim was both incredible and impossible at the same time. He was remarkably humble about his abilities and his origin, almost as though he were unaware of the amazing power he possessed. Furthermore, she could hardly imagine why he had failed to tell them outright that he was from the imperial family. It made her extremely jealous that this unassuming human was someone of such import.

Even though she had been born into a relatively renowned family line, her own deficiency related to her rune had ensured that she would never be more than a low-ranking captain of a special operations squad. Much of seerrine culture was paired with song, and all of it remained elusive to her, in terms of the kinds of oral tests that were a component of societal advancement. She did have the advantage of her rune being highly functional as a weapon, but this was of almost no benefit among her own people.

Nirim was her only hope for retaining the honor of her family name. If he proved capable of rescuing her people, it would be she that would be remembered as the one who brought about such a historic deliverance. She felt a strange affinity for Nirim, and she could not decide if that was revolting or wonderful. The more she learned about him, the more concerned she became that he would consider her so far below him that she would be but an annoyance to him. Her fears were compounded by the fact that her same deficiency was hindering Nirim in his completely nonsensical quest. That he would flaunt her weakness so flagrantly hurt and angered her. Yet while she wanted to stay mad at him, she was already regretting getting in the first boat.

She sighed and asked across the skimmer, "Hinna, why are you following Nirim around?"

Hinna perked up and responded firmly. "Because he is my source of human history, something of which there is a dearth among the isper libraries."

"So you're a scholar?"

"Yes. Technically, I am a records keeper of the second degree, but until I publish a great work in my discipline, I will not receive any recognition for my title."

Animus broached her next question as casually as she could. "You wouldn't say that you are . . . uh . . . attracted to him at all, would you?"

Hinna laughed and shook her head. "Oh, no, not at all. I mean, he is of imperial lineage from a time at the pinnacle of human society, and he is surprisingly nice for a human. Thoughtful most of the time, generally sensitive, strong, handsome . . . ."

Hinna's voice trailed off, and she looked away quickly, a slight rosy color rising in her cheeks. Animus watched her with a wry smile but said nothing.

After a moment, Hinna added, "Whatever else

he is, he is still just a primitive human, so I guess I would compare him to a nice dog. No matter how endearing he might be, he is still a dog at the end of the day."

Animus chuckled. "I suppose that is true. What do you say that we agree to help one another avoid his sinister charms?"

Hinna gave her a mischievous grin. "That sounds like an excellent idea."

***

Nirim sat across from Astroligin as they rushed along the waterway. Though they sat slightly below ground level, he still caught glimpses of large, majestic trees and equally impressive buildings. At several places they passed through villages where some structures were built over the waterway, with what amounted to sidings where they could exit the waterway if they desired. However, he was mostly distracted by his thoughts on what Animus had said.

He had not stopped to consider it, but it was true that Miralla would not necessarily have been aware of the nature of the person who would deliver the message that she had given to Spite. Miralla had never really explained the extent of her abilities to see the future, nor was there any precedent to go on; she had been the first formal seer in the empire's history. He knew there was some link to the great mystic Alurim Conder, whose family had long held the secrets of the rune of time, but most of that knowledge had been lost by the time the great empress ruled the empire.

As far as he knew, Miralla's perception of things yet future was not directly tied to her iether runes. Miralla was born with the blue iether rune of rest, and she had been inscribed with the red iether rune of healing, which was a practical rune like his own. None of this information provided him the answer to Animus's perceptive question—unless the whole thing was an elaborate joke at his expense. He shook his head unconsciously. While Miralla loved a good joke, he felt that his current mission had to be something far more important.

Astroligin interrupted his ponderings by asking smugly, "There is no faster, smoother way to travel than the seerrine waterways, wouldn't you agree?"

Nirim brought his thoughts back to the present. "I would say it is much faster than traveling by horseback or carriage, but it's substantially slower than traveling by trackkus." Nirim saw Astroligin's questioning look and provided a brief explanation. "The trackkus system was developed by the human empire. It harnessed the power of blue iether to propel a series of metal carriages along a metal-clad stone dike. It could reach incredible speeds."

"And here I thought the only thing humans used blue iether for was slaughtering people."

"Well, I can't speak for all humans, but the empire used it for a wide array of things that did not involve weapons."

Nirim glanced at the boat in front of them and caught Animus and Hinna watching him with what he considered to be disconcerting expressions on their faces. They both looked quickly back at one another, and then broke out into spontaneous laughter. He turned toward Astroligin. "I don't suppose you could convince a seerrine warrior and an isper historian to stay here with you?" Astroligin chuckled, shaking his head.

Nirim sighed and changed the subject to something only slightly related. "Why is Animus so sensitive about her memory issues?"

Astroligin's face became serious, and he spoke

grimly. "It is the thing that holds her back from rising above obscurity, as her family's name practically demands."

Nirim raised his hand, as though presenting his confusion physically. "But why? It seems like such a bizarre and tangential problem."

"Animus has the makings of a truly great seerrine, but one of the qualifications for advancement in our society is the memorization of the ritual songs that tell our history, and since Animus is unable to remember that type of information on command, she is stuck in her current position. Should she become paired with a mate, her family's name would be lost forever."

From Astroligin's tone and expression, Nirim suspected that this was like a fate worse than death for a seerrine, even if it would not make much of a difference in human culture. Nirim tried to follow Hinna's advice and be sensitive of the seerrine's seemingly pointless cultural requirements. He asked gently, "That seems a little harsh. Couldn't her mate simply take her name instead of her taking his?"

His companion shook his head firmly. "No. Our laws require that the family name of the individual with higher standing remains, while that of the lower standing is struck from the record of extant families."

Nirim looked back at the scenery as he murmured, "That seems rather sad."

Astroligin agreed softly as he joined Nirim in watching the terrain fly past. "Yes, yes, it is."

Nirim was glad that the seerrine missed his double meaning. It was sad for Animus that she faced an unsolvable problem, but it was far sadder that their culture was so inflexible that no obvious solution existed. He contemplated if there were aspects of his own culture that caused similar types of problems. He grimaced as he remembered that from the seerrine perspective, human culture was barely recognizable as culture at all.

They rode on silently for hours, and soon the sun began to set. Nirim wondered if they were close to the capital yet. The boat in front of them shifted to a side channel, and theirs followed. They rapidly slowed down and came to a stop by a small village.

Nirim looked at Astroligin in curiosity. The seerrine explained as he gestured toward the lights of the city. "This is Frialddimire. It lies about halfway between Gerialin and our destination of the central city, Kristigia. We will stay here tonight and leave first thing tomorrow." He helped Nirim stand, and they disembarked and made their way up a ramp that led to the street level of the village.

They traveled down the main street to a large, three-story building. A relatively regal seerrine appeared at the door, and Astroligin began to converse with him, with no small amount of pointing toward Nirim.

Nirim could not hear their conversation from where he stood with the others, but he had another matter to handle. He turned to Animus and bowed politely. "Please forgive me, Animus. I spoke unkindly to you earlier, and it was wrong of me to do so."

When he returned to an upright position, Animus was staring at him wide-eyed and speechless. After an awkward moment, he returned to watching Astroligin, trying to decide if she was scared, angry, frustrated, or perhaps offended.

He glanced back when he heard Hinna making vaguely dog-like noises. Animus muttered, "Thanks," as she looked intently at the ground.

Nirim merely nodded, ostensibly waiting for the two seerrine at the door to finish their conversation, but he was once again unsettled by the degree to which his traveling companions made absolutely no sense. Was apologizing something forbidden in seerrine culture? But if so, what would happen if he apologized for apologizing? Would it be an infinite, self-canceling loop that would culminate in his personal annihilation?

A chill ran down his spine, and he trembled unconsciously for a second as he considered the possibility that this continued irrationalism was eating away at the soundness of his mind. Perhaps it was only a matter of time before he, too, started barking like a dog, and thinking of humans as despicable creatures not worth the food it takes to keep one.

Astroligin returned to their group and communicated the situation. “Nirim, this is a warriors’ barracks. They will provide us with food and lodging, but they refuse to allow a filthy human to sleep in the same room, so you will be assigned a spot in the loft.” Nirim did not even bother responding; it would not alter anything. Astroligin led them inside, and his “honor guard” dispersed into the building, while they continued to a table at one end of the large dining area.

They sat down, and a young seerrine woman served them individually. She set a large bowl of some kind of soup in front of Nirim. It looked like it contained fruit, and maybe dumplings. Nirim was not impressed. It was tangy, and sweet, and had a strange bitter aftertaste that made him thirsty.

Hinna asked Astroligin about the village and the area surrounding it, and Astroligin explained that the area was a central orchard, but this particular village was known for its production of medicinal plants. Nirim only half-listened as he began to remove from his soup the small red flower buds that were the source of the bitterness. He was halfway through his meal when Astroligin stopped mid-sentence to stare at him and the small pile of red buds next to Nirim’s bowl. The seerrine asked breathlessly, “Where did those come from!”

Nirim groaned internally as he realized he was probably badly violating some unspoken etiquette. He tried for a smooth recovery. "I am sorry, Astroligin, but they are terribly bitter to me, so I had to take them out of the soup."

Astroligin appeared on the verge of panic, so Nirim brought his hands up apologetically as he said quickly, "You can have them if you want. I only ate a few." He noticed that Animus had turned white as a sheet, and for a moment, he wondered at just how twisted their culture must be.

Astroligin spoke gravely. "Nirim, I hate to be the one to tell you this, but those are blood rose buds, and they are among the most poisonous plants that grow in our lands. If the Creator has mercy on you, you will live for another hour, but if not, your heart will explode in a matter of minutes."

Hinna bolted from her chair and threw her arms around Nirim. "Please don't die, Nirim!"

He glanced at Animus and noted that her face looked wet. "Why would someone poison me?"

Astroligin answered in a low voice. "Because there are some who disagree with the elders that the solution to our problem is human."

Nirim shrugged and ate another spoonful of his soup. Animus yelled at him in what bordered on despair. "Are you crazy! Didn't you hear him say that stuff is going to kill you already!"

He thought about taking another bite of the soup, whose flavor was starting to grow on him, but he decided that would just be cruel. He put the spoon down and raised his arms as best as he could, with Hinna still holding to him tightly. He paused as red iether filled the otherwise invisible rune on the surface of his right arm. "Those of us who have drawn upon the red iether cannot be harmed by either poison or disease, as the iether purges it from the blood, even when not directly drawn."

Astroligin sighed heavily with relief, but continued to eye him warily for signs of poisoning. Animus buried her face in her hands and muttered loudly, "You're really mean, Nirim."

After a long pause, she made a sound almost like a dog whimpering, and Hinna let go of him and kicked him in the leg. He jerked back sharply at the pain. "What was that for?" She said nothing but returned to her seat next to Animus. He looked at Astroligin for guidance, but the seerrine simply shrugged.

They ate the rest of their meal in silence. Or rather, everyone else ate. Nirim merely watched, as they took his bowl away from him as a precautionary measure. Starving him to protect him from being poisoned was a lousy way of delaying the inevitable, in his opinion.

After their meal, he was brought to what was essentially an attic that was half the height of a normal room. The long, narrow space had nothing in it but a simple stack of fresh blankets that he presumed to be his bed. Nirim turned to thank Astroligin for such wonderful accommodations, but the seerrine had already descended to the floor below. He made his way to the makeshift mattress and laid down on it. It did little to hide the hard floor beneath it, but he had to admit it was far better than sleeping out on the ground. He thought briefly that he should check the stack of blankets for a hidden dagger or some other such trap, but then he remembered that it was Animus who had retrieved them for him, so it was slightly less likely to be so rigged.

Nirim sighed slowly as he relaxed. In some ways he was glad for his isolated sleeping arrangement. It afforded him peace and quiet, freedom from his shackles. Not the physical ones, of course, but the seerrine and the isper. Animus was odd, and Hinna was odder. He did not want to admit it, but it seemed like they were working together against him. But for what reason, he could not even imagine. It was like they wanted him as an entity, but they did not want him as a person. He shook his head as he closed his eyes. Maybe he was just imagining things.

He let his mind wander to his days with the other guardians. Spite was first guardian, and their bowman, while he had been second guardian, holding dual roles as tactician and scout. The third guardian, Friska, was a kobay who served as their primary front-line fighter. The fourth and last guardian was Ista's brother Rim, who was a multi-role fighter.

Nirim considered himself a poor replacement for Spite in terms of leadership, and he had no idea what to think of Animus as a replacement for himself as second guardian. He wondered who the other two would be. As he drifted off to sleep, he pushed the thought away, lest he be plunged into despair by the contrast between his imagined ideal and, in all likelihood, the highly dysfunctional reality.

Chapter 12

Nirim woke with the rising sun, partially from sleeping in a new place, and partially from a soft, regular noise that was not annoying, but certainly unfamiliar. He turned his head to one side and opened his eyes. He blinked, bleary-eyed, at what looked like an elongate lump between him and the ramp leading to the lower levels. He sat up, rubbing the sleep from his eyes.

A faint smile ran across his face as he realized Animus and Hinna were sleeping in his little accommodations as well. He momentarily wondered what had possessed them to join him, but it was likely that he did not really want to know. His lack of a desire to know their reasoning did not stop him from rapidly learning it, as a voice behind him commented, "They were worried that an assassin might try to sneak up here and kill you in your sleep, so they chose to stay up here and watch you through the night."

Nirim grinned and shook his head as he turned to face Astroligin, noting the seerrine's sleeping mat on the other side of his own. "And were you also deeply worried about my safety?"

Astroligin shrugged. "No. There was substantial concern that something lewd, and likely non-consensual, would occur if you were left unattended. Hence, I am your chaperone."

Nirim frowned as he looked back at the other

two, who were beginning to stir, and muttered, "Nothing like being treated like a base animal to make you feel especially welcome."

Soon they were all awake, and grabbed a quick breakfast before they made their way to the boats. While they were climbing aboard, Astroligin spoke solemnly to Nirim. "I did a little digging, but I was not able to discover who poisoned your food. I do not believe it is one of your honor guard, but you must be careful. Your continued survival means they failed this attempt, but I doubt they will give up."

Nirim thought ruefully that Astroligin's use of the singular made it clear that he was the only person who had anything to be worried about. On the skimmer, Hinna and Animus sat on either side of him, and Astroligin sat across the way. Soon they were back out in the waterway, zipping along with the swift current.

Nirim asked Animus with mild humor, "So dare I ask how long you actually stayed awake protecting me?"

Her cheeks reddened slightly as she tried to look dignified. "We watched over you deep into the night."

Hinna chimed in with what he assumed was supposed to be as serious a tone as Animus's, but it failed, and her words came across as comical. "Yes, we must have stayed up for at least an hour!"

"Hinna! It had to be much longer than that. It certainly felt like an eternity watching him sleep like a rock."

Astroligin brought in his superior knowledge. "It was almost exactly an hour and ten minutes."

Nirim laughed. "It's a good thing seerrine assassins don't work night shifts." Animus and Hinna gave him sullen looks, but Astroligin smiled.

Nirim changed the direction of their conversation. "Tell me more about this problem I am supposed to solve."

Astroligin sighed and leaned back, closing his eyes as he spoke reflectively. "For as long as the seerrine have inhabited this valley, the climate has always been stable, warm, and wet. This is primarily due to the incredible network of hot springs that runs extensively through most of our land. Places where the springs do not run, we built channels to maintain the same climate artificially. For many years now, some have suggested that these hot springs have been cooling. At first, a number of explanations were put forward, and it was generally accepted that this was temporary, exaggerated, or even imagined. However, the problem has accelerated in recent years, and now it threatens to undo our very way of life. Without the hot springs, the temperature will drop severely, likely below the point of freezing, if the effects at the far reaches of our lands are any indication of what lies in store for us. We will be forced to move, probably into the human lands, which would be the worst calamity our race has ever faced."

Nirim refrained from smiling at the way Astroligin insinuated that the bad part of the whole situation was the one involving humans. He gestured broadly to include the passing surroundings. "What exactly do the elders expect me to do about the cooling of hot springs?"

"They expect you to stop it, and possibly reverse it."

"And how do they expect me to accomplish such a feat?"

Astroligin met his gaze soberly. "I have no idea."

Nirim muttered, "Well, then, that makes two of us."

Animus studied their faces for a moment. "So what makes the hot springs hot? Can't you just make them hot again?"

Nirim shook his head slowly. "Such a phenomenon did not exist in the empire, and my abilities do not include anything related to heating large amounts of water."

Animus frowned, but Hinna spoke up calmly. "Hot springs are usually heated deep underground by magma flows and rise to the surface, often under pressure and at high temperatures as a consequence of their proximity to the heat."

The others stared at her with mild disbelief, and Nirim found himself surprised that she had contributed something meaningful to the conversation. Astroligin asked with curiosity, "Magma?"

"Magma is essentially rock heated and pressurized to the point that it is a liquid. It occurs deep underground in various places around the world, or at the surface inside of volcanoes."

Fearing what she might answer, Nirim asked hesitantly, "How deep?"

Hinna looked up at the sky as though she were calculating the answer to his question. "Well, if I am understanding things correctly, it would be farther down than most mountains are up."

Nirim rolled his eyes as he sighed. "I was afraid you were going to say something like that."

"Why is that?"

"Because it means that what the seerrine are asking of me cannot be done. Even if I had the power to fix the problem, it would take years to dig down there to even find out what the problem is. And what if I were to get down there and find out that the magma flow was cooling? Would anyone know how they are heated, or how they could be reheated? It seems to me that it's no more fixable than a lightning strike or a hurricane."

Astroligin frowned. "If that is the case, things

may end badly for you."

Nirim looked at him wryly, arching one eyebrow. "And they haven't already? I am in chains, without my weapon, and someone has attempted to take my life. Time does not permit me to list everything else that could be lumped into being removed from everything I once knew in an instant." No one said a word more, and Nirim was glad for it. The thoughts made him want to simply give up on helping anyone and start his career as a hermit immediately.

The rest of the trip occurred mostly in silence, and without event. As the spire rose up into the horizon ahead of them, they entered a lighted, covered portion of the waterway that led into a large complex, and, to Nirim, a bewilderingly confusing routing hub where numerous waterways converged. There were boats and seerrine everywhere, and a number of docks for mooring the strange elongate craft. Nirim wondered how anyone knew what they were doing, among all of what looked to him to be a convoluted mess from which there was no escape.

They disembarked, and he was led to another type of waterway that was much shallower, and ran in a barely elevated stone aqueduct. They boarded a boat that was similar in shape to the others, but flatter and thinner. This other waterway afforded a good view of its surroundings and traveled at about half the speed of the larger ones.

Nirim watched with a sense of wonder as majestic buildings and intricate structures flew by while they wound their way through the city on the canal. Nirim turned to Astroligin. "So what is the spire in the center of the city?"

Astroligin watched as they rapidly approached the object in question. "It is the spire of unity that was built to commemorate the unification of the seerrine tribes. It is the site of our government's operations, and our current destination." Nirim hoped that the magnificent yet imposing structure was not a harbinger of what he would face before the seerrine elders.

They arrived at another docking area that was near the spire, but underneath a large, complex building that seemed to completely surround the spire. Once again they disembarked, and once again he was led up a long ramp into a spacious atrium with vaulted ceilings and prismatic skylights that filled the area with soft, multi-hued light. They were met halfway through the area by a contingent of formally dressed seerrine soldiers, and someone whom Nirim could only guess was some kind of government official.

The official glanced at him with disdain, and then addressed Astroligin. "The elders are convening now in preparation for dealing with . . . it." The official did not wait for any response, instead saying, "This way, please," while turning and moving toward one of the many exits to the large room. The guards with him formed a circle around them.

Nirim found it mildly funny that they wanted a really powerful human to help them with their problems, but this seemed to equate him with being a really dangerous criminal. He wondered if there was some disconnect in their minds concerning the power it would take to solve their problem, and how many seerrine guards it would take to keep him from going on a deadly rampage. Then again, he had to remember that none of the seerrine possessed weaponizable iether runes.

There were, of course, a few of them who found some means of using their runes in a roundabout way that was essentially a weapon, such as Animus's amplification of sound. But they would not necessarily connect his iether power with his potential to do them harm. This was in stark contrast with the way the humans in general, and even he, generally measured iether power.

None of this changed the fact that he lacked the power they were looking for; they just did not know it yet. His hands were beginning to sweat as he considered that the seerrine elders were not going to be happy when they discovered this for themselves.

He was led down a hall and through a series of rooms before they entered an antechamber to the expansive, crescent-shaped, tiered council room. The council room sloped from the second level at the back to a dais that was set below level at the front of the room. He could see the elders, who appeared to number over fifty, through the glass-paneled wall of the antechamber.

The official stopped and turned to Nirim. “This is how the meeting will proceed, human. We will take our place on the dais, and they will address me, and I in turn will address you. You, for your part, will speak only to me, as it would be grossly inappropriate for a seerrine elder to speak to the likes of you.”

Much to the official’s obvious surprise, Nirim bowed politely and said calmly, “As you wish.”

The official turned to his traveling companions and honor guard, and with a wave of his hand, said, “You are dismissed.”

Astroligin looked a little reluctant, and Animus more so, but they proceeded toward the exit. Hinna did not move, and her face looked resolute as she gripped the inconspicuously cloth-wrapped blade staff tightly. Animus, realizing that she was not coming, took her hand, urging her to follow them. “Let’s go, Hinna. We will see him afterwards.”

Nirim had no doubt she would not budge without his intervention, so he addressed her softly. “Please, Hinna, they don’t understand about us. You need to go with the others.”

He regretted his phrasing the moment he spoke, as it engendered a wrathful look from Animus, and one of sheer revulsion from the seerrine official. Hinna, for her part, only smiled faintly at his reassurance and left with Astroligin and Animus. So it was in a state of unsettledness from his verbal blunder that Nirim watched two attendants open the large double door to the spacious meeting room. The official cleared his throat loudly, and Nirim followed him into the room and out onto the dais.

Nirim was annoyed by the seerrine official's less-than-flattering introduction for him, but years of training allowed him to retain a calm composure.

"I present today for your discussion, a disgusting and despicable human who, certainly by no effort of its own, possesses the power of the iether. Now lay upon his frail soul whatever charge you may."

Nirim wondered if that was supposed to be a call for questions, or a challenge for them to attempt to ruin said "frail soul."

One of the elders, who appeared to be rather respected based on his central positioning, asked calmly, "What is its name?"

The official turned to him and nearly demanded, "What is your name, human?"

Nirim sighed internally; this was clearly going to take the entirety of the day. But if there was anything he had learned from his position as a member of the imperial household, it was that one had to play by the formal rules if any ground was to be gained. He answered the official. "I am Nirim—"

The official swiveled away from him before he could even give the full part of his first name. "It goes by the name 'Nirim,' Elder Roshivalin."

Another elder raised her hand and, apparently ignoring the fact that he had a name, asked pointedly,

"What kind of white iether rune does it possess?"

The official turned to Nirim and repeated the question in his demanding tone. Nirim replied levelly, "I do not possess a white iether rune, but rather a blue—"

He was cut off again, but not by the official. The elders gathered before him broke out into various forms of incredulous gasps and began to argue among themselves.

"What good is the horrid creature to us if he lacks the white iether?"

"We have no shortage of blue iether wielders! What help can it possibly be?"

The elder that had addressed him initially rose, and the room instantly went silent. He fixed his gaze directly on Nirim. "Human, your power is of no use to us in our plight, and it was a mistake to have you brought here. We would release you back into your own lands, but we cannot let your despicable crimes go unpunished."

Nirim leaned toward the official and asked cautiously, "Crimes?"

The elder did not wait for the message to be relayed, though he certainly appeared surprised that the human, of all people, was the only one maintaining proper decorum. "We have heard from our agent of your vileness, and the disgusting form of slavery that you have forced upon the innocent isper girl."

Before Nirim could recover from his outrage at such serious charges against his character, the seerrine guards that had escorted him to the room appeared out of nowhere and hauled him forcefully away. They promptly clamped a strange casing on his left arm and carried him roughly through a side door and down several ramps. He was hurled none too gently into one of a row of metal-barred confinement cells. The official watched him rise to his feet, calmly brushing himself off.

After a moment, the official spoke with renewed disdain, "Prepare yourself to meet the Creator, human. You will be executed for your crimes at the end of the week." With that, he and the guards left him there to contemplate his fate.

Nirim looked up and down the row of cells, noting that he was alone. Apparently few seerrine were troublesome enough to end up awaiting execution. He looked down at the metal object that had been locked onto his left arm. It was heavily studded with the black stones that the empire referred to as ward stone. Ward stone completely sapped iether when it was drawn, rendering iether useless when the ward stone was present in sufficient quantity. The rune of second sight was probably not going to help him in this state. It only made sense that in a society where everyone had some inborn iether power, it would be necessary to subdue the unruly or insane.

In some ways, he was relieved that he had not had to let the seerrine down by informing them he could not do what they requested of him. Opposing his feeling of relief was one of frustration that someone had apparently been telling tall tales about him, and the list of suspects was rather small. He sat on the floor, leaned back against the metal bars, and let his anger fade away. It was hard to be genuinely angry at Animus for merely propagating and expanding the rumors that he himself had started.

A seerrine guard passed by, glanced at him, and shuddered before continuing his route. Nirim watched and waited. He would need to memorize their movements if he were to escape before the execution day. He tried not to think about how incredibly hard it would be to evade detection in a land where he was nearly the only biped. Worse, he had to find Animus if he was to have any hope of retrieving the rest of

Miralla's stupid song. For a moment, he again considered that his cousin could be paying him back for some joke when they were young, though this made little sense, if for no other reason than it was far and away more drastic than anything he had ever done at her expense.

Nirim looked down at his shackles and the iether-blocking device on his arm. The escape plan he had in mind was dependent on the device having a short range; otherwise, he was not going anywhere. The more he thought about it, the more it dawned on him that his life was also dependent on the same reality. Should the iether block drain the red iether of the flux rune, it could easily kill him. A small test would be in order, but he would have to wait till he had a better grasp of the guards' schedules. So Nirim waited, finding that the peace and quiet was rather pleasant, even if the looming threat of death was not.

Chapter 13

Hinna sat, waiting as patiently as possible, staring out the full-length window at the busy circular courtyard below. Animus moved up and down the room nervously, and Astroligin perched in the corner of the room, contemplative but tense. He had dismissed their honor guard to the central city's barracks for rest and food, so it was just the three of them in one of the private lounges for guests at the unity spire.

Animus muttered out loud, "What is taking them so long!"

Astroligin looked at her curiously. "Do be calm, my friend. You know how they like to deliberate." She relaxed a little, but only temporarily. Hinna had noticed that she had been angrier than normal following Nirim's request that she acquiesce to the seerrine official. Though she could not conceive of why, she still felt somehow responsible for Animus's bad mood.

She had been traveling with them long enough that she had detected in them the animosity that she frequently inspired in others, a rather strange phenomenon that meant she had never formed close friendships. None of the books on relationships or social functioning that she read seemed to explain why people got so upset with her. Her job as a records keeper had benefited from it, since she could work without the distractions of social interaction. However, she would be dishonest not to admit she disliked the loneliness this incurred.

Despite his deficiencies, being a human and all, Nirim was different. He never seemed to be angry with her, though he did often look bewildered, like a lost puppy. She smiled reflexively as she thought of him as a domesticated pet. The image suited him. He was kind, noble, loyal, and mostly all bark and no bite. She caught Astroligin's eye on her and rapidly forced the thoughts out of her head, fervently hoping he could not read her mind.

After several more minutes of watching Animus wear a hole in the floor, Astroligin suggested, "Let's go get something to eat."

Animus frowned, like she was not interested in food, and Hinna did not want to be away when the verdict concerning Nirim was handed down, but it did seem better than sitting around doing nothing. Hinna stood up, and Animus sighed. "Fine. Let's go."

They followed Astroligin through the maze-like interior of the spire's lower levels to emerge onto a brick courtyard that opened up onto a public thoroughfare. He led them down the street, past shops and garden terraces. Everywhere there were carefully manicured plants of all kinds. They stopped under an enormous tree whose branches spread out over most of the width of the side street. A small shop was built around the tree, and Hinna and Animus sat at one of the outdoor tables while Astroligin went to purchase their food. Hinna watched the modestly busy street absentmindedly.

After a couple moments, Animus asked, "Hinna, is there anything about you and Nirim you haven't told me yet?"

Hinna reflected for a moment. "Why, yes, there probably are a few things."

Animus's eyes narrowed. "Oh? Do tell."

"Well, I suppose you don't know about all the times we slept together, or . . ."

"WHAT!?"

Those nearby looked sharply in their direction, and Animus lowered her voice as she blushed slightly from her undue outburst. "Hinna, please tell me that isn't appropriate for isper culture?"

Hinna stared at her, feeling very confused. "Don't most traveling groups sleep together? I mean, didn't we sleep with him when we were trying to protect him from potential assassins?"

"Oh, right. Ha, ha, sorry about that."

"Why? What did you think I meant?"

Animus's face turned beet red, and she did not raise her eyes from intently studying the tabletop. "N-never mind. I, uhhh, must have misheard you. So was there anything else you were going to say?"

Hinna watched her with some concern. She had no desire to upset her seerrine traveling companion any further, but she continued slowly, "As I was saying, he also rescued me from some human soldiers who had captured me and were threatening to make me a slave. But other than that, I can't think of anything that I haven't told you." Animus appeared to be mulling this over, and Hinna took the opportunity to ask her own question. "Animus, why are you mad at me?"

Animus straightened in surprise. "Mad at you? Hinna, I am not mad at you. It's just that Nirim is so frustrating."

Hinna returned to watching the bustling streets. "I don't find him frustrating exactly, but he is hard to understand."

Animus added, almost to herself, "Nirim isn't the only person who is hard to understand."

"Oh? You've known other people who are hard

to understand?"

Animus sighed. "You have no idea."

Feeling a little lost with their conversation, Hinna shrugged. "No, I guess I don't."

She wanted to ask more about the other people who were hard to understand, but Astroligin returned with ample quantities of bread and fresh fruit. While they ate, Astroligin noted almost as an aside, "Did you ladies hear some crazy woman screaming a few moments ago?"

Animus rolled her eyes. "Wow, who would do such a thing?"

Hinna paused, food in hand. "But, Animus, weren't you the only one screaming?"

Animus buried her face in her hands under Astroligin's suspicious gaze as she muttered, "You know, Hinna, not every question demands an immediate and specific answer."

Hinna frowned. "Yes, I have heard of this, the rhetorical question."

"But?" Astroligin prompted.

Hinna felt surprised at his perception. "But I can never tell when people use them."

Astroligin smiled at her. "Hinna, did you know people speak in a wide array of different tones to indicate what they are feeling, or how they intend for you to understand their statements?"

Hinna ran the idea through her mind, but came up with no examples. "No, no, I don't think they do. I have never heard anything of the sort."

Astroligin was undaunted. "Yes, they do. You are unable to hear it."

Hinna bit her lip, considering the ramifications of what the seerrine was saying. "I guess that could explain why people get so angry around me, but I am not sure I believe it, and even if I did, there is nothing I can do about it."

Animus asked Astroligin, "How can you be so sure that's the problem here? How would you even know that?"

"I know because I had a close friend who had a similar problem. She was completely deaf to the tonal variations in speech, forever unable to hear people's emotions in their voices."

Animus stared at him. "That's terrible. How could such a person even function in regular society?"

Astroligin looked back at Hinna soberly. "Typically they can't. They remain on the fringe, drifting like a leaf in a stream."

Hinna felt a swirl of emotion she struggled to identify, but she merely smiled and shrugged. "We isper are generally more emotionally reserved than the other races, so I may not have many friends, but I am hardly a social outcast." Astroligin was about to say something further, but he stopped, staring down the street behind Hinna. He rapidly rose, excusing himself and darting off.

Animus turned in her direction and said sheepishly, "I am sorry, Hinna. I didn't know you had such a problem. I just thought you were, well, insensitive."

"Thank you, but I don't really have a problem—maybe only a little. My people don't have problems, at least not most of us . . . ."

She trailed off, looking down at the crumbs that remained of her food. Was it truly she who had the problem? Astroligin may not have meant it, but he had just turned her whole world upside down. It was like thinking everyone was a bully, only to realize it was you who bullied everyone else. Worse, she knew well that her people so rarely suffered from inborn maladies that it was considered a mark of the Creator's disfavor to have one. Still, she supposed it did not really change anything, other than to clarify one of the nagging oddities in her life.

The more she thought about it, the more her supposition failed to hold water. She began to feel self-conscious just thinking about it. Would she have to second guess everything anyone said? Should she ask people to tell her what they meant when they said anything? But who could carry on a conversation like that? Maybe she would never talk to anyone—yet that was no solution at all. Her troubled thoughts were interrupted by Astroligin's return.

He looked stern and grim. Animus asked him, "Was that the intermediary for Nirim's meeting with the elders?"

Astroligin nodded his head but said nothing. Hinna prodded, "It's bad news, isn't it?"

"Unfortunately, yes."

Animus rose quickly. "Okay, what did that dolt do now?"

"It started with a miscommunication, it seems. The elders were looking for a human who could wield white iether, but Nirim is not such a one. They were decidedly displeased when they learned this while he was on the stand."

Animus threw her arms up in the air in exaggerated disgust. "Great! He has singlehandedly ruined my life!"

Hinna studied her carefully, trying to gauge what she meant, and offered gently, "Don't you think that is a little harsh?"

Astroligin did not laugh, however, and Animus gave him a concerned look before he continued. "It seems yours isn't the only one. They decried his criminal behavior that they received word of in the official report, and sentenced him to death."

Hinna jumped up. "What! Now he has ruined

my life too!"

Astroligin raised an eyebrow at them both. "Sit down, you two. Nobody's life is ruined. Yet." Hinna and Animus sat promptly.

"You are probably not going to be welcome back in the city for this, but obviously we can't let them just kill him, especially not considering the charges."

Hinna nodded. "Yes, what charges were brought up against him that they decided he needed to be executed?"

Astroligin paused briefly before responding. "Apparently he was accused of acting indecently toward one of his traveling companions, as well as being described as villainous scum."

Animus shook her head in disbelief. "But who would—?" Her eyes grew wide, and she said, with no attempt to conceal her regret, "Oops!"

Astroligin rolled his eyes. "You could say that again."

Animus covered her face with her hands. "I am such an idiot! I knew I shouldn't have been so generous with my elaboration of the situation, but I—"

"You can beat yourself up over it later. Right now, we need to devise a way to get one filthy human out of the city's prisons, and, for that matter, smuggled out of the seerrine lands."

Hinna tried to understand his statement. "Are the prisons that dirty?"

Animus and Astroligin simply stared at her, and she hunched her shoulders sheepishly and whispered, "Sorry."

All three of them burst into laughter. Hinna did not know how, or entirely why, but she felt confident that they would rescue Nirim from his intended fate.

Chapter 14

Nirim lay on the floor of his cell with his eyes closed, thinking through his options. He had the guard rotation memorized, and he knew where the nearest exit was. He knew that he needed to ascend a certain number of floors to reach his previous location, but he was at a loss as to where he would find his friends. Would they still be in the spire? Would they be staying nearby? He wondered if they had even heard of his plight; for that matter, the cynical side of him could not help but wonder if they cared.

He tried not to think negatively as he focused on the more immediate problem. The fused metal shackles on his wrists made it difficult to sustain enough red iether to manipulate the locks because it forced his red iether rune to be close to the iether-draining ward stones on the contraption attached to his left arm. He figured that he should be able to open the cell door, but there was nothing he could do for the shackles. He muttered to himself, “And that won’t make me look suspicious!”

The guard passed by, and the moment he vanished, Nirim leapt to his feet. The guard would be gone for a minimum of fifteen minutes, and that would give him enough time to escape his cell and determine if the exit really was where he remembered it being. He pressed his hands against the cell door and looked down at the lock. He hesitated; there would be only one shot at charging his runes and forcing the lock before he was weakened greatly by the use of his red iether.

Suddenly, he thought he heard something faint, an odd airy sound out in the darkness. He froze. Had they changed the rotation? Had the guard decided to come back for some sensible reason? He looked up and had to muffle his own scream, as there was a face inches from his own. It took him only a moment to realize it was Animus staring at him in the dim light. He shook himself, trying to recover from his adrenaline surge, and whispered, "Animus! What are you doing here?"

She smiled, though it seemed a little forced, and said rather importantly, "I am here to rescue you, silly."

Nirim detected a slight sadness in her eyes. He determined that they had no time for apologies. "Animus, I . . . ."

She held up her hand, cutting him off. "We have only a few minutes before the guard comes back."

"Fourteen minutes to be exact, and I forgive you. Now please tell me you have the key to these?" He held up his hands with the shackles on them.

She blinked rapidly as surprise and guilt traveled in quick succession across her face. "But aren't you mad? Shouldn't you at least rebuke me harshly or something?"

While Nirim found her invitation particularly alluring, he was painfully aware of his own participation in the situation, and rebuke seemed blatantly inappropriate under the current circumstances. He merely reiterated, "Key?"

A second face appeared as Hinna materialized out of the shadows. "Did you kiss him yet?"

Animus turned crimson and gave Hinna a reproving look as she gasped, "Hinna! Weren't you supposed to wait, and what on earth makes you say that?"

Hinna crossed her arms defensively. "I did wait, at least a whole minute, and it was you who said you were going to have to kiss and make up."

Nirim was thinking that execution was sounding better by the minute. He cleared his throat softly. "Um, I would like to be rescued now." Animus's hand shook slightly as she pushed her arm through the bars, holding out the key to the shackles. He held his hands up, and she unlocked them. Nirim sighed with relief. Now things would be much easier.

Hinna spoke apologetically. "Sorry, Nirim, but we will have to wait for the guard if we are to unlock the door."

Nirim smiled. "Thankfully not." He held his palm against the lock, and red iether surged down his right arm. There was a soft click, and he swung the door open.

Hinna was clearly impressed as she whispered, "Is there anything you can't do?"

"Yes, it seems that I can't reheat hot springs."

Hinna looked at him seriously, but to his surprise, she said nothing patently misinterpretive. Animus glanced toward the far hallway and murmured, "We still need to get that iether restraint off of you, so we need to ambush the guard."

Nirim had a better solution. He held his hand out toward Hinna, and she gave him the cloth-wrapped blade staff. He untied the cord holding the cloth in place, threw the cloth into the bed in his cell, and attempted to make it look like he was lying under the blanket. Taking the tip of the blade staff, he cut down the length of the iether restraint in a single motion, as though it were made of paper. He pulled it free and tossed it toward the wall.

"Let's hope the rumpled cloth is sufficient to buy us some time." Nirim gestured toward the hallway.

"Come on, we can't just stand here. Lead the way."

Animus and Hinna nodded in unison and began to make a swift exit. Nirim followed them, and they took a long and circuitous route that seemed to him to descend lower instead of ascending to the surface where the exits were. While he certainly would not say so out loud, he was really hoping that their escape had been formulated by Astroligin. They stopped in some small side hallway while Animus peered through the crack in the frame into the room beyond.

Nirim glanced at Hinna and asked, "So what is the plan?"

"We are going to put you in a box and take you to the border." Nirim decided that with as few options as he had, he could not afford to be picky.

They entered a large storage space with a waterway running through the middle of it. A few seerrine guards stood at one end of the room, talking casually. They crept quietly behind a proverbial tower of wooden boxes awaiting shipment. He whispered to Animus, "Now what?" She simply raised her hand for him to be silent. After they had waited for a few minutes, Nirim heard a bell chime several times off in the distance, and the guards made their way calmly from the room.

Animus and Hinna wasted no time in lowering a skimmer into the water. Animus grabbed the nearest box and practically tossed it into the skimmer. Nirim scratched his head doubtfully as he observed, "That box is half full of feathers, and it's kind of small, don't you think?"

The mischievous grin on Animus's face should have been a clear warning to him, but by the time his mind informed him that something less than desirable was about to occur, Animus had already grabbed him and stuffed him into the box. Nirim had rather forgotten about the seerrine's superior strength, which meant it was a trivial matter for her to manhandle him into the box. He flailed helplessly and complained as discreetly as his pride would allow him, but neither prevented him from being dumped into the feather-laden box and being squished down as the lid was quickly hammered into place.

Animus slid into the back of the skimmer where the steering mechanism was, and Hinna sat with her back against the crate, facing her. They were picking up speed in the waterway, nearly out of the room, when Nirim could hear the guards yelling for them to stop. At first he thought they had been discovered, but then he heard them yelling the words "paperwork" and "permission of goods," or something like that. He heard the splash of at least one other skimmer being committed to the waterway, and knew that a chase was about to ensue. He peered through a knothole in the wood, but he could not see much from his crumpled horizontal position inside the terribly stuffy box.

***

Animus glanced back as they exited the room, seeing two other skimmers filled with guards preparing for pursuit down the dimly lit subterranean waterway. Their being discovered meant a change of plans was in order. The guards would certainly relay their message to the next exchange dock, and soldiers would be waiting. Astroligin had prematurely activated the guard rotation bell, but apparently this group of guards had returned to their post after finding no replacements at the guard station.

"Stupid diligent guards!" she muttered, wondering where all the lazy slouches were when she needed them. The guards tailing them would also likely be a problem. If they were strictly dependent on the waterway for motion, they would of course remain at a distance, but should one of their group possess the appropriate kind of rune, they could easily catch up. Chances were good that such would be the case.

While she was considering their options, they shot out of the enclosed part of the waterway into the bright morning light. As they made a sharp turn, Animus caught sight of their pursuers, who were indeed gaining on them. She spoke loudly over the sound of rushing air. "Hinna! I am going to try to jump into the parallel waterway by forcing the skimmer up the side. Hold on, because it will be a rough ride!"

She thought she heard Nirim scream some kind of objection regarding his undue concerns about what would happen should his temporary hiding place plummet into the water. Animus ignored him and grabbed the rudder with both hands. She was about to ram the side of the canal when Hinna's eyes widened, and she waved frantically to get Animus to stop. She looked at the isper girl, concerned they might be giving up their only chance to evade capture, but relaxed her grip on the rudder.

Hinna grabbed the sides of the skimmer. Radiant gold iether burst from her back as Hinna spread her wings out to their full extent, and Animus clung tightly to the edge of the skimmer to prevent her own dismounting as the craft literally flew out of the water through the air and landed smoothly in the next canal over.

Animus sighed with relief, glad she had been born a seerrine, as the sensation of flying was not one she wanted to repeat. She was also berating herself mentally for forgetting Hinna was not without her own iether powers. The seerrine hardly thought of the isper as bearing runes because their wing marks were merely uniform parallel patterns on their backs, and lacked the diversity and variable forms of the seerrine runes. Despite her lack of interest in being off the ground, Animus could not help but be a little jealous. Hinna's wings were incredibly beautiful, with their illuminating gold light, crystalline-like translucence, and majestic size, spanning a width greater than that of the skimmer.

Animus shook her head as she tried to focus; they were not out of this yet, though looking around she could see that they were nearly out of the city. She directed them to the right at one of the many junctions. They would be cutting straight east towards the mountains, where there was a lesser-known way into the human lands. Actually, if the information that Astroligin provided was correct, it was an unfinished part of the waterway that was intended to connect the human lands with the seerrine lands back during a time when humans were less bestial and savage.

Hinna leaned toward the wooden crate and put her ear to it. She turned to Animus and said, "He wants to know when he can come out?"

Animus smiled mischievously. "When it is dark out, or when he can look like a seerrine, whichever comes first."

Animus arched one eyebrow as Hinna merely patted the box, saying, "She says you can't come out." Animus thought that was a bit of a harsh interpretation of what she had said, but it was close enough.

She watched the low walls of the waterway fly by in a blur of textures as the reality of her situation began to sink in. It was likely that she would never be able to return to her own people. Even if they never discovered her role in helping the convict human escape, she would still go down as the worst special forces leader in history. Her blunder in misunderstanding precisely what the elders wanted had given them a momentary false hope concerning their dire situation, and they would not quickly forget how they felt when it became obvious that she had let them down. To make matters worse, their plight remained unresolved, with no particular hope for any future resolution.

Animus felt quite guilty about leaving her people behind, but the hard fact was that she was not losing much. This loss amounted to her deranged father, her mother's grave, her friend Astroligin, and the seerrine under her command, with whom she had never really formed a bond. She supposed it also included her chances at finding a mate, not that such a thing was beneficial in her case. Marriage would mean the end of her family's name, and that was something she simply could not accept. Now, however, she was unsure what, if anything, she could do about it.

She reached behind her back and touched the silver metal of her father's astral bow. What was she supposed to do as the second guardian? Surely it would be better to look forward to what lay ahead, instead of fixating on things left behind. But what exactly was ahead? What were they guardians of? Why was she second, and what did that even mean? She looked at the box that sat in the middle of the skimmer. Why did the first guardian have to be so strange and unpredictable?

They traveled on without stopping, initially passing familiar landmarks, but her surroundings rapidly transitioned into places and structures she had not seen before. They were well on their way to the mountains when night fell and they let Nirim out of his box. Hinna was as tactful as usual as she commented about how bad he smelled. Animus smiled softly as he, being the good human he was, blamed the feathers for making his ride practically sweltering.

They ate some fruit and drank some water as they discussed their next course of action. Nirim listened as Animus explained. "We are going to travel without stopping until we reach the eastern mountains."

"I assume you mean the mountain range I crossed to get here?"

Animus was about to snap at him for being dense when Hinna interjected, "They are the western mountains from his perspective."

She replied simply, "Yes, those mountains. Now pay attention. The waterway cuts through the mountains to exit on the human side, but we don't know how complete it is. So we will need to stop and investigate things at the last exchange dock on that branch of the waterway."

Nirim looked concerned as he asked, "So where is this relative to the pass?"

Animus thought for a moment and then answered, "It's a long ways north of the pass, maybe even a couple weeks of travel over land."

Nirim sighed with some relief. "At least it's within Imperia territory." He looked thoughtfully at her. "You know, I have no memory of the seerrine ever building any connections to the empire through the mountains, other than the one natural pass."

Hinna chimed in, "Maybe it happened later."

Nirim looked doubtful. "Maybe." He stopped and turned to Animus. "Where is Astroligin?"

Animus waved her hand dismissively. "He returned to the pass. I mean, a city overseer can't just abandon his post. Though he did plan most of our escape, and aid us with a few parts of it."

"Most of our escape?"

Animus put her hand to her chest proudly. "Yes, hiding you in the box was my idea."

His expression softened, and he said with surprising sincerity, "Animus, I am sorry for your loss. I can't imagine your people will be particularly happy when they find out you helped me escape."

Animus was taken back that he was so thoughtful, to the point that she thought he was teasing her initially. After a moment, she blushed slightly and said, "Oh, don't worry about it. I am glad I could help you. Besides, we are traveling together from here on out."

She found it odd that Nirim's face went slack at her comments, but she thought nothing more of it, other than reiterating to herself that he was a human after all. Hinna's whimpering noises brought her back to the task at hand, and she cleared her throat loudly, while Nirim stared at Hinna with concern. Animus continued, back on topic. "So at sunup, Nirim has to go back into the box until we reach the human lands."

Nirim frowned, while Hinna rubbed her hands together gleefully. "This is so exciting!" Nirim gave her a dour expression but kept his peace. Animus thought that Hinna was right. It really was exciting, but perhaps Nirim did not like the excitement all that much.

Chapter 15

Despite his vehement opposition to the notion, and his pathetic alternative suggestions, Animus stuffed Nirim back inside the box at sunup. "Silly human, people could see you from the waterway's overbridges even if you laid down in the bottom of the skimmer."

Their trip was relatively smooth. They saw the occasional soldier or guard who eyed them suspiciously, but no one attempted to stop them, nor did any pursuers show up behind them. Hinna was content to watch the passing scenery, and to ask a question now and then. Animus thought Nirim probably was not content, but at the moment she did not really care. There was a sense in which she felt freed of her social obligations, and it was exhilarating.

They passed a low-hanging sign that showed a skull and crossbones painted on top of one branch of the upcoming fork in the waterway. Hinna asked bluntly, "Animus, did that sign say that there is death on this route?"

Animus ignored the muffled sarcastic response that emanated from the box. "Probably not. I am sure it's just to scare people away from the unused part of the waterway."

As they approached the fork, Animus shouted, "Get down!" They both ducked, and the boards intended to prevent travelers from accessing the closed portion of the waterway scraped across the top of the box, much to Nirim's vocal consternation. They traveled along a part of the canal that had been long abandoned. It had green algae growing on its sides, the occasional fallen tree across the top of its low walls, and a few snags that Animus had to weave around. After what Animus considered to be a harrowing obstacle course, they shot out of the canal into what would have once been an exchange dock at the base of the mountain. There was, of course, a return canal that led back into the seerrine lands, but Animus scanned the area, looking for one that ran into the mountain. Hinna pointed suddenly with an excited shout. "There!"

Animus looked carefully at the canal that was on the other side of the long-disintegrated docks. It appeared to be isolated from the one they were on, and it looked like it was fed with water directly from a mountain river. This was good, in that it meant the canal actually had an exit somewhere, but it was bad, in that it meant that there probably wasn't much progress on the other end of the canal. Animus looked at Hinna, gestured toward the canal, and asked politely, "Hinna, if you please."

Hinna nodded. "Right!" She spread her wings and lifted the whole skimmer through the air over the dock to land them into the unfinished canal. Animus had to remind herself that it was not by muscular strength that Hinna could accomplish such a feat, but by the power of the gold iether to impart near weightlessness and motion to whatever it interacted with.

Hinna expressed her concern as they entered the unlighted, rough-hewn tunnel that led through the mountains. "I don't know about this, Animus. This canal doesn't seem as safe as the others."

Animus spoke calmly to assuage Hinna's fears. "It wasn't completed, but I am sure it's perfectly safe."

Animus doubted the truthfulness of her words as her own fear began to eat at her. She held up her left arm, shedding bright blue light on to their surroundings. The tunnel walls still bore the raw gouge marks from where it had been carved out of solid rock. Animus wasn't sure, but they seemed to be picking up speed, far faster than she remembered the other canals ever moving. It was like the canal was sloped, or maybe it was too narrow. She tried to convince herself, rather unsuccessfully, that it was just her imagination.

Nirim made some comment, disparaging from the sound of his tone, and Hinna looked at her seriously. "Nirim says we are all going to die. Is he joking?"

Animus laughed with mock confidence. "Of course he is. What could possibly go wrong?" Nirim started to say something, but Animus snapped, "Don't answer that!" Of all the people she expected to respond to her rhetorical question like a dummy, it was Hinna, not Nirim.

They raced through the tunnel for what had to be at least an hour. Occasionally they would pass through caves either on a suspended aqueduct or along the cave floor. Animus tried not to think about what would happen should they find a collapsed aqueduct halfway through one of the larger caverns. She shivered at the thought of plummeting through the darkness to sure death on top of large stalagmites. Animus was pondering such grim possibilities when Hinna called out sharply, nearly causing her to fall out of the skimmer. "Look! Up there!"

Animus peered around the wooden box that obscured much of her view and saw what appeared to be daylight. She breathed a sigh of relief. Finally they were through the mountain. She noticed that her estimation of their speed was probably accurate, as they were approaching the exit quite rapidly.

Moments before they shot out of the tunnel, Animus could tell that something was wrong. No matter where she looked at the exit, she could see nothing but clear blue sky. Then they were in that sky, poised over a modestly sized mountain lake. Hinna and Animus gasped audibly in unison. Hinna took to the air instantly, grabbing Animus's hand, and the two exchanged brief looks of gratitude that rapidly turned into ones of horror as they watched the skimmer and its cargo plummet to the lake below.

The exit of the unfinished waterway canal came out of the middle of a cliff face, far above the lake. The skimmer plunged beneath the water at high speed, resurfacing like a harpoon over a hundred paces away. The wooden box, on the other hand, seemed to explode into a cloud of white fluff when it hit the water. Feathers went everywhere, leaving a strange, white, rippling pattern on the surface of the lake. The two of them waited breathlessly as Hinna's wings beat rhythmically to keep them suspended in midair. A moment later, Nirim burst through the fluffy patch of water and began to swim toward the nearest shoreline.

Animus and Hinna sighed in unison, and Hinna remarked soberly, "At least he isn't hot and smelly anymore."

Animus wrinkled her nose. "Somehow I doubt that is among his highest priorities right now." Hinna glided to the shore and landed gently. They both stood feeling guilty and helpless as Nirim finished swimming toward them. Animus glanced at Hinna. "You know, you could . . ."

She trailed off as Hinna shook her head. "No, he probably needs to vent his frustration on the water first." Animus looked back at Nirim as he reached shallow water and stood up, wading slowly towards them. It seemed that Hinna was more crafty than she let on.

Nirim reached them on the shore and stopped there, breathing heavily while water dripped from every part of his body. Animus smiled weakly as she said with exaggerated humor, "See! We made it alive . . . heh heh ehhh . . . ."

She could not make herself continue, and Nirim said nothing. He raised his right hand sharply, and both Hinna and Animus flinched. He paused, looking a little disappointed. "Have I ever hit anyone since we have been traveling together?" They both shook their heads silently. He muttered something unintelligible.

Red iether ran the length of his arm, and he swung his hand out slowly. The water in his clothes and hair was drawn away as a suspended cloud of droplets that coalesced and fell to the ground with a splash. He studied their surroundings as he fished out the map that the Imperian border captain Baldric had given him. The wax-soaked parchment remained unharmed by his fall into the lake. His eyes ran over it momentarily before he raised them toward Hinna and Animus, who continued to stare at him, huddled over like small children waiting for a parent's verdict concerning some grievous offense.

"Look, we can't function as travelers with a common goal if you expect me to explode with rage at every ill turn. Don't misunderstand me—I am not getting in another box ever again—but we can't stand here out on the open shore and not draw attention to ourselves." Animus heaved a sigh of relief, Hinna relaxed and nodded, and they followed Nirim as he led them into the tree line.

This part of the human lands was heavily forested, unlike the more arid foothills of the rest of the western mountains. Animus hoped that they would not run into too many of the locals, but then she almost chuckled at the notion. Nirim was different than she expected a human to be, to the point she scarcely thought of him as a human. For that matter, he was typically so reserved that she wondered if he was even a mortal. Had she been in the box, she would have been livid. Someone would have been made to pay for such an offense against her, and yet he seemed to be his normal calm self.

For that matter, now that she thought about it, if she had been forcefully required to save an entire people, and then cast into prison to be executed as a criminal, she would personally lay waste to those responsible. Yet Nirim never even mentioned it. What was with him? Was he hiding some great secret about his past? Was he really who he said he was? With her imagination the only limit, she began to watch him carefully, as though she expected him to transform into some magnificent being at any moment.

***

After nightfall, they sat around a small firepit that Nirim had dug in the woods. Its warmth was welcome in the cool air of the foothills. Nirim stared at the flames, trying not to think too hard about the events of the past few days. Frankly, he was intensely frustrated at the seerrine's complete bullheadedness. Beings of knowledge, his boot!

Then there was the whole abandonment to a watery grave situation. Though he was no longer wet, he was still picking feathers off his clothes. He had to resist the urge to hurl certain individuals off the next cliff they encountered, as a form of ironic just desserts. The longer he considered it, however, the more he decided that serendipitously, this would not help with his would-be historian.

He breathed deeply, slowly calming himself. None of it mattered at the end of the day. Something substantially bigger than himself was in motion, and he had only so much time to figure out exactly what it was. Miralla would not have put him into such a situation without a reason, and if he knew her as well as he thought, the reason was incredibly serious.

Knowing how sensitive a topic it was, Nirim tried to broach the subject carefully. "Animus?"

She glanced up from an apparently deep contemplation. "Yes?"

"Have you thought any more about Miralla's song?"

"Uh, um, M-miralla's song?"

Nirim refrained from showing his exasperation and muttered, "Never mind."

"Wait! I do remember more of it." Nirim looked at her with some skepticism, and Hinna looked at her expectantly.

Animus scrunched her face, as though recalling the words took substantial amounts of physical effort. She spoke slowly. "The next part goes, 'To the first who is here to stay, go to Airili, to the city of the red. The third is the citizen who remains un-dead.'"

Nirim waited until the silence was almost unbearable. "So I guess that isn't the last of the song?"

Animus crossed her arms defensively. "I am trying my hardest here. Why can't you be satisfied with what I can remember?"

Nirim raised his hand in appeasement. "Sorry, I was just wanting to be sure." He cleared his throat and said, nodding politely, "Thank you, Animus."

Hinna asked curiously, "So where is Airili?"

Nirim laughed, but she merely looked puzzled. He hesitated, and then spoke with some surprise, "Oh, I thought you would know about one of the few kobay cities. It's a relatively large city in the lower plains of the kobay lands. It is quite a fascinating place, as most of the buildings are made with a red clay dug from the plains."

"I guess I don't know. Where is this city?"

Nirim dug out his map, unfolded it, and poked at a particular spot. "It's right—"

Animus and Hinna leaned close, but where Nirim held his finger, there was nothing. In fact, there were no markers on the map in the entire lower plains. He shook his head. "I don't understand. How could they leave such an important landmark off the map? Unless—"

Hinna finished his sentence grimly. "Unless it is no longer there."

Nirim silently berated himself for delusionally thinking this would be a much simpler task. He glanced up from the map to see his companions watching him with concern. "Sorry, I guess I got my hopes up that this would be easy. Now, it looks like we will have to stop at Mibi." He gestured to a small town on the border of the lower plains. "And try to figure out if anyone knows where the citizens of Airili have gone."

Animus leaned toward the map. "That's a long way to travel without a waterway."

"Yes, it will probably take more than three weeks to reach it on foot."

"Three weeks?! Are you that slow? That's practically forever on the road!"

Nirim smiled wryly. "Isn't it, though?"

Hinna spoke softly, as if she were thinking out loud, but Nirim was impressed that at least this time she seemed to be aware of her confusion. "Three weeks is forever? That doesn't make any sense."

Nirim smiled and replied, "Well, sometimes things feel like they take a really long time when they are done under unpleasant circumstances."

"That would be terrible! I'm glad we're not in such a circumstance, right?"

Nirim grinned in spite of himself and said,

"Right!"

Animus shook her head, muttering, "Don't encourage her, Nirim. It's bad for morale."

Chapter 16

Nirim enjoyed the mostly peaceful travel down through the foothills. True, the previous day had been a nightmare, but with the bright sun, the pleasant weather, and no sign of terror on the horizon, he was fairly certain this day would be a relaxing stroll compared to the last.

That thought made him rethink wryly that surely it would be only moments before some horrible fate befell him. People often spoke of looking back and laughing at personal disasters, but he felt they only had a tendency toward self-deception, though perhaps that level of insanity was appropriate for the current world. Focusing on the negative, however, would not improve his mood, or his day, so he focused instead on the picturesque countryside as they proceeded on a southward trajectory, angling slightly away from the western mountains.

Hinna and Animus trailed behind him, talking in hushed tones. He was trying not to be suspicious, but he very much doubted that he wanted to know their topic. It fell somewhere between a relief and a worry that they were now getting along fairly well. He sighed unconsciously; surely he was making too much of too little, and he needed to decide what their approach was going to be for finding the third guardian.

Hinna and Animus sidled up on either side of him, and Hinna asked him bluntly, "Nirim, did you have a wife in your past life?"

Nirim took the odd question in stride. "No, I did not."

Hinna pressed further. "Why not?"

He glanced at her, attempting to gauge her intentions, but was met with her usual innocent look. "Uh, well, the imperial family had a custom that out of respect for the rising empress, no close family member of a given cohort would marry until the empress had. Since Ista had not yet married, none of her cousins had either. Of course, we could pursue potential spouses. We just needed to put off the wedding until after the empress's."

Animus leaned toward him and asked curiously, "And did you pursue a potential mate?"

Nirim wanted to correct her for confusing seerrine culture with human culture, but he was more concerned about the direction the conversation was going than with the accuracy of her terminology. He looked at Hinna, who looked equally interested in hearing the answer to Animus's question. Nirim cleared his throat uncomfortably. "No, I never pursued that kind of relationship."

Before he could attempt to change the subject, Hinna asked with what he considered an inappropriate level of excitement, "Why not? Couldn't you find a human woman you liked?"

"I was busy doing other things, and I am not some weak-kneed sop who staggers after every pretty face that passes by. Now, why are we talking about this?"

Rather than offering a normal answer, his companions exchanged a knowing look and retreated back to their previous position out of earshot, with Animus waving her hand dismissively, saying sweetly, "Oh, no reason at all, Nirim. Don't be so suspicious."

He glanced back at them, laughing and giggling, and shook his head in dismay. He admitted that perhaps it was a neglected aspect of his life, but he was starting to suspect his traveling companions were no longer viewing him as simply a means to an end. Or rather, the end was not the one they had started with. He had no desire to enter into any kind of serious relationships. He just wanted to go home to his own time, and he had not given up hope that Miralla might have set up a return trip for him beyond all this madness. The past seemed a perfect dream compared to the twisted nightmare of the present, where few things were predictable, and nothing was reasonable.

Nirim considered telling them flatly that he was not available. But that would sound vainglorious, and especially so if he were incorrect about their shift of intentions. Unfortunately, for a long while, he had viewed the pursuit of the fairer sex as a kind of vice that was a common weakness of the human race, one that he had personally overcome. He had experienced a number of lessons in humility, and now knew that he had been wrong, but some thinking patterns were hard to break. His unsuspecting traveling companions were probably going to find out just how strong such habitual patterns were.

He also might be being presumptuous. It was unlikely the two of them would be working together to pursue him. After all, none of their cultures practiced or accepted polygamy. Still, he would have to consider how to communicate to them his lack of interest in a way that was neither self-extolling nor hurtful, though he had not the faintest idea how that could be accomplished.

Indeed, it seemed to be another cruel paradox handed down by the Creator himself. He knew better than to blame the Creator for his problems. But where were the shades, the fellbeasts, and all the other things he was trained for? Complex relational dynamics was not part of his training, nor had he any interest in adding it to his repertoire. If the next guardian were also female, he was going to resign his guardianship immediately and live in a cave.

As Nirim was thinking, he was scanning the surroundings for any sign of trouble, or at least any sign of trouble that he could address. He caught sight of a tall, long, and rectangular building in the valley below them. It was heavily overgrown, and looked to be falling in on itself, but he stopped to consider it.

Animus and Hinna peered around him, and Hinna asked, "What is it?"

Nirim studied it for a moment longer, and then said, "It appears to be an old sideline house."

Animus rolled her eyes. "Thanks, Nirim, now we know exactly what it is."

Before he could add more details, Hinna looked reprovingly at Animus. "No, that's not true. I still don't know what it is."

Animus gave her a level stare, and Hinna gazed dejectedly at the ground. "Oh, sorry."

She looked pitiful enough that Nirim had to resist the sudden urge to give her a reassuring hug as he explained. "It was part of the trackkus system, where a trackkus could be refueled and loaded or unloaded in a covered building. Like the docks in the seerrine waterways."

Animus commented disparagingly, "It isn't that much like the waterway system. We would never put a dock in the middle of nowhere."

Nirim frowned with annoyance, but refrained from speaking unkindly. "I doubt this was the middle of nowhere when the trackkus was still running."

Hinna pointed. "Look, there are humans down there."

Nirim squinted in the bright daylight, trying to decide if the people who appeared to have taken up residence at the sideline house were likely to be friendly. Animus shuddered. "Ugh, filthy humans. Please tell me we can avoid them?"

Hinna's hands trembled slightly. "I hope the savages don't try to eat us."

Nirim arched an eyebrow at them. "You do realize that most humans aren't even remotely like that, right?" he asked.

They both stared wide-eyed at him as they answered in perfect unison, "No." Nirim shook his head as he proceeded down the hill toward the decrepit structure and its accompanying human encampment.

As they got closer, shouts went up from the camp's watch, and half a dozen burly, disheveled fellows came out to meet them. Nirim realized far too late that they could not turn back now. These were clearly some kind of bandits or a gang. It was especially regrettable that they looked like they had not bathed in weeks, a feature that did not escape Animus's notice. "Hmm! Filthy!"

The one at the front of the group bellowed out, "Well, looky what we got here, boys. Some fresh meat!"

Nirim glanced at Hinna, whose eyes were huge in her pale face. "It's just an expression. Don't worry." Or at least, he hoped it was. Nirim faked a reasonable smile. "Hello there. We are just passing through. Don't want any trouble, you know."

The fellow grinned viciously. "You think you can tipsy-toe through our hideout with two exotic beauties hanging on your arms and be on your way?" He and his men laughed, a ruckus laughter, as though the unspoken answer to his question were especially funny.

Nirim wanted to object to the man's insinuation concerning his association with Hinna and Animus, but at the moment, they were quite literally gripping his arms tightly. Additionally, he had to squash the temptation to tell the guy that the two nuisances were all his. "Fine! You win! These humans are completely filthy savages." Hinna did not look reassured by this admission, but Animus seemed particularly smug.

The leader snarled angrily, "What was that you said, pretty boy?"

Nirim watched the man, suppressing his rising sense of humor. "Nothing unfactual, I assure you." More of the thugs were gathering, and they looked rather agitated. Nirim met Animus's gaze and gestured toward the bandits. "If you please."

Animus let go of his arm and pulled out the simple whistle that hung on a cord around her neck. Nirim raised his right arm, and, using the red iether, solidified the air immediately around Hinna and himself as Animus unleashed the bone-numbing tone, exponentially amplified by her iether, that resulted in a debilitating and painful disruption of the brain in humans.

Every thug fell to the ground, writhing. Animus tucked the pipe away, and Nirim dropped his arm to his side. He looked at Hinna for a moment, but after she failed to get his message, he said, "Hinna, you can let go of my arm now." She jerked away from him reflexively, shaking herself and apologizing profusely.

Nirim started walking toward the sideline house. Animus raised her hand as though objecting. "Hey! Where are you going?"

"To satisfy my curiosity."

Hinna ran to catch up with him and Animus sighed disdainfully, but she also hurried to stay with them.

Inside the deteriorated structure, piles of assorted objects sat around everywhere. It appeared as though anything the bandits thought might be valuable was hoarded up inside the sideline house. Nirim waded through trinkets and baubles, ignoring Animus's berating. "Just look at all this junk. Like a rat's nest, don't you think?"

Hinna affirmed her opinion. "Yes, it really is like a rat's nest."

He stopped and looked thoughtfully at a large metal object in the center of the building. It stood easily three times taller than he did, with its peak forming a pointed, sloping roof. It had numerous metal ridges that stuck out like fins on a fish, and it was pointed at both ends with a constriction in the middle. The whole structure measured some seventy paces long. Animus and Hinna came up next to him, and Hinna commented, "Oh, an enormous piece of junk!"

Animus chimed in, "But how did they move it here?"

Nirim gave them both a long look before he put his right hand against the door of the trackkus. He turned his hand slowly, and they heard an audible clank as the door unlocked. He released the exterior safety latch and pulled the door down. They were hit with a blast of stale air as Nirim lowered the door to the ground. The inside surface of the door formed a sort of gangplank up into the trackkus.

Nirim gestured broadly to the door. "Ladies first!"

Hinna smiled and curtsied. "Thank you, sir." She walked up the ramp, already glancing around curiously.

When Animus did not immediately follow, Nirim turned back in her direction. She waited a little ways away, arms crossed, staring dubiously at the trackkus. She met his gaze and stated adamantly, "I am not getting inside a large, stinky, metal box."

Nirim narrowed his eyes at her as he said sharply, "Well, at least it isn't full of feathers!"

Animus cringed, and then with an exaggerated sigh, started toward the ramp. "You'd better not send us flying off a cliff just to even the score."

Nirim shook his head as she boarded, saying mostly to himself, "If there was a score, I would have already lost."

Nirim also boarded and then latched the door behind them around the time the first of the bandits were staggering back to their feet. He walked down the central narrow hallway of the trackkus, noting that the inside was essentially untouched, remaining pristine despite the decades. Actually, it appeared to be new, possibly even unused. That struck him as odd, since most trackkuses had been assembled at the machine yards east of the capital, not here on the north-western edge of the empire.

He entered the forward control room to see Animus frantically trying to restrain Hinna. "Hinna! Don't touch that. You don't know what it does! No, no, not that either. Hey, just leave this thing alone!"

Nirim chuckled as he walked up to the control panel. Hinna was not in danger of activating the sleeping hunk of metal. It took a specialized key to ignite the iether drive in a trackkus, assuming any iether was left. He looked up at the small name plate just above the large, square viewing ports whose metal shutters were currently closed. A grin spread across his face, and he spoke out loud in amazement. "They actually built it!"

Animus stopped trying to keep Hinna from fiddling with every one of the numerous switches and levers in the control room, and looked at him with some exasperation. "Nirim, would you stop talking nonsense and help me keep Hinna from blowing up this contraption before we can get out of it?"

Nirim ignored her, rereading the name plate as

though he doubted what he saw, and reassured himself that it was real. There was no question about it; this was the iether bloom.

The guardians had talked extensively of the need for something capable of dealing with threats from the darkness that were more formidable than individual guardians could deal with alone. The outcome of these discussions was the commissioning of the imperial engineers to create a weapon of unprecedented size. They referred to it as the iether bloom project, and it was conducted mostly in secrecy, to avoid causing concern among those both inside and outside of the empire who doubted the necessity of a defense against an enemy that had not shown itself in generations. As far as Nirim was aware, the design stage of the weapon had been incomplete at the point of his being subjected to the time lock. He considered the control room thoughtfully. This explained why it was out here in the middle of nowhere, and why it looked new.

"Hinna! Stop! Just stop!"

Hinna responded without pausing, pushing a series of buttons before flipping a switch. "But how does it work? This is a historical moment. I just have to see it move."

"It doesn't work! It won't move, so just stop it, or you're going to blow us up before we can get back to our long walk to the kobay lands!"

Nirim interrupted them, and this time Hinna did stop, as she joined Animus in staring at him with a wide-eyed expression, albeit one of wonder instead of Animus's one of trepidation.

"Not only will it move, but we won't be walking to the kobay lands now."

Chapter 17

Animus looked alarmed. “Please tell me this thing doesn’t still work?”

Hinna looked delighted. “Please tell me that it does!”

Nirim took a cylindrical object, somewhat longer than his palm, out of a small drawer in the console. He slid the rune-covered object into a hole in the console. Rune traces shot out from the spot as they were filled with bright blue iether. The light flooded the console and the dim room. Nirim smiled at their expressions, but only for a moment, as he realized that half of the settings on the control console were skewed randomly. He sighed, unsure if he wished that Hinna were less curious, or Animus more adamant.

Hinna was mesmerized by the various mechanical gauges and illuminated rune traces that formed an intricate pattern across the whole console. Nirim spoke as gently as he could manage. “Hinna, please don’t touch anything now that it is on. It could be very bad.”

Her smile was innocent, but her eyes were bright with excitement. “All right, Nirim. If you don’t want me to, I won’t touch anything.” Animus made a strange sort of growling noise, but Hinna merely shrugged and put her hands behind her back, as though it were the only way to keep herself from grabbing the trackkus's numerous levers.

Nirim studied the panel before him, well aware of how very little he knew about a trackkus's fine-tuning. He was disturbed by the fact that he could not recognize half the things on the panel that Hinna had been fiddling with, but after a moment he felt a wash of relief as he realized that those settings were dedicated to the weapon, which was why they were unfamiliar.

He reached out and set several of the switches that he was familiar with. Technically he had never trained as a trackkus operator, but he had received some basic training as an exercise in satiating his own curiosity about their functioning. He slowly turned the central dial that controlled the iether drive's output power. Subtle vibrations ran through the trackkus as the long-dormant quad-turbine drive mechanism began its spin-up cycle.

Hinna clasped her hands in joy, but Animus, of all people, clung to him tightly. Nirim wanted to tell her to stop being so silly about it, but he decided that it would be better to let her work it out. He just hoped she figured out that the trackkus was completely safe before she permanently constricted his waist.

He pulled the long, thin chain that opened the metal shutters, allowing them to see through the generous glass ports of the control room. Nirim smirked at the various thugs who were scouring the area in a vain attempt to locate the disappearing interlopers. Several were gape-jawed, pointing at the trackkus that had seemingly come alive under its own power.

Nirim watched the needle of a gauge on the console slowly rise toward a blue-shaded section. The trackkus operated by forcing iether-heated air into a large, narrow, fluted chamber that then abruptly expanded just prior to exiting the rear. This created the thrust that propelled the trackkus along the rail. Sustained movement was relatively efficient, but getting started was rather difficult. Considering how long the trackkus had been sitting here, it was going to take one incredible burst of iether to send it into motion.

He looked at Hinna. "You might want to hold on to something." Hinna nodded and grabbed one of the vertical metal rails along the side of the room designed for that very purpose. He looked down and back at Animus, who held tightly to his waist, with part of her tail wrapped around one of his legs, her eyes squeezed shut. "Uh, that goes for you, too, Animus."

Her quivering voice was muffled due to her face being nearly buried into the back of his tunic. "I am holding on to something!"

He shook his head as he reached out and gripped the nearest railing as well as he could. If Animus's added weight resulted in his injury, he would have no one to blame but himself for not making her find a more substantial and sturdy handhold.

Nirim slammed the boost lever forward, which probably was more an act of showmanship than one of necessity. The bandits screamed, but Nirim could barely hear it over Animus's vocalizations as the iether bloom jumped into action, sending debris flying in all directions. Nirim braced again as they burst through the closed door of the sideline house. He sighed with relief, and turned the iether drive dial further until it sat at the halfway point. For a moment he could feel the backwards pull of their acceleration, and then it leveled off as they reached full travel speed. He was curious just how fast the iether bloom could go, but it seemed like that could wait for another time.

He smiled at Hinna, who clapped with delight. Nirim cleared his throat as he spoke. "Animus, you can let go of me now." She said nothing, but merely shook her head. Hinna emitted a bark-like sound twice, and Animus gave her a rather sullen look before she slowly extricated herself. Nirim could not help but ask, "Hinna, were you barking?" Hinna only shrugged and then watched the trees racing by the window. He felt like the longer they traveled together, the less he understood the pretty but odd isper girl.

Nirim strode toward the connecting hallway that led to the rest of the iether bloom's compartments. Animus let out a yelp as she expressed her dire concern. "Nirim! You can't just leave it run aimlessly! Don't you have to steer or something?"

"Animus, we are on a track. There is nothing to steer."

"But—but—but what if there is a tree growing in the way? It has been many years, after all."

Nirim entered a small room on the left that was immediately behind the control room. "The rail is built on top of a wide and deep stone base. No large trees will be growing in the way."

"But what if a tree has fallen across the rail?"

Nirim leaned forward to study the large map that covered the entire back wall of the small room as he answered absently, "Animus, it will be fine. The trackkus is equipped with a shock-absorbing scoop that will throw debris off the rail."

Hinna, trailing behind Animus, marveled, "That's amazing. It's like they thought of everything!"

Animus still looked worried, but seemed to be out of end-game scenarios. Nirim hoped to avoid her coming up with something legitimate, like what would happen if the rail were simply missing at some point, or a bridge out, or if there had been a cave-in somewhere. So he offered her a reassuring smile. "Animus, please don't worry. I will keep you safe."

He had intended to say that he would ensure

their safety, but what came out was close enough that by the time he realized he should have said something less personal, it was too late to reword his statement. Animus looked at him, wide-eyed, and then smiled sheepishly. "Really? Thank you, Nirim."

Somehow using the trackkus to reach their destination now seemed less of a good idea with its relatively tightly enclosed quarters. Rather than figuring out what had just happened, he turned back to the map that hung on the wall of the navigation room. If the map was reasonably current, then they were on the outer imperial loop. They could travel directly to the kobay lands without passing through any civilized areas. This would be advantageous, as he could only imagine what people would try to use the trackkus rail for in an urban context. He hoped no one had built a house on the outer loop rail. The trackkus could clear one or two houses from the rail easily, but a whole line of them would probably result in a full stop.

He pulled out his modern map and compared it to the old trackkus rail map. As far as he could tell, no new cities had sprung up on top of the outer loop rail. That was not especially surprising, because the outer loop really did run through relatively remote territory.

Nirim turned back to his companions, and, pointing at the map, showed them the route they were taking. Animus had little interest in the details and said rather nervously, "That's great. So when can we get off this thing?"

Nirim could have calculated the precise interval with his rune, but instead he just gave a generic figure. "We should be there some time tomorrow."

Hinna looked impressed. "That really is fast."

He nodded and said, "Right. Now let's go see what else is here."

They followed Nirim as he went from room to

room along the hallway. There were two sleeping rooms with two beds apiece, a small storage space, a dining booth designed for four, and a small kitchen space. This was all neatly packed into the front half of the iether bloom. The back half did not appear to be accessible from within. Nirim presumed that was where the weapon was stored.

Hinna gently touched the blank wall. "What's in the back part?"

He decided that it would be best not to tell them about the weapon, after all the disparaging comments he had heard about humans doing nothing but making weapons out of the iether. "It's just mechanisms related to how the trackkus works."

Hinna looked a little disappointed, but seemed to accept his generic oversimplification. He walked back to the kitchen area and checked the water reservoir, where a large metal tank in the top portion of the iether bloom supplied water via gravity to the small kitchen basin for cooking and drinking, and to the emergency braking system for cooling. When he pulled the stop out, clean water flowed freely into the basin. He tasted it and grimaced. It was generally fine, if he ignored the metallic aftertaste.

He rummaged around the cabinet above the basin and pulled out a threaded filter and attached it to the waterspout and tried the water again. The metal taste was gone, though the water had clearly sat unattended for some time. He stepped back from it, speaking for the benefit of the others. "The water is safe, even if it is a little stale."

Hinna spoke excitedly as she grabbed Animus's arm and dragged her toward the kitchen alcove. "Come on! Let's make lunch while we travel at death-defying speeds!" Animus did not appear to be particularly encouraged by Hinna's exaggerated description and unnecessary exuberance.

Nirim waved at them as he headed back to the navigation room. “I will be with the maps.”

Nirim sat down at the small table in the navigation room and tried to determine their best course of action. He did not want to leave the iether bloom sitting out in the open, where it might attract undue attention, and possibly even disappear if it were discovered by a resourceful individual. He checked the rail map again to be sure. It looked like there was a sideline house in a secluded canyon only a day’s journey from Mibi, which lay on the edge of the lower plains. It would add to their travel time, but he could not see a better option.

He leaned against the wall and closed his eyes. He had half-expected to find a note from Miralla hidden somewhere in the iether bloom. Would she have seen that he would be using it? Or was it built with the four guardians in mind? Miralla had rarely known the full context of her visions, merely that certain things were true. He wondered if she knew that her message would be transmitted by Animus, or if she simply knew that she had to give her message to Spite. The former case felt like a joke; the latter case made him wonder if he was locked out of time far longer than Miralla had anticipated. Perhaps things were not as clear as he had originally assumed. The Creator was working out a plan, and it was more intricate and complicated than either he or Miralla could understand.

Was Hinna part of this plan? What about the iether bloom? Surely they did not stumble upon it apart from the Creator’s unseen hand. It seemed that a series of negative events had culminated in their unreasonable success. This thought bothered him, as he did not want to experience any more failures if he could help it.

A cheerful voice interrupted him. “Nirim? Are

you sleeping? It's time to eat."

He sat forward and opened his eyes to see Hinna's smile from barely a hand's breadth away. He would have been startled had it been anyone else. "No, I am not sleeping, just thinking."

She examined his face for a second, and then turned and made her way to the small, partially enclosed dining booth. Nirim followed and took a seat next to her. Animus sat across from them, looking a little uncomfortable on what was to her a strange seat. Nirim shrugged apologetically. "Sorry, Animus, they weren't designed with a mind towards seerrine." She grumbled wordlessly and looked at the shuttered glass port in the wall.

Nirim reached around Hinna and pulled the chain that opened the metal shutter, allowing them to see the scenery slip past. Animus frowned. "I am not sure that helps." He was about to close the shutter when she returned to watching the window, with actual interest this time. Nirim set about eating his simple meal, mostly composed of dried fruit and dried fish that his traveling companions had packed in preparation for their flight from the seerrine lands.

Without any warning, Hinna asked bluntly, "Nirim, if you had to spend the rest of your life with either me or Animus, whom would you choose?"

Nirim choked on a mouthful of chewy fruit. It took him a few moments to recover before he swallowed successfully. He could not tell if Animus was glaring at him or at Hinna. He cleared his suddenly dry throat. "What a fascinating question. Let me think about it for an extended period of time."

Nirim rose from his seat and Animus asked suspiciously, "Where are you going, Nirim?"

"Oh, uh, just checking on the control room. Wouldn't want something to happen."

He made his way up to the control room and closed the door behind him. The paradox he had hoped to ignore was coming back to bite him. He tried to rationalize that with Hinna, it was probably a completely random question that was unrelated to anything. However, no amount of brute force logic could definitively convince him that this was the case, not to mention he hated the false dilemma the question created. A quick mental analysis told him that Animus would offer normal conversational abilities, but he did find Hinna's personality to be more endearing.

Nirim shook his head violently and muttered, "What am I doing, falling prey to this trap!" He hoped, meagerly at any rate, that Hinna would forget about her question altogether. Yet he felt like he still needed to have an answer. "I don't know" sounded rather dumb, but it was probably his best recourse. He might also say something about spending a lifetime with himself, but that sounded bad on several levels.

Nirim sighed and calmed himself. The silly things faded from his concern as he reminded himself that there were more important tasks to accomplish than addressing what was likely just an innocent musing.

Chapter 18

Animus stared at Hinna, frustrated partially at the isper's lack of tact, and partially at the seeming boldness that she herself was lacking. As the door to the control room closed, she spoke sharply to Hinna. "What are you doing, Hinna!?"

"Doing? I wasn't doing anything. I was curious. Don't you want to know which of the two of us he likes better?"

Animus shook her head. "That is beside the point. You practically asked him which of us he was going to marry!"

Hinna's eyes widened in shock as her face slowly turned red at the thought. She muttered, "It doesn't work that way among the isper."

Animus crossed her arms with a huff. "Honestly, I would think you had forgotten that we are talking about the human dog."

Hinna glanced sheepishly down at her food. "I don't want to think of him in that way anymore."

Animus feigned exaggerated outrage. "What do you mean! I thought your goals were important here." She did not really want to admit that she did not want to think about Nirim like that either.

Hinna stared out the window as she spoke in a small, soft voice. "He is just too likable really, almost as though he were made for the purpose of getting along with people no one else could get along with."

Animus wanted to deride her for being so naïve, but she could not bring herself to say anything. Hinna was right; Nirim was far too likable, and seemingly undaunted by repeated failure, his or otherwise. She decided on another course of action. "Hinna, let's agree to stop treating Nirim poorly, and to not press him into awkward situations. We are going to have to travel together, and it creates undue tension."

Hinna seemed deep in contemplation, but to Animus's relief, she simply nodded and said, "I agree."

Animus knew that Hinna had the advantages of her direct methods and her undeniable beauty. However, from Animus's perspective, Hinna lacked two rather important things: namely, usefulness and social aptitude. She wondered how someone as nice as Nirim could have evaded the attention of females of his race.

Hinna apparently was reflecting on something similar, as she asked, "Do you suppose that Nirim had many admirers back in his time?"

"I don't know. All he said was that he was too busy for such things."

"Too busy? It's a wonder his race procreates at all."

Animus gasped. "Hinna! Don't say that so loudly! What if Nirim heard you?"

"Was something I said inappropriate?"

"Substantially so."

Hinna looked glumly back towards the window. "Oh. Sorry."

***

The iether bloom shot swiftly along the rail as the morning mist faded away with the rising sun's heat. The previous day had been uneventful, with the iether bloom only scraping an occasional branch or throwing some minor debris off the rail. The previous night would have been uneventful as well, were it not for the large fallen tree that they hit after midnight. Of course, the tree had not stood a chance, and the iether bloom was unharmed. However, following the deafening bang and the sharp shudder that shook the whole metal frame, Animus had appeared in his sleeping room and dragged him bodily from his bunk, demanding reassurance that they were not about to die. It took an hour to assure her that there was nothing to be concerned about.

Nirim now lay in his bunk, watching the sunlight filter through the slits of the closed metal shutter. He felt tired, despite having done nothing strenuous the past day. His brain hurt from thinking in circles about things that probably were not worth thinking about.

A tail hung down from the bunk above him, meaning someone had switched sleeping quarters during the second half of the night. He glanced at the floor. Hinna lay on a makeshift bed of her own design on the floor of the narrow room. He knew what excuse Animus would give him, but he would not be asking why Hinna had thought it necessary for her to be in the same room. He found it mildly humorous that they had been worried about assassins sneaking up on him when they were the only ones who seemed to do any sneaking.

He crawled out of his bunk and stepped over Hinna on his way to the control room. The forward windows revealed the savannah that made up the majority of the kobay lands. They looked substantially drier than he remembered. He could not recall having visited during the peak of the dry season.

Nirim slid a lever forward to guide the iether bloom into taking the side rail at the next junction. He watched for about an hour before he saw the stone marker that indicated the coming junction. He dialed the iether drive back to a mere ten percent of its capacity and let the air resistance slow them down. He could brake hard and probably throw both of his companions out of their respective sleeping positions, but he resisted the urge to be mean. The iether bloom would fail to change rails if it were moving too fast. It slid effortlessly onto the side rail and slowly drifted away from the main rail over a substantial distance.

As they descended into a canyon, Nirim shut off the iether drive and began to slowly apply the brakes. He was surprised as the old sideline house came into view. It appeared to be relatively intact, despite its age; sitting in a narrow canyon had likely protected it from the elements. The iether bloom rode smoothly through the large doorway that had long since lost its door, and Nirim brought it to a complete stop. He withdrew the ignition key and tucked it into his belt. He did not want to risk Hinna's curiosity resulting in her driving off without him. Nirim went through the iether bloom, closing the shutters. He glanced back into the sleeping quarters to see his companions still motionless. Nirim smiled at how peaceful they looked.

He walked to the exit, picking up the blade staff as he went. He lowered the hatch and exited into the dim interior of the empty sideline house. At least he hoped it was empty, which was what he was about to determine. He closed the hatch behind himself. Nirim walked cautiously through the large building. He saw a stack of dry but mostly decomposed wooden crates that were now little more than a pile of dirt. In another corner, he saw scrap metal, maybe old trackkus parts. He entered the small office space that would house the supporting staff of the trackkus system, but saw nothing of interest inside.

He stepped back into the main part of the

sideline house, and was feeling confident that they were pleasantly alone. He was nearly halfway back to the iether bloom when a deep voice spoke softly.

"What brings you to this decrepit place, human?"

Nirim turned slowly, every part of his body tensed for action. A large kobay stood no more than ten paces away. He wore a black cloak that concealed most of his features. The small amount of his hair that Nirim could see was a ruddy color, which was quite unusual for kobay, whose hair colors typically did not stray far from black or dark brown. The kobay was substantially larger than he, standing a full head taller, and he appeared to be built entirely of sinew and muscle. Nirim stared at him, and the kobay asked, "Is your hearing as weak as your body, human?"

Instead of answering what seemed like a trick question, Nirim asked his own question. "Who are you?"

The kobay watched him calmly for a moment before he replied. "I am Red, and you are?"

Nirim shifted his weight a little uneasily. "I am Nirim, but Red doesn't sound like a kobay name."

"And what gives you the right to decide what a name is, Nirm?"

The kobay sounded a little agitated, or maybe it was his imagination. Nirim raised his blade staff preemptively as he reiterated, "It's Nirim."

The kobay gestured casually at the blade staff. "There is no need for that, Nrim, as I am a pacifist of the highest degree."

Nirim did not lower his weapon. "Of course. You just happen to look like a highly toned warrior, and my name is Nirim, not Nrim."

Red shrugged casually. "Well, you don't have to believe me, Neerum, and I do apologize. I am terrible with names."

Nirim decided it wasn't worth the effort to correct him again. "So what are you doing here, Red?"

Red gestured toward the iether bloom. "Oh, I was just on my way home when I heard an unfamiliar sound and tracked it here. What are you doing here, Niroom?"

Nirim felt like something was off with the kobay, but he could not put his finger on it. Red seemed to be entirely genuine in every regard, even if his story and vague statements were highly suspect. Nirim relaxed a little but continued to watch Red warily. "My companions and I have stopped here, and will be traveling to Mibi for some information."

"Why, we share the same general travel direction. I don't suppose you would like company?"

Nirim had as much traveling company as he could handle, but he also knew that if this was the peak of the dry season, a guide would be indispensable. After mulling it over for a moment, he decided that the benefits outweighed the risks. "Sure, you can accompany us, but you will have to wait for my companions to wake up."

"I am in no hurry." The kobay turned his gaze to the iether bloom, following its various contours with his eyes.

Nirim swept his hand toward the door. "I don't suppose you would like to come in and have a seat while we wait?"

"I would be delighted to, Narum. Thank you."

Nirim resisted shaking his head as he returned to the iether bloom and opened the hatch.

Red ducked his head as he entered the doorway and followed Nirim to the back, where they sat down at the booth in the dining area. Red looked around curiously as he noted, "What an incredible machine! You humans sure are a crafty lot."

Nirim smiled wryly. “Thanks, Red.” The kobay pulled his hood back, and Nirim could see the source of his name. His hair and the mane that ran along his neck and upper back were indeed a hearty red color. “So how is life as a pacifist among a people whose predominant pastime is warfare?”

Red looked at him carefully before he gave a calm answer. “Difficult, lonely, and ofttimes unfulfilling, but well worth the peace. How is your life, Narem?”

“Mostly insane, but occasionally funny.”

Red looked rather curious. “And what occupation do you have that brings about such occasional jocularious psychosis?”

Nirim contemplated just what kind of kobay would be so well spoken. “I am a guardian.”

Red looked around, then asked, “And what is it you are guarding?”

“I stand against the tide of the darkness, should it rise again.”

Red blinked, and then pondered out loud, “Ah, so you try to prevent nightfall. Well, that certainly explains the insanity portion of your life.”

Nirim was about to correct him when Animus appeared around the corner, rubbing her eyes. She muttered, still somewhat dazed, “Nirim, it’s still dark out. Shouldn’t it be morning?”

Red turned toward her and marveled, “Why, I have never seen a seerrine before! Good morning to you, Mrs. Nirim!”

Nirim thought it was unfortunately convenient that Red got his name right that time. He cleared his throat. “Please don’t give her any strange ideas.”

For her part, Animus seemed unaware of the exchange, recoiling slightly with her left arm raised. “And who is this?”

"This is Red. He will be accompanying us to Mibi."

Animus eyed him warily. "Is that your real name?"

"It is the only name I know."

Nirim peered at him curiously. "But surely you have a surname, or a tribal designation."

"I don't know why you care, but no, I am Red, nothing more, nothing less." Animus sat next to Nirim as she muttered, "You don't say."

Red looked at Animus. "May I have the pleasure of knowing your name?"

Animus hesitated, so Nirim answered for her. "This is Animus. She is also a guardian."

"Ah, twice the madness. Well, each to their own, I suppose."

"The only crazy one here is Nirim, but I must ask, what are you doing here?"

Red shrugged. "I am just passing through, and your friend here intrigued me, so I supposed he would like company."

Hinna came around the corner, complaining slightly. "Nirim, why didn't you wake us up when you got up? We could have started already." She stopped suddenly upon seeing the stranger.

Red did a double take, sounding more surprised than before. "An isper? I apologize, Nirim, for intruding on your complex personal life. I didn't think such . . . ."

Nirim raised his hand sharply. "Red, these two are my traveling companions, and we are doing nothing but traveling together."

Red watched Nirim with mild concern. "You are a very troubled man."

Nirim sighed with exasperation as he muttered, "You don't know the half of it."

Animus gestured to Hinna. "This is Hinna."

Red looked at her and nodded politely. “Good morning, Hinna. And are you a guardian as well?”

Hinna looked wide-eyed and turned to Nirim. “I never thought of it. Am I, Nirim?”

Nirim struggled to find a nice way to let her down, but there was no way out of this particular situation. “Ah, no, Hinna, you are not.”

Her face fell, and she slid into the seat next to Red. “Oh, sure.” Nirim believed she was better off not being a guardian, but he did wonder why disappointing her made him feel so bad.

Red announced spontaneously, “All right then, your friends are gathered. Shall we proceed on our way?”

They filed out of the iether bloom, and Nirim locked it behind them. By now it was starting to become hot in the sideline house, and as Nirim had anticipated, it was even hotter outside the sideline house. Nirim turned to Red and asked, “Red, is this the dry season?”

Red looked around at the surprisingly arid savannah landscape as he responded. “Well, yes. It isn’t the peak of the season yet, but it seems the water in this land is fading away.”

Nirim straightened in surprise. “Say what?”

“Yes, there are nearly no oases left, and a number of the rivers have dried up. Many of my people have migrated to where the water is, while others have built stone cisterns to hold water that collects during the rainy season.” Nirim shuddered as he imagined the kobay and the seerrine converging on the human lands in a large mass. Even if they avoided war, it would be confusion and chaos.

Animus asked, “Did you seek help from the humans with this problem?”

Red looked as though he thought her crazy. “Help from the humans? We kobay are the most powerful of the four races. Why would we seek help from weak humans?"

Animus tossed her head to one side. "Clearly you aren't that strong, or you would have solved the problem yourselves."

"Stronger than you, anyway."

Nirim thought they were approaching the truest test of Red's pacifism in just a matter of moments. Animus turned sharply toward Red, rising to what Nirim assumed was the seerrine equivalent to standing on tiptoe, though she was still shorter than he was. "Do you want to try saying that to my face?"

Red shrugged, stating without hesitation, "I am stronger than you are by a substantial margin."

"You obviously have no idea what you are talking about! I challenge you to a contest of strength. Martial combat, right here and right now."

Nirim was about to intervene, but Red beat him to it. "Very well. I challenge you to a feat of strength. We will each take turns carrying the other, and the one who tires first loses."

"Ca-ca-carry you? That's ridiculous, and I am certainly not letting you carry me!"

"Then if you will not accept my challenge, neither will I accept yours."

Animus glared at the big kobay sullenly. "Fine! Be that way."

Nirim chuckled as he continued on, with the rest of them trailing behind him. Red was certainly a formidable character, physically and mentally.

Chapter 19

As the sun set, Nirim stopped their small party at a slightly concealed ravine that would afford them protection for the night. It had been a long and hot day's trek, and Nirim had to remind his companions that their journey was too important to wait for traveling at night.

Nirim decided to use the evening to help Animus become more familiar with her father's astral bow. Red and Hinna watched in amazement as Animus drew her hand from the silver bow's grip to the shimmering white iether string, leaving a brilliant white shaft of light in the path her hand had taken. She drew the iether string back and fired. The iether shaft flashed through the canyon in a near perfect line, faster than a lightning strike.

Nirim thought it was rather ironic for that metaphor to be the one that came to mind, as it fit well with the old adage that lightning never strikes twice. Animus's father had been a dead-eye with the legendary bow—which is to say, he never missed a shot. Animus, on the other hand, shot like she had no eyes. It made Nirim wonder if she were certain of her parentage.

He tried to be gentle. "Well, that time it was a little wide, so let's try again. Remember, you are trying to hit that giant boulder in the middle of the canyon."

Animus nodded as she stared down her target with renewed purpose. She drew the bow back and fired another luminescent shot. Nirim groaned internally as it arched wide of what he would have sworn was a target too big to be missed. Hinna added her usual charm to the situation by observing all too loudly, "Oh, you missed again!"

Animus lowered the bow, pursing her lips. "At least I am not useless!"

Hinna's eyes grew wide, and Nirim said sharply, "Animus! Hinna isn't useless." Animus looked at Nirim with a level gaze, raising one eyebrow.

Hinna spoke resolutely. "Yes, please tell her how useful I am, Nirim."

Nirim blinked and tried to think as he spoke, which was, as could be expected, rather disastrous. "Right. Hinna is useful in lots of ways! She helps with the. . . uhhh . . . and then she is also great for. . . ummm . . . I mean, she keeps things interesting."

Animus laughed, and Hinna looked dejectedly at the ground as she muttered, "Thanks, Nirim."

Red mused out loud, "Not everyone's value is weighed by their practical skills."

Hinna looked at him with big eyes as she said in a small voice, "Are you saying I am not practical?"

Red leaned back as he tried without success to answer her. "Uh, well, no, that isn't . . . um . . . ."

Nirim and Animus both broke into laughter at the big kobay being effectively stopped by the diminutive isper woman. They retired for the night shortly thereafter, but Nirim could not help feeling sorry for Hinna. It was apparent to all of them that Hinna had no real function among them. Even Red, who was practically a stranger, was currently an asset. Hinna, on the other hand, was merely present. He enjoyed her company, but he was not going to pretend that her social ineptitude did not irritate him.

Nirim gave his thoughts a pause as he

considered what Red had said. Maybe he was looking at things incorrectly. Hinna was remarkably engaging, despite her shortcomings, and she seemed to hang on every word in her conversations. Her innocent demeanor was charming, and he admired her positive spirit, though she was frequently the recipient of anger and disdain for her unintentional blunders. However, he was concerned that she might be more of a liability than an asset, not to mention he had no idea how he could communicate that he appreciated her for who she was without giving her the wrong impression. He sighed; maybe somehow he could get Red to say such things to her, and thus avoid implicating himself.

***

Nirim awoke to two faces looking down at him. They were such a sneaky lot. Animus spoke first. "Red is gone, and we are about to have company."

Hinna nodded and said with a slight frown, "And he didn't even say goodbye."

Nirim stood up quickly, just in time to see four well-armed kobay sauntering toward them with unpleasant expressions on their faces. The one in the front eyed them carefully. "Good morning there, human. What ya doing in a remote place like this?"

"Passing through. And what are you up to this fine day?"

The kobay grinned slyly. "Oh, mugging hapless travelers. You haven't seen any, have ya?"

"Only four of them, just now."

The kobay cackled and called to his comrades, "Boys, we got ourselves a funny human here." He looked back at Nirim. "I don't suppose you would be willing to trade that pretty little isper for safe passage?"

Stepping directly between Hinna and the kobay,

Nirim replied calmly, "Not unless you think she is worth dying for."

"And what, you do?"

Nirim was no longer thinking about anything but the battle he was about to be engaged in as he slid one foot back and brought the blade staff to bear. He spoke grimly. "As a matter of fact, I do."

At that moment, Red came ambling around the corner of the canyon behind them, calling out, "I found us some more wat—"

He cut off abruptly at the scene in front of him. The leader of the kobay thieves shrieked like a small child. "It's HIM!"

One of the others cried out in despair. "Run for your lives!" Substantially faster than they had appeared, they fled like their very lives depended on it.

Nirim relaxed from his battle posture, grinning wryly at Red. "It seems you're rather scary for a pacifist."

Hinna looked at Red as though seeing him for the first time, and shook her head. "I don't think Red is scary, Nirim. Are you sure you're not thinking of those other kobay?"

Nirim let out a small sigh as Red chuckled and said, "Well, maybe they thought I was someone else."

Animus muttered under her breath, "Somehow I doubt it."

Red held up a large drinking gourd as he repeated his initial statement. "Anyway, I found fresh water for us."

They traveled for several hours before they reached a fork in the path, with one branch leading to the town of Mibi, which was just visible from the intersection, and the other winding off toward the lower plains. Red turned to them and bowed politely. "Thank you for your company, friends, but we part ways here."

Animus smiled broadly at him and bowed in return. “Well met, kobay. Fair travels before you.” Nirim and Hinna stared at her for a moment before simply waving. Red proceeded down the path away from them.

Animus watched him leave. “Do you think we will see him again?”

Hinna spoke confidently. “I am sure we will. He was too nice for us not to.”

Nirim shook his head. “Hopefully we won’t. He was more than he pretended to be.”

Animus waved her hand dismissively. “Oh, Nirim, you’re just jealous.”

Nirim raised an eyebrow. “You would say that.”

Hinna defended him, however unnecessarily, blushing slightly. “Nirim, you don’t have anything to be jealous of.”

He put his hand to his face as he glanced at Animus, who appeared to be enjoying his suffering. “Let’s just go see if anyone in Mibi knows about Airili’s denizens.”

They made their way to the city, and Nirim noted that it was a rather dense place, with the tan stone buildings built close together and even on top of one another. It was moderately busy, with kobay engaged in diverse tasks busily roaming the streets. Nirim quickly saw that he was very nearly the only human, and without doubt Hinna and Animus were unique here. They drew numerous curious expressions from the passing kobay. Nirim wondered if it would have been a better idea for him to do this particular task by himself. Actually, if he thought about it, this was probably true of almost everything he had experienced in this time so far.

Nirim assumed they needed to head to the large building on one side of town if they wanted to talk to anyone knowledgeable, and he only had to ask four different kobay before he got an answer, or at least an answer more than a vague grunting noise that seemed to mean he was considered an annoyance.

He was walking down the street when someone ran into him from the side, sending him reeling, though he managed to avoid falling over. He swiveled to see the kobay who had practically crashed into him. The tall, darker-skinned kobay muttered some kind of apology that included a derogatory comment about weak humans, and continued on his way down the cross street. Hinna asked anxiously, "Nirim, are you okay?"

Nirim spoke absently as he watched the kobay disappear around the corner of a building. "I am fine."

He turned and continued toward the large building that was the guild hall. As far as he could tell from conversations with Red, and his own past experience, the kobay government was a loose coalition of warriors' guilds. Weight of authority was determined by the number and strength of the warriors in a guild. Essentially every town operated autonomously, with its guild serving as civil law enforcement, military, and bureaucratic body. Nirim was impressed that the kobay could get anything done with such a haphazard system. They entered the guild hall, and Nirim looked around at the various burly warriors milling about.

A younger kobay woman with a long blond streak in her black hair and mane came up to them and greeted them. "Hello, strangers. I am Ziase, attendant for the Tyque guild. How may I assist you?"

Nirim thought this was too easy, and that some horrendous altercation was inbound to correct for the unreasonable rationality of the situation. Nirim suppressed his cynicism as he said, "We are interested in learning about the fate of Airili and its people."

Ziase eyed them skeptically for a moment. "Well, you are foreigners." She cleared her throat and spoke briskly. "I will provide you with the information you seek in exchange for a favor."

Nirim sighed as he muttered under his breath, "Horrendous." He then stood up straighter and asked, "Sure. What is this favor that you would ask of us?"

Ziase smirked darkly as she said, without any tonal inflection, "I want you to rid the ruins of Airili of the blood-cursed demon."

Hinna's mouth fell open, and Animus swung her gaze toward Nirim with a look that spoke volumes of her desire to avoid attempting such a task. Nirim smiled and tossed his hands in the air. "Oh, is that all you need?"

Ziase's eyes narrowed. "Yes. I should warn you that it has been killed before without lasting success."

"And is there anything else we should know?"

"Bring me the city's scepter as proof that you have slain this horror. You will find it in the subterranean levels of the old library. Now be off with you, human. I have better things to do than babysit your kind."

She turned and walked off. Nirim wasted no time in walking back out to the street. Animus spoke a little nervously. "Please tell me you aren't considering doing this? Maybe someone else knows about Airili."

Hinna tugged on his arm to get his attention and said to him with great concern, "Nirim, please let's not do this."

Nirim said nothing for a moment as he continued down the street, his companions anxiously awaiting his response. He stopped at the city's gate and said calmly, "We have to do this, not for information about Airili as much as information about that thief who stole the key to the iether bloom."

They both looked at him in shock. Nirim had not noticed the absence of the key until after their conversation with Ziase, but he was certain that the tall, dark kobay had taken it. Animus scolded him. "You were pickpocketed? Nirim, you're still an idiot."

"Thanks, Animus. Your kind words are bolstering my delicate ego." Hinna stared at them, but surprisingly said nothing.

Nirim started down the road in the direction of the ruins of Airili as he said, "Besides, there is no demon."

Animus called after him as she and Hinna hurried to catch up. "Wh-what? How do you know?"

"Because they don't exist. There is no record of any such being in all the histories of our peoples, at least not such that would remotely fit the description that Ziase gave us."

Hinna sighed with relief. "And here I thought we were going to have to fight some enormous monstrosity."

"Oh, that we will probably have to do, but it won't be some undying supernatural being, even if it is a monster."

Animus complained, "Somehow I don't find that particularly reassuring, Nirim."

Nirim glanced at Hinna, who looked worried again, and said reassuringly, "Look at the bright side, Hinna. You can see the ancient site of Airili for yourself."

She appeared to be considering that idea, but her expression returned to one of anxious anticipation as Animus added, "You just have to watch out for murderous monsters behind every rock, that's all."

Nirim frowned at Animus, while Hinna grabbed tightly to his arm like her life depended on it. "Animus, that really wasn't necessary."

Animus shrugged innocently, as though she had no idea what he was talking about. He worried about where the previous unity between his two companions had gone. They now seemed to be at odds with one another. If this continued, he was going to have to have an unpleasant talk with them.

Chapter 20

Hinna trudged silently alongside Nirim, the question consuming her mind since Animus had brought it up so unceremoniously the night before. What use was she? Animus's words struck a strange truth that she had not wanted to consider. Nirim was an incredible warrior from the past, on a mission that she only partially understood. But what she did know was that she had no apparent function as one of his traveling companions.

If it were just her own opinion, she would have dismissed it as the ramblings of her mind. But since it was an opinion shared by Animus, Nirim, and even their brief friend Red, it was a rather undeniable reality. What made it even harder to clear from her mind was Nirim's surprisingly strong stance the next morning, where he had implied that her value exceeded his own. But how could that be? If she were useless, how could she be valuable? It seemed a sheer contradiction.

She pondered asking Nirim directly for some clarification, but she remembered the trouble she had skirted when she asked him her last direct question. She could, of course, ask Animus, but she dreaded being put down, as Animus seemed more hostile again.

She knew some fear as her thoughts turned to what they would find in the ruins of Airili. What was she to make of Nirim's statements about the demon not being real, but also being real? It was merely confusing, and not less scary than saying nothing at all. Of course, Nirim was a formidable warrior, and he could deal with whatever evil awaited them. She found this thought, too, to be comforting, though since they had started traveling together, she had never seen him directly fight anyone, which seemed odd for a warrior. But then again, Nirim was probably the oddest person she had ever known, so it fit him perfectly.

She studied his face as they walked along. He looked cautious, yet calm. Nirim always seemed calm. It was this feature of his character that made her continue following him even when things seemed particularly distressing. True, she still wanted to write her summary of human history, but this was becoming less of a motivating force. Nirim glanced at her, and she quickly turned away, feeling the heat rise in her face as she realized she had been staring at him the whole time. She completely missed Nirim's rolling his eyes and shaking his head.

Animus's voice broke into her contemplations. "We have been traveling for hours, and it's starting to get dark. How far away is this place?"

Nirim shrugged. "I don't know." He stopped walking and held up his left arm, and his blue iether rune began to glow with a dim light. After a quiet moment, he smiled wryly at them. "We have arrived at our destination."

Hinna swept her eyes across the inhospitable wilderness landscape. "Nirim, this doesn't look like anything."

Animus crossed her arms. "You're lost, aren't you, Nirim? Males are all the same, regardless of race. You're just flat unwilling to admit to needing directions."

Nirim ignored them and surveyed the area

instead. He pointed to a large, elongate area that was easily more than a thousand paces long. "That is what used to be the lake of Airili," he clarified. He then pointed off to the right. "And that there would have been the town center." Turning further to the right, he gestured triumphantly. "And that there must have been the great library."

Hinna looked doubtfully at the large pile of stones dotted with brush and small trees. Nirim walked purposefully toward the rock pile, blade staff in hand. Animus muttered almost to herself as she followed. "Maybe the heat is getting to his head."

Hinna thought she saw something move in the shadow of a large rock and hurried to catch up. "W-wait for me!"

Nirim stopped and looked curiously at the doorway-shaped opening on the far side of the large rock pile. Animus grinned. "Dark, monster-infested demon lair, here we come!"

Hinna shuddered and grabbed Nirim's arm tightly. Without turning, he spoke to Animus. "You really don't need to be so descriptive here, you know?"

The seerrine was hardly repentant. "I just tell it like it is. It's not my fault that some of us here are defenseless."

Nirim shook his head and looked at Hinna. "You will be fine, but I do need my arm free if I am to successfully engage any . . . enemies." She let go of him reluctantly.

Animus turned her head sharply. "Did you hear something?" Hinna jumped and darted her eyes quickly back and forth over the rocks.

Nirim took a harsher tack with Animus. "I will make you ride on the roof of the iether bloom if you keep this up."

Animus recoiled with a fearful look. "All right,

all right, but seriously, I thought I heard something." With a slight nod, Nirim entered the opening in the rock pile. Hinna and Animus hurried after him.

They passed along a corridor that was clearly the remnants of an old hallway. Nirim held up his left arm and used his rune to light the way. At the end of the hall, Nirim turned and walked down a second corridor that ended at a large double door. It was opened just a crack, and light was visible on the other side.

Nirim reached for the door, and Animus whispered urgently, "Wait! What if it's the demon?"

Nirim whispered back, "If it is, he will be in for a surprise."

Hinna added, "And if it's not?"

"Then someone else will be in for a surprise."

Nirim swung the door open and stepped inside without hesitation. Hinna gasped in delight. Nearly everywhere she looked, there were stacks of books. Shelves lined the large cylindrical room, and they had to look down to see the main level. They stood on a balcony platform that opened immediately onto a staircase that ran down along the wall to the lower floor. Down in the central room, there was a glowing fire pit with several old stuffed chairs arrayed around it.

Nirim's eyes narrowed as he focused on the back of a figure who sat reading in one of the chairs. Nirim slowly descended the stairs, and as they reached the bottom, the figure said in a loud voice, "So they finally found someone brave enough to challenge the demon of Airili?"

Hinna trembled and reflexively grabbed Nirim's arm, but to her confusion, he seemed quite relaxed, and he did not object to what he had told her could be a hindrance. Instead, he simply waited silently. The figure rose and turned to face them.

Animus gasped. "Red!"

Red blinked, his mouth opening slightly. Obviously they were not the people he was suspecting had come. The ruddy kobay looked a little embarrassed. "Well, if I had known you were coming, I would have put on more tea." He turned to the metal pot that hung over the fire pit, used a hooked metal rod to retrieve it, and busied himself with filling it with more water.

Nirim muttered out loud, "Why am I not surprised." He walked forward slowly, Animus and Hinna trailing behind. "So, Red, how long have you been living in this place?"

Hinna thought this was an odd question, considering the seeming sameness of the demon Ziase spoke of and the kobay they knew as Red. Red considered it, and then said with confidence, "I have been here precisely ten years and one day." Nirim laughed so suddenly and loudly that Animus flinched and Hinna let out a startled yelp. Red simply stared at him and asked, "Is your psychosis acting up?"

Nirim sighed and took a seat in one of the chairs by the fire. "What are you reading, Red?"

Red glanced back at his chair a little sheepishly and said, "Oh, it's nothing really, just something light after the systematic treatment of minerals that I finished earlier."

Nirim looked over at Hinna and Animus and reassured them, "You might as well come over here and have some tea. Red probably won't get murderous anytime soon."

Hinna walked slowly toward Nirim, while Animus shrugged and made her way over to where Red had been sitting and took his seat. Hinna sat next to Nirim and watched patiently as Red poured them each a cup of tea and served it to them. Red stared a little oddly at Animus, who practically lounged in his chair reading his book; however, he merely handed her some tea and said, "Don't lose my place."

Red turned to look at Nirim and asked, "Was there something that you wanted, Nirim?"

"The fine guild at Mibi requested your eradication, but that really isn't what I wanted."

Red sighed wistfully. "There are things that simply cannot be run from, I suppose." He paused, looking thoughtful for a moment, and then asked, "What is it that you did want?"

Nirim chuckled. "I wanted to learn more about what happened to the people of Airili."

"Now that is simple. There was a terrible earthquake that destroyed most of the city, and resulted in the lake draining away. With neither water nor homes, the people of Airili left this place, and many of them founded Mibi."

Nirim nodded knowingly. "And those people are probably long dead by now."

"Yes, likely so, as it was quite some time ago."

Animus lowered the book that Hinna was fairly sure she was not actually reading and said, "So basically, your crazy cousin has us looking for someone who can't possibly exist."

"Miralla was a little eccentric, but no, she knew I would understand the situation here, which is why we don't need to look any further."

Red looked perplexed. "You are on a mission for your cousin?"

Hinna tried to explain. "Yes. You see, Nirim's cousin was a seer, but she has likely been dead for years."

Animus rebuked her. "Hinna! Not everyone we come across knows about Nirim."

Hinna stared at the floor, embarrassed that she had made yet another mistake. Nirim relieved her of some of her guilt when he said, "It's fine, Hinna. Red is going to figure it out sooner or later."

Red looked even more perplexed. "At this moment, I am just confused."

Nirim sipped his tea and stood up as he explained to everyone. "Airili was one of the earliest kobay settlements, so citizenship had a single requirement. One needed to live within the city for at least ten years. Since Red has met such a requirement, that makes him a citizen by default, probably the first in a generation or more. Therefore, he must be the third guardian." Nirim glanced around and added, "And though I don't see it, I suspect the red iether astral rod is not far away."

Hinna was surprised that Animus seemed rather excited about the prospect. "Ah, so Red will be joining us on our strange venture?" Hinna looked at Red, who appeared contemplative. Nirim said nothing, waiting silently.

"I hate to disappoint you, but I am not interested in joining you."

Animus jerked upright. "What! You can't just abandon us to fight the darkness alone!"

Red shook his head. "I am a pacifist. What good would I be to you? And I rather like my life of solitude here."

Animus was about to say something else when Nirim raised his hand. "I respect your desires, and we will not force you to accompany us, but I would request that you think it over tonight."

"Very well, Neerum, please stay the night here with me, and I will let you know tomorrow if my opinion has changed."

Animus protested, "Nirim, he has to come with us. Can't you just beat him up and make him come?"

Nirim looked at her with his strange, serious expression. "Animus, there are other ways to deal with people, and besides, I didn't force you to come along. Why would I force him?"

Animus slumped back into her chair. "Because your cousin said he was supposed to."

Hinna wondered why Animus was acting so strongly about the whole thing. If Red did not want to come with them, then they could do nothing about it. Honestly, she thought Red was nice, but she was concerned that her own position among them might be lowered by the presence of another formidable fighter. One could tell she was especially useless when her status was threatened by a pacifist warrior. Then again, Red was nice enough that she was not opposed to him traveling with them, just a little leery.

Nirim glanced around the room and said casually, "So I guess you read a lot?"

Red nodded. "Yes, it is my regular pastime, other than occasional forays out into the surrounding areas to see what the current state of the world is."

Animus interjected bluntly, "So you do nothing but read books and take walks in the wilderness?"

Red gazed at her for a long moment before he said with some resignation, "You could say it that way, I guess."

Animus shook her head. "Somehow you managed to be substantially weirder than Nirim. A true feat, I assure you."

Red raised an eyebrow and asked Nirim, "Is she always like this?"

Nirim sighed. "Yes, especially when she is upset."

Red nodded knowingly. "I see. Well, this does explain your mental problem."

Animus objected loudly, "Excuse me! I am sitting right here!"

Hinna simply watched. It was quite frustrating,

really. She could tell that at some level they were bantering back and forth, but from her perspective, she could not tell where they were speaking seriously, and where they were merely jesting. It was one of those situations where, regardless of the number of people in the room, she felt very, very alone.

Chapter 21

Nirim lay on the makeshift mat that Red had provided for him, located a handful of paces away from the fire pit. The others slept on the compass points around the fire. The more he thought about it, the more he had to agree with Red that it made no sense for him to accompany them. Sure, he had shown them the astral rod that Friska had carried long before as the previous third guardian. But what good was such a weapon in the hands of someone committed to pacifism?

Nirim got the distinct impression that Red had not always been that way. And if there was a shred of truth to what Ziase had implied, his past was probably about as far as one could go from pacifism. The response of the kobay thieves also suggested he still had quite the reputation even after years of his new lifestyle. Nirim shuddered to think what might happen to Red if the guild at Mibi knew of his non-threatening ways. While it might be interesting to see how far Red's pacifism went under the threat of death, Nirim decidedly did not want to see if the savagery of the kobay had changed much since his time.

The whole thing felt like an utter waste of time and effort. He appreciated the fact that it kept him occupied, but it was far too elaborate for his tastes, and made him somewhat ambivalent about Red's company. What did it matter if a long-defunct, elite group of warriors, trained to fight an enemy that seemed to no longer exist and belonging to a government that was but a whisper of memory, had the right number of members?

Nirim rolled restlessly onto his side and looked across the faintly glowing fire pit at Animus, who was curled into a ball under her traveling cloak. He wondered why she was acting more outrageous than normal. It seemed senseless to him, and it created unnecessary friction.

Thinking about Animus reminded him of the unfortunate reality that he would need to find the iether bloom's ignition mechanism. Because it was not a mechanical key, he could not operate the iether bloom without it. While it looked rather interesting, it was not made of precious metals, nor was it an item in demand. He tried to envision where a thief would fence such an object. He chuckled quietly to himself, as the only thing that he could think of was either a museum or a junkyard. He reached out and touched the rune of second sight as it occurred to him that finding the ignition mechanism would not be particularly challenging. Retrieving it might be the hard part.

He closed his eyes and willed himself to sleep. It worked perfectly, if one discounted the hour that passed between the willing and the sleeping.

***

"It was Red's decision to stay, and we are going to abide by that decision, regardless of its logic." Nirim was starting to feel impatient with Animus as he addressed the issue for the fourth time during their walk back toward Mibi.

"But . . . but what about—?"

"Animus, please. I know you wanted him to come with us, but we can't force him to come."

Animus looked sullenly at the ground as she muttered, "I didn't want him to come that much."

Nirim rolled his eyes. She was acting like they had left a close personal friend of hers rather than some random kobay that they had met two days before.

As Mibi came into sight, Nirim spotted a familiar-looking kobay walking toward them. It was the pickpocket, or at least the kobay that he was fairly confident had been the pickpocket. He had not yet seemed to notice that other people were approaching. Nirim turned to Animus and said, "That's the guy who stole the iether bloom's key. If you would be so kind as to apprehend him, we might be able to save ourselves a great deal of time in tracking it down."

Animus smiled grimly. "I got this." She darted down the road at the unsuspecting kobay at full speed. Technically kobay were physically stronger than the other races, but the speed and dexterity of the seerrine was legendary.

By the time the kobay looked up and realized his day was about to get worse, it was too late. Animus struck him to the ground with a powerful blow from her tail and, coiling it around him, held him tightly. He struggled pointlessly against Animus's iron grip. Nirim and Hinna caught up. Nirim peered down at the gasping kobay and asked, "I don't suppose you would like to tell me what has become of the object you unceremoniously retrieved from my belt?"

The kobay practically spat at him. "I don't know whatcha talking 'bout."

Hinna looked at Nirim and said with genuine concern, "What do we do if he won't talk to us?"

"It's simple, really. I just make his eyes explode." Nirim raised his right arm, and red iether began to glow brightly through his rune.

The thief was beside himself in his hurry to

speak. “Ya-ya-you’re crazy, human! I sold it here in town to a loopy woman who lives in a remote place to the northeast.”

Animus gave him a hard look. “Like I believe that. What was her name? And just how far away is this?”

The kobay whined, “Please spare my eyes! I am a thief, not a liar! Her name is Vesa, and she lives in the old junkyard that is on the other side of the human rail. Please, you gotta believe me!”

Nirim plucked the kobay’s money bag from his belt as he said, “Well, looks like we are going to have to buy it back.”

Animus looked at him, waiting for further instruction. Nirim flicked his hand. “Just toss that garbage off the road. We don’t need it anymore.” Animus shrugged and hurled the kobay fifty paces through the air to land with a crunch in a ditch. The kobay wasted no time in jumping to his feet and running back toward Mibi. Nirim watched with a bit of satisfaction before he said, “Let’s go find this scrapyard.”

As they walked, Hinna asked a little nervously, “You weren’t really going to make his eyes explode, were you?”

“Of course not. That would have been Animus’s job.”

Animus glared at him. “And what makes you think I would do it?”

***

It was not difficult to find the old scrapyard that had served as a repository for the dead husks of the retired trackkuses. It was also conveniently close to where the iether bloom lay hidden, meaning it had still taken them the better part of two days to get there. Nirim surveyed the area, then gestured to his companions. "Come on. Let's go find out how much it is going to cost us to get the iether bloom's ignition mechanism back."

They proceeded down the steep decline that led to the small, flat depression where the scrapyard was. There were only a few modestly intact trackkuses; the rest were bits and pieces, old rail cladding, and other junk dumped there out of convenience. The scrapyard's small office had obviously been converted into someone's home.

Nirim knocked on the door and waited. After some footsteps, the door opened, and an older kobay woman looked at them suspiciously. "What do you want?" she snapped, with some irritation at being interrupted from the meal that was plainly visible on the table behind her.

Nirim bowed politely and began, "Pardon our intrusion, but a fellow of questionable character claims to have sold you an odd-looking—"

"A trackkus ignition mechanism. Now what of it?"

The woman held up the item in front of him. Nirim looked at her shrewdly. Apparently her choice of dwelling location was not by coincidence. He cleared his throat. "It was stolen from us, and we need it back."

She looked at them as though seeing them for the first time, muttering, "An isper, a seerrine, and a weak human." Nirim was not particularly impressed by being the only one with an adjective, but before he could say anything, the woman wheeled to the side and bluntly commanded, "Come in!"

They entered, and the woman closed the door behind her, intoning sarcastically, "So where is the kobay?"

Animus huffed with exasperation. "The kobay

was too fond of his solitary life among the books to come with us."

The woman stared at her for a long moment before she said, "I am Vesa. Now please have a seat and tell me more about why you need this."

Nirim and the others sat at the table, and Vesa began to serve them some of the soup she had prepared. Nirim raised his hand in objection. "You don't have to feed us."

She looked at him like he was out of his mind and snapped, "Just shut up and eat it!"

Nirim blinked and wondered if this was standard kobay hospitality. Hinna spoke softly. "Wow, I guess she told you."

He gritted his teeth. "Thank you for bringing that to my attention, Hinna."

She smiled warmly at him. "You're welcome."

Nirim let out a long breath. It had been a long trek in the burning sun, and he was not really in a mood for this. He reminded himself that Hinna did not know she had done anything annoying, but that did nothing to make it less annoying. They ate silently for several moments, then the woman looked at Animus and asked, "Tell me about this kobay who refused to join your diverse little group."

Animus glanced at Nirim, but he simply shrugged, so she answered for them. "Well, we were hoping to recruit a kobay to assist us on our journeyings, but the one we found turned out to be a pacifist, and he didn't really want to travel with us."

Nirim closed his eyes and took a deep breath. "And this is why I do most of the talking."

Hinna attempted to continue. "His name is Red, and he looks big and strong, but he's a bit strange, and quiet and nice."

Vesa shook her head. "Red never would commit

to anything after his break with the Tyque guild. It's too bad really. He has so much potential."

They all stared at her for a second before Animus asked rhetorically, "You know Red?"

Hinna looked at Animus in surprise. "Animus, isn't that clear from what she said?" The seerrine's expression became rather sour, but she refrained from upbraiding Hinna for her social non-comprehension.

Vesa eyed them like they were deranged, which Nirim felt might be more accurate than he cared to admit. "Red is my son."

Animus nearly fell out of her chair. "What!"

Vesa cupped her chin thoughtfully as she clarified. "I suppose 'adopted son' would be more accurate. I found a small kobay child in the ruins of the city of Airili while I was looking for more information on the mechanical human constructs. I felt pity for him, and took him home. I never had a partner, so I raised him by myself. When he was older, he wanted to join the Tyque guild." She paused, frowning slightly. "I never should have let him go. He was too young to know how to deal with those fiends."

Hinna's eyes got wide, and she whispered, "They attacked him?"

Vesa stared at her and said pointedly, "You're not running at full capacity, are you?"

Hinna leaned back, looking pensive and a bit uncertain. Nirim brought the attention back to Vesa's story. "Please, continue."

Vesa arched one eyebrow at him, but followed his prompting. "Anyway, the Tyque guild saw that he had the making of an incredible warrior, and so they manipulated him with flattery and vain promises. He became their best assassin, a kobay of blood and terror for any who would oppose their guild. Some claimed that he was a demon, cursed to walk among mortals, spilling the blood of any that dared cross his path." Vesa sighed. "I thought he was gone, that bloodlust would forever be his anthem, that killing the unfortunate targets of the Tyque guild would be his lot in life. A sad existence, all in all. I longed for the Creator to save him from such a terrible end, but I knew he was on an unalterable trajectory."

Vesa paused and looked out the small window in the converted home, as though recollecting the past with great difficulty. At the point where Nirim was about to interrupt her thoughts, she spoke again. "Then out of nowhere, Red came by to visit me, something he had long given up on, since I would give him an earful of my opinion of his bloodthirsty ways. He told me he had chosen to become a pacifist and was no longer a member of the Tyque guild.

"At first, I presumed it was some kind of joke, and that he was mocking me. But he continued to visit regularly, and I could see that he was changed. He spent nearly every moment reading in the ruined library of Airili, and he would often tell me of what new things he had learned. I still don't know what happened to him that caused such a pronounced and sudden change, but as far as I can tell, it started in that same library." She shrugged. "I never asked, and he never said."

Animus looked skeptical. "Sounds like he went crazy, if you ask me."

Hinna said with an air of self-confidence, "Reading the right kinds of things can really change people." She gave Animus a friendly smile. "Perhaps you could try it, too!"

Animus's eyes narrowed and her iether rune blazed with blue light, so Nirim quickly interposed himself between the two of them as he spoke to Vesa. "Ahem, well, interesting to know, but I don't suppose you're inclined to let us buy the ignition mechanism back from you?"

Vesa simply tossed it to him, and Nirim caught it out of the air. "I don't understand. Why did you buy it, only to give it away?"

"I only needed its design. The object itself is useless for my work."

Nirim was satisfied with her answer, but Hinna was unafraid to voice her curiosity. "And what is that?" Vesa studied them for a moment, then rose from her seat and beckoned them to follow her.

She stepped out the back door with them trailing behind her. She walked past several piles of junk to a large, open-sided building. Inside was an ominous metal contraption that had been a trackkus in its previous life, but now it was something far different. Nirim was at a loss as to what it was, actually. Rather than being vertically tall and horizontally narrow, it was wide and moderately flattened. It was still quite large, perhaps half the length of the iether bloom.

Vesa gestured to it with great pride. "This is my life's work!"

Animus tried to sound impressed but somewhat failed. "Wow, that's a nice . . . errr . . . whatever it is."

Hinna looked puzzled but then said, "I don't think that would stay on a rail very well."

Vesa laughed loudly, and, shaking her head, she said with a certain mischievous gleam in her eye, "Ah, but it doesn't run on a rail."

Nirim stared at it in disbelief as he slowly comprehended the object before him. The empire had tried to create exactly such a thing, but nothing had ever worked. The blue iether was too volatile to propel something in a safe manner without a restraint of some kind, like the trackkus rail. Nirim finally stated his doubt. "How does it function? I thought blue iether was too unstable for such a task."

Vesa frowned, as though she had never considered the possibility. "Yes, I do believe that is correct. The blue iether is quite unstable." Then she grinned fiendishly as she added, "But my machine doesn't run on blue iether." They all just stared at her. She waved her hand dismissively. "It's not like black magic or anything. It runs off of red iether, which restricts the pilot to a select few individuals, but still, it should work."

Hinna spoke hesitantly. "I have never heard of something mechanical running off of red iether."

"Of course not, but in principle it should be possible, and I will be the first to demonstrate it."

Animus questioned, "Should be?"

Vesa looked a tad embarrassed. "Well, I haven't exactly got it running just yet, but I am very close."

Nirim let his eyes rest on every detail he could see. "So it's a mode of transportation that moves without the need of a rail?"

"Oh, no, it is more than a mode of transportation. It is a weapon."

Nirim felt that this was no surprise coming from a kobay, and had not his own people tried to push the boundaries of how blue iether could be weaponized? Vesa was not unaware of his mild mental consternation and said rather slyly, "Aren't you going to ask me why I am building a weapon, human?"

"Okay, Vesa, why are you building a weapon?"

She turned back to look at the thing as she spoke softly with a grim tone. "Because when the world falls into chaos, I don't want to be a victim."

Nirim looked at the machine for a moment before he answered. "Vesa, do you think that the world will really get that bad before the Creator intervenes?"

"I don't know, but I do know that my people cannot resist the changing landscape. It will not be long before they sweep north to find land that is plentiful with water, land that is not theirs."

Nirim muttered, "Sounds like things might be getting crowded pretty soon."

Vesa looked at him with some curiosity, but it was Animus who clarified, saying, "The seerrine lands are under threat of freezing over, so our people may be pushed to migrate east into the human lands."

Vesa looked thoughtful as she mused, mostly to herself, "Hmm, I suppose so long as the seerrine keep to the northeast, there shouldn't really be a problem."

Nirim merely rolled his eyes, but Hinna spoke up almost vehemently. "What about all the humans living there now?!"

Animus looked away, not willing to address the reality of the question. Vesa answered flatly, "What about them?"

Chapter 22

Vesa had provided them with lodging in her home for the night. They had given her their thanks, and were on their way back toward the iether bloom, hidden in the canyon.

Animus felt unsettled. She had not thought much about what Red's past could be like, but now that she knew he had been a murderer by profession, she felt a little off at having found his company so enjoyable. It was like eating some sweet fruit, only to later find out that it was actually poisonous, and a near brush with death.

She wondered if a person like that could really change. What if he had come with them and gone berserk? What if he had hurt one of them? Of course the only person she could imagine getting hurt was Hinna, which made her particularly angry. Hinna could be annoying, but she carried an innocent persona that made hurting her seem especially sinister. Animus sighed; maybe it was for the best that Red had not accompanied them.

She watched Nirim. She had come to respect his unnerving ability to make the best decisions in the worst circumstances. Hinna was walking so close to Nirim that he had to be careful not to trip over her. Normally Animus would be bothered by the silly interloper, but at the moment, she wanted to brood alone. And if Nirim was attracted to Hinna by her mere proximity, then he really did deserve her.

Animus wished Red had been a little more transparent. It soured her whole mental image of him as a rare, bookish kobay who was not a bloodthirsty killer at heart. She had found it sweet that the book he had been reading was a touching romance between a peasant and a princess. Now she felt it would have been more apt for him to have been reading a brutal encounter between an executioner and a prisoner.

"Are you all right, Animus?"

Startled, she glared at Nirim, as though he had been reading her private thoughts, and snapped at him, "I am fine. Now leave me alone!"

Nirim recoiled slightly at finding her moody, and muttered, "Sorry I asked."

They walked along the rail down into the canyon and entered the sideline house. Nirim stopped abruptly, and Hinna, sounding a little nervous, asked, "What is it? Monsters?"

Nirim gave her a crooked grin. "Almost."

Just then, Red stepped from the shadows, the astral rod loosely in his grasp, and said apologetically, "Do forgive me showing up like this, but I don't suppose you are still willing to let me come with you, Narum?"

Nirim held out his hand in a gesture of generosity. "Of course—"

"NO!"

Hinna and Nirim turned toward Animus, surprised at her outburst. Red appeared slightly concerned. "Animus, I would not have suspected you of all people would turn me away."

Nirim muttered, "Why can't he get my name straight?"

Animus flushed slightly, saying, "No, Red, you

are a threat to our group. You cannot come."

"Sorry, Red. She has been a little testy since we visited Vesa."

Red looked thoughtful. "Hmmm. Well, then, I guess she told you about my former life, though I suppose it is no secret to anyone." Red hesitated a moment, and Animus thought he looked a little nervous himself. "Would you let me travel with you at least until your next stop then?"

Animus suppressed her revulsion. "Why don't you just go back to your dead library." It was more of a subtle command than a question.

"Well, I . . . uhhhh . . . I can't, you see."

Nirim's expression grew serious. "Why not?"

Red was struggling through a stuttered answer when Nirim simply turned and raised his right arm, unlocking the iether bloom with his red iether. Hinna grew wide-eyed and asked, "What's going on, Nirim?"

Red finally tumbled into his response. "You see, it's—it's because the library was burned and they are quite intent on ending my life, so I was rather hoping that you would be so kind as to let me at least travel with you a little bit?"

Animus opened her mouth to voice her unchanged opinion, but Nirim spoke sternly over the top of her. "We go now. You can debate the appropriateness of our new traveling companion on the rail, but I don't want to be overrun by hundreds of angry kobay warriors."

At that very moment, Ziase leapt through the air, blade out, screaming, "Diiieeee!" She lunged with full force at Red. Red did not have time to react, but he did not need it. Nirim's red iether rune burst in brilliant red light in the dim sideline house, and the air around Ziase became thick to the point that she hung suspended in the super-dense medium.

Nirim shouted sharply, "In. Now!"

Not one person hesitated as they rushed aboard the iether bloom. Nirim closed and locked the door and ran toward the control room. They could hear incessant banging along the iether bloom's metal hull. Nirim staggered to the console and slammed the ignition mechanism into place.

Red watched him with curiosity as the console came alive with blue iether. "Impressive."

Animus shook her head and grabbed tightly to one of the handrails as she quipped honestly, "No, it's about to be sickening." Red looked questioningly at her, but got no answer.

Nirim turned the iether drive power dial, and the iether bloom roared to life. He waited for just a second and then threw the booster lever forward. The iether bloom fairly flew down the rail, scattering the kobay warriors that were swarming it, looking for a way in. Nirim was thrown back into Hinna, who caught him rather deftly. Animus did not have as good of a grip as she thought and was hurled into Red, who barely caught her at all, and both of them went down into a heap. She scowled at him. "If you kill me, I will hate you forever."

Red nodded enthusiastically. "Yes, that would make two of us."

As the iether bloom's speed leveled out, Red asked politely, "Would you mind getting off me so that I can get up?" She got up, watching him warily.

Red dusted himself off and looked over to Hinna, who stood staring wide-eyed at Nirim, who was limp in her arms. Animus moved closer. She put her hand to his neck as Hinna asked, "W-what happened? I mean, I know that he didn't hit his head." Animus was likewise unsure, as he looked reasonably unharmed.

Red answered them as he peered around Animus at Nirim. "He must have expended his energy protecting me with the red iether. Its use by humans can often have severe consequences."

Animus studied him grimly. "So it's like you nearly killed him without lifting a finger?"

Red looked at her for a long moment before he responded. "You have a most wonderful outlook on things, Animus, but I would appreciate it if you could keep some of your animosity to yourself."

Hinna interrupted them hesitantly. "Uh, could you help me put him in a bed?"

Red nodded, but Animus spoke defensively, "Don't touch him, Red. You have done enough damage already." Animus picked him up and carried him to the sleeping area, depositing him in a bottom bunk. They then retired to the dining booth, where Animus sat silently, glaring at Red as he was investigating the window shutter mechanism with great interest.

Hinna stared at the table contemplatively before she asked, "So if humans don't have any iether of their own, and they aren't particularly strong, fast, or smart, what are they for?"

Animus looked at her with mild frustration, but she had not the faintest idea how to respond. Red answered her softly. "Humans are for love."

Hinna blushed heavily and stammered, "O-o-o-oh, if you say so."

Despite her desire to remain angry at Red, Animus burst out laughing, while Red raised his hands quickly in a manner that suggested he was trying to halt Hinna's mind from wandering further down that particular thought path. He spoke, a little embarrassed himself. "No, no, not like that. It's more of a reflection of the Creator's own love, as an aspect of character."

Hinna scrunched her face in mild consternation. "Well, they seem to be rather terrible at reflecting that as a whole."

"I suppose that is true."

Animus asked, "And how do you know this information?"

"I read it in a book, of course."

Animus rolled her eyes as she said pointedly, "Are you sure you didn't murder someone for it?"

Hinna frowned at Animus and spoke with an atypical firmness. "Animus, it isn't appropriate to so insult our new traveling companion. Besides, you know very well that Nirim holds nothing against us for our past failures. Why should we hold Red to his?"

Animus turned sharply to rebuke her, and caught sight of Nirim, watching them silently while leaning against the back wall. His expression was mildly disapproving, sufficiently so to cause her to draw up short. She muttered with some frustration, "Shouldn't you still be unconscious, Nirim?"

Hinna looked quite uncomfortable at his sudden appearance. "Why, Nirim, h-h-h-how long have you been standing there?"

Nirim took a seat next to Red and slowly put his hand to his face as he sighed. Animus had noticed that he did this a lot; surely their company was not that exasperating. Nirim spoke with mild resignation. "Please don't tell me what you were talking about that would cause you such distress at the possibility of my having heard."

Red mercifully changed the subject. "So tell me more about this psychosis of yours that involves ending nightfall." Nirim did not look particularly excited about the way Red had taken the conversation, but he proceeded to explain anyway.

"A long time ago, before our races existed, the Creator formed an extremely powerful entity for his own benevolent purpose. This entity became envious of the Creator, and sought to supplant the Creator's position.

This, of course, ended badly, and it was inflicted with an indelible blackness to mark it as a rebel. Since that time, it has been known simply as the darkness, and it has long schemed and manipulated the races into turning away from the Creator. Those who would not turn away became targets for destruction. Now, it seems the darkness has not been seen by any of the races since even before my time, when the great empress banished it from both the human and the isper lands. I belonged to, and now lead, a group of elite warriors trained specifically to combat this insidious threat, should it show itself."

Red mused, "I have read of this darkness, though it seemed fictional to me. But isn't it a non-issue if the darkness isn't around anymore?"

Nirim shook his head. "No, it's not that simple. The darkness is still a serious threat, and its complete absence is more worrying than reassuring. It has been known to develop intricate schemes over the course of hundreds of years, and it is only the Creator's intervention that ultimately foils its plots. Actually, I suspect that my purpose in being kept until this time is a direct counter to some move the darkness is going to make. Miralla was a seer, and the things she saw were often visions of the future. Yet, most of those visions were more like instructions as to what she needed to do, rather than things she needed to do something about."

Hinna furrowed her brow. "Now I am confused. Miralla saw the future, but not the future?"

"None of us really understood much of what she said or how it worked. What we did know is that what she saw was never wrong."

Red looked thoughtful. "Maybe she was always right, but she does seem to have chosen a rather unlikely group of individuals for stopping such a severe threat."

Nirim smiled wryly. "Tell me about it." Hinna

had just opened her mouth to speak when he turned and said as gently as possible, “Sorry, Hinna, that was rhetorical.” Hinna dropped her eyes to the table, trying to hide her shame at being called out for not being able to follow the conversation correctly.

Red rescued her again by asking, “So where are we going next?”

Nirim answered. “An excellent question.” He turned to Animus. For her part, Animus felt self-conscious with all three of them suddenly looking at her, though Red’s glance was inquisitive, not knowing why she was the center of attention.

She cleared her throat. “I did remember the rest of Miralla’s song a little while back, but I have since forgotten it.”

Nirim slumped over and murmured, “Why am I not surprised.”

Animus tossed her head and crossed her arms. “Fine. If you’re going to be so insulting, I won’t read it to you.”

“Sorry. You should have said that you had written it down.”

Red arced an eyebrow at Animus. “I am sorry, but how old are you?”

Annoyed at his insinuating that she was childish, she fixed an angry glare upon him. “Just keep pushing your luck, cat-breath.”

Nirim cleared his throat loudly and threatened, “Okay, you two, don’t make me put you on the roof.” Red chuckled, but Animus felt a jolt of fear merely at the thought of riding on the iether bloom’s roof.

Hinna’s curiosity had reached the point of overflowing, and she interrupted. “So? What does the rest of the song say?”

Animus fished out the scrap of parchment that she had written the last part of the song on while it was lucid in her mind and read, “East you have been, and south, and now the last, but not least. For the fourth, go west, to the land of the glorious. Find the one who is reborn in the light of the sun.”

Red wore a confused expression. “That’s interesting, but it has no meaning to me.”

Animus could not agree more, and they all turned this time to look expectantly at Nirim. He appeared particularly sheepish as he stroked his chin and said, “Uh, well, so we have to go to the isper lands. And then we need to . . . do . . . something. I have no idea.”

Animus found the lack of his usual certainty amusing and erupted into laughter. Nirim gave her a narrow look. “Thank you for that vote of confidence, Animus.”

Hinna, of course, began to express her confusion over why he was grateful for Animus’s blatant guffawing at his atypical difficulty with this new riddle. He merely sighed, and Red said with some humor, “Well, at least you’re not a boring lot, eh?”

Nirim chuckled lightly. “It’s amazing the things you miss when you no longer experience them.”

Animus teased, “Oh, come on, Nirim, you know that you love us!”

He nodded and said with great sarcasm, “Yes, deep down. Very deep down.”

Nirim paused and looked quickly at Hinna, whose face had taken on a rosy shade, her eyes gone soft and dreamy. However, rather than try to correct his mistake, he simply got up and walked back toward the front of the iether bloom. Red called after him. “Where are you going, Neeram?”

“Back to sleep, where it is safer.”

Red looked at Animus with a perplexed expression. “Safer? Is he in some kind of danger?”

Animus slid her eyes slyly in Hinna’s direction.

"Substantial danger that threatens his very soul."

At first Red glanced around as though he expected some enemy to emerge and pounce for Nirim's life, but then he stopped, his eyes resting on Hinna. "Oh! I see."

Hinna watched them with consternation, the subtleties of their meaning lost in the tonelessness with which she heard them. "What danger?" To her chagrin, this only resulted in both Red and Animus breaking out into the mutual laughter of friends sharing an inside joke. Hinna studied the table's surface, looking a little dejected. "I am sorry. I just don't understand what you are talking about."

CHAPTER 23

Later that day, with the iether bloom flying smoothly along the rail, Nirim sat in the small logistics room pouring over the various charts and maps, trying to decide which was most accurate, and where the best point of departure would be. They would have to stop near the river and take a boat into the isper lands. And then they would have to somehow deal with the enormous wall the isper had erected. He briefly contemplated enlisting Hinna's help, but then he realized that there was probably a reason she had been operating outside the wall when she had been captured by the human raiding party.

Once they got through the wall, the problems were not over. Nirim had not the slightest clue how they were supposed to find this enigmatic individual who was "reborn in the light of the sun." It was very likely an isper, as the others had been citizens of their respective lands, but he supposed it was not a given. Was the rebirth figurative, or was it a literal reincarnation? The latter sounded crazy. Maybe it would be easier to work from the sunny side of things. Nirim chuckled to himself for a moment at how humorous that sounded, but lost sight of the humor as he realized that was no more helpful in understanding what Miralla meant than the rebirth ideas.

Nirim leaned back in his chair and tried to

envision what kind of person this fourth guardian would be. He took stock of the current guardians. Himself, a homeless warrior noble without any marketable skills. Then there was the seerrine warrior leader who could not shoot a bow to save her life. Highly unfortunate, given that the astral weapon was her only real defense against minions of the darkness. Red was third, the skilled assassin who had taken an oath of pacifism. This rendered him useless in a fight, which seemed to negate the whole point of his being a guardian.

Based on the current average of their group's dysfunctional state, Nirim predicted that the fourth member would have to be someone relatively defective. Maybe they would be crippled, unable to walk? Or perhaps so grotesquely ugly that they always had to hide their face?

Nirim shook his head, as he knew with certainty that neither of those would be the case. No, their next guardian would have to have some kind of severe personality quirk to fit well with the rest of them. Probably an agoraphobe, or a sufferer from spontaneous panic attacks. Even better, maybe they could have a demented fascination with crawling things.

He sighed; it would all have been funny, except for the lingering dread that his line of thought was most likely completely true.

Nirim glanced up to see Hinna standing in the doorway, eyes downcast, waiting silently for him to finish his brooding. Nirim cleared his throat softly, and she looked up, startled. "Hinna. What can I help you with?"

Hinna hesitated, but then took a deep breath and asked, "Are you busy?"

"Not really. Please have a seat, and tell me what's on your mind."

Hinna walked gingerly over to one of the other

seats that was bolted to the floor and slid into it. She rested both elbows on the table and put her chin in her hands as she gazed at him across the table, with a sort of nervous, furtive expression that told him he would have been better off telling her that he was exceedingly busy. He hoped Red or Animus was about, because their timely appearance might be a welcome escape from whatever trouble was about to come from giving his socially incompetent historian isper an open invitation. Actually, what worried him most was the fact that she seemed less and less interested in human history in general, and more and more interested in Nirim history specifically. The last couple of questions she had asked him had been a little personal for his comfort.

He could not deny she was incredibly beautiful; even in the muted lighting of the logistics room, her long, colorful hair framed her face like varying hues of tiny flowers flowing down onto the table and into her lap. Regardless, he still held out hope for a means of returning to his own time. Surely if he could be held till a future time, he could be sent back. Nirim spoke as calmly as he could manage, and was grateful in this moment that Hinna could not hear the plainly awkward variation in his tone. “What did you want?”

Nirim already knew exactly what she was going to say. That question any girl would ask of her love interest. As far as he could tell, women were mostly similar in their concerns and aspirations, so she was obviously going to ask if he found her beautiful, and he was going to be honest, but follow up with something about beauty being dissociated from actual relationships.

“Nirim, do you think that I am . . .”

“Yes.”

“. . . useless?”

They both stared at each other for the briefest of seconds, looking surprised to hear what the other said.

Nirim quickly tried to recover. "Uhh . . . NO, I mean . . . no, you are not useless, Hinna."

She sighed and looked down at the table, her voice barely audible. "Nirim, I was thinking that since we will be in the isper lands, it might be best for me to return home, and . . . stay home."

Mentally, Nirim was immediately opposed to the idea, and he could think of dozens of reasons why this would be a bad thing. However, he caught himself and considered that this might be the out he was looking for. Yet the more he thought about it, the more guilt he felt at a passive abandoning of his most faithful traveling companion.

Nirim decided that he would leave this decision squarely in Hinna's lap. "Well, I am sure we would all love to see your home, but whether you stay there or continue traveling is up to you."

"But Nirim, if I am not useful, why should I slow you down on your quest?"

Nirim was deeply regretting his earlier presumption as he reiterated, "Hinna, you are not useless, and you certainly aren't slowing down anything. Besides that, your knowledge of your homeland is bound to be invaluable for the next leg of our journey."

Hinna appeared doubtful. "Maybe, but after that, won't I just be in the way? I mean, do you even want me around?"

Nirim hardly knew how to answer such direct questions that seemed to have little bearing on the current circumstances. He attempted to sound confident. "Of course we want you around, Hinna. Who wouldn't? You are pleasant, knowledgeable, and funny."

Hinna rose slowly, looking far more dejected than Nirim would have anticipated from what he had said. Her shoulders were slumped, and her words forlorn. "So I am just comic relief? At least it's better than being useless."

Nirim was too shocked by the sheer pitifulness of her demeanor and expression to respond. Instead, like a man trapped in a block of ice, he simply watched, mortified, as Hinna turned slowly and walked back out into the hallway and toward the dining area.

As though a bell had summoned her presence, Animus entered the logistics room in a chatty mood, saying, "So, Nirim, I was thinking that—"

She stopped as she saw his expression, and she glanced back at the hallway with a smirk. "Have you been talking with Hinna again?"

Nirim threw his hands up in the air with exasperation. "She is impossible to communicate with. It's like she only hears a third of what I say!"

Animus laughed. "Yes, you're much the same way."

Nirim frowned at her, but she gave him no room for rebuttal as she continued. "So anyway, I was wondering how much longer before we get off of this thing?"

Nirim reviewed the map as he estimated the distance and time in his head. "Hmm, we should be there tomorrow sometime." He looked back at her and asked, "Have you come to peaceable terms with our new member?"

She seemed to consider the question for a moment before she said thoughtfully, "He does seem far too polite to be a real threat, but if you wake up with a dagger in your chest, don't come crying to me."

"Would that be his dagger or yours?"

For reasons beyond his understanding, Animus blushed slightly and tossed her head to one side as she said coldly, "Nirim, you really are an insensitive idiot." She turned briskly and rapidly disappeared through the doorway.

Nirim sat still, wondering where he had gone wrong, when Red poked his head in the room and looked at him with some concern. He said nothing, so Nirim asked cautiously, "Yes?"

"Oh, I observed the isper girl looking quite mournful, so I thought I would suggest that you cheer her up, but then I passed Animus, who appeared to be unhappy about something, and since both of them came from this direction, I could only guess that you had died in here. As that is clearly not the case, I am at a loss as to the problem."

Nirim was not sure if Red's comments made him want to laugh or cry. He shrugged and said, "Why don't you try encouraging Hinna?"

Red looked both ways down the hallway as though he feared someone might see him, and then entered and sat at the table across from Nirim. Red leaned forward and spoke in a low tone, as if sharing some grave secret. "To be honest, I find the isper to be a rather unnerving group, what with all this flying nonsense, and Henna is no exception. So I don't really feel comfortable talking to her, even if her clear social disability were not a factor."

"You do realize we are headed straight for the heart of the lands of the isper, right?"

Red sat back sharply and licked his lips. "We?"

Nirim restrained the smile that crept across his face. "Yes, 'we,' or did you forget you voluntarily joined us as a guardian?"

"Ah, yes, I suppose I did, didn't I. But what of Animus? Doesn't she despise my very presence?"

"No, not really. She just hasn't quite come to grips with your past. You know, maybe you should go talk to her about it. To clear the air, as it were."

Red stood up and spoke rather loudly, which made Nirim feel a little uneasy with what he said. "An excellent idea, Nirrum! I will talk with Animus while you cheer Hunni up!"

Nirim heaved a deep sigh. "Why me?"

It was a standard rhetorical question, so he was surprised when Red said matter-of-factly, "Because she adores you, of course!"

Nirim doubted that Red could possibly know that from having traveled with them for a handful of days, and besides, it was a substantial exaggeration of Hinna's mild interest in him. However, Red was convinced of the fact, and did not wait to hear what Nirim had to say about it, as he walked away in pursuit of Animus, the only person whose name he seemed capable of remembering reliably.

Nirim gazed around the logistics room suspiciously. He was not superstitious, but he could not help thinking the room was cursed. If there had been a fourth person to enter, no matter what he said, the conversation would leave him feeling like it had been a disaster.

He followed his companions' examples and promptly left the room, heading for the control room. He casually skimmed over the various switches and buttons that comprised the weapon controls of the iether bloom. It was a fairly sophisticated control system that anticipated the operator having an assistant to do the vector calculations necessary for getting the weapon's attack to hit a designated target. If it was as powerful as the guardians of his time had originally discussed, then missing by even a little could be catastrophic. Nirim doubted that it was meant to be fired while in motion, as this would make calculating the correct vectors nearly impossible.

However, Nirim's mind was not really on vectors or weapons, but rather on whether he wanted Hinna to stay with them, or remain in her homeland when they left. He knew without doubt which would be easier, at least logistically. Leaving her would be harder emotionally. Just the thought of it, and her sad, pitiful expression, made him feel especially guilty. He stared out the forward viewing ports as he mulled over what particular course of action they would follow after they found the fourth guardian.

Nirim's churning thoughts halted instantly. The rail through the open savannah ran to a bridge that was rapidly approaching. It was not so much the bridge that caught his attention, but the part of the bridge that was conspicuously absent. There was a gap in the closer side of the bridge, where a section of rail nearly as long as the iether bloom had collapsed. Within a few seconds, his brain informed him that at their current speed, they would slip off the rail and plummet to the bottom of what looked to be a deep canyon.

His knee-jerk response was to stop the iether bloom immediately, but a moment's reflection told him that their journey would instantly become a long, arduous one on foot. He raised his left arm, and the rune of second sight gave him sufficient information to know that they could jump the gap if they reached a high enough speed before they got there. He knew what speed they needed, but he did not know what speeds were realistically achievable by the iether bloom; the rune of second sight afforded him no information from tertiary calculations.

Animus encroached on his life-and-death decision-making as she entered the control room calling out with a sing-song voice. "Oh, N-i-r-i-m, Red is being especially annoying, and I think you're to b-l-a-a-m-e."

Noticing that he was deeply concentrating on something particular ahead of them, she glanced out the window, and her tone completely changed. "Is that bridge out?"

Nirim merely muttered as he went back over his calculations again. "Maybe."

"Maybe?! Obviously it is. Open the door now!"

"What! Why?"

"Because I want off before you do whatever idiotic thing you're contemplating. The only person who gets to risk my life is me, thank you very much."

Nirim put his hand on the iether drive power control as he said, "Sorry, Animus. If I open the door now, it will slow us down."

Red stepped into the control room and asked, "What is going on here?"

"Nirim is trying to kill us in the most creative way possible!"

Red turned to Nirim and said with a completely straight face, "Really?"

Hinna joined the growing number of commentators, and, taking one look out the view port, pointed urgently and said, "Nirim! The bridge is out!"

Distracted by the situation, Nirim spoke sarcastically without thinking. "Thank you for pointing that out, Hinna. I would never have noticed."

She smiled proudly. "You're welcome. I'm trying to be useful." Animus simply rolled her eyes, and Red just stared at her, scarcely believing that she was serious.

Hinna's eyes got wide, and she announced, "I know! We'll just jump off and glide safely to the ground before the iether bloom falls off . . ." She stopped when she saw the incredulous looks on their faces. She hunched her shoulders apologetically. "Oh, uh, I am the only one who can fly, and I can't carry more than two people."

Nirim grinned mischievously as he pushed the iether drive's main power up to its limit. "You're not the only one who can fly around here."

Red's face filled with trepidation as he begged, "Please tell me you're not going to do what I think you're going to do?"

Red's question was answered by the iether bloom's surging ahead with enough increased acceleration that grabbing the nearest handrail was the only thing that could prevent a forced relocation into the hallway. The iether bloom shot towards the bridge much faster than Nirim had anticipated it would go. No other trackkus he had ridden on could move this fast. He called out loudly, and likely unnecessarily, "BRACE!" just before the iether bloom hit the short slope immediately before the gap in the bridge.

There was an infinitesimally short period of time where they felt weightless as they left the rail and sailed through the air. At their current speed, the force of impact when they landed back on the rail could be great enough to crush them into the floor. Against his better judgment, Nirim threw his right arm forward, and the air in the control room gelled as the iether bloom slammed into the rail on the other side of the gap in the bridge.

Nirim thought he heard someone yelling, but he did not know who or what, as he wrenched the iether drive control back to something more reasonable before he blacked out from the strain of the red iether.

Chapter 24

Nirim awoke to someone sharply yanking him out of his bed, talking to him with playful exasperation. "Come on, Nirim! You're going to miss the whole ceremony at this rate!"

Nirim pulled himself groggily out of the bed and stared in disbelief. "Ista! What are you doing here?"

His cousin's amused face filled his frame of view. "Trying to keep you from embarrassing yourself. What else would I be doing?" It quickly dawned on him that he was no longer aboard the iether bloom, but in his own bedroom in the imperial residence. Ista grabbed his hand and brought him instantly into a quick walk.

Nirim was entirely unsure what was going on, so he asked as casually as possible, "So, uh, what ceremony is this?"

Ista laughed and gave him one of her you-are-a-dunce-Nirim looks as she teased, "The wedding, of course! Sometimes I wonder if you forget more than you even knew in the first place."

Nirim laughed uneasily. "Right, of course!"

They hurried through the familiar halls to the great banquet room where such events were held. Nirim noticed that he was wearing the finest formalwear that the empire had to offer. While Ista wore something quite nice, it was not on the same level as his own clothes.

Two imperial guards opened the double doors to

the great room, and Ista rushed him into the beautifully lit space. It was packed with people, many of them known to him. A long, thin section of carpeting ran from the door all the way to a makeshift dais, where two beautiful young women in white dresses stood waiting for their grooms. Nirim looked at Ista, and she answered his unspoken question with a giddy level of excitement. "It's a double wedding!"

Nirim tried to drag her off to one side as he said, "Come on, Ista. We don't want to be standing in the way when the two lucky grooms come through the door."

To his complete bafflement, she resisted him, and instead pulled him to the center of the aisle with a muffled chuckle, "Oh, silly! You are the lucky groom!" Nirim jerked his gaze back toward the dais reflexively and took a step backwards as he realized that the two young women were none other than Animus and Hinna.

At that moment, he sat straight up in his bunk on the iether bloom and smacked his head loudly into the bunk above his. Nirim winced at the throbbing pain and put his hand to his head, tenderly massaging the spot he had hit.

Red popped into the doorway and looked at him with concern. "What happened? Are you okay?"

Nirim waved away Red's concern with his free hand as he said, "It's nothing. Just a horrible nightmare, that's all."

He thought he caught a little movement out of the corner of his eye and glanced down. He smiled faintly as he saw Hinna kneeling at his bedside, slumped over on his bed, sleeping soundly. Red spoke softly. "She's been there all night."

Nirim looked up at the viewing port in the room to see sunlight streaming through the small gaps in the closed shutters. "All night? How long have I been out?"

"Since yesterday evening."

Nirim climbed out of his bunk, being careful not to disturb Hinna. He was about to proceed to the control room when he stopped and turned to look back at the isper girl, whose only motion was the gentle rhythmic movement of her breathing. Red spoke slowly, as though he feared interrupting something. "Are you sure you're all right?"

Nirim shook himself as he said, "I am fine. I just can't leave her like that." He momentarily thought about carrying her to the other room, but that seemed unnecessary, and so he picked her up and gently set her in his own bed. He wondered if she was having a similar dream to his own. She had a small but silly smile on her face, which would accurately contrast with his own response.

Nirim was acutely aware that Red was still in the doorway watching him. He stood and walked to the door. Red's expression was hard to describe, but Nirim was certain the wheels were turning beyond what was reality. "Where is Animus?" Nirim asked, as more of a distraction for Red than out of any real concern at not having seen her yet.

Red nodded and said, "Ah, yes, she is sleeping in the other room, after being up the first half of the night watching the route ahead of us to make sure there weren't any more surprises." Nirim did not need to ask who watched the rail for the other half of the night, and he did not want to ask what they thought they were going to do should there actually be a problem.

They entered the control room, and Nirim turned to watch the scenery to check their bearings. He was not a moment too soon, as he got a good, if brief, look at a marker stone that told him they were nearly to their destination, at least as far as the iether bloom was concerned. As Nirim reduced their speed in anticipation of changing rails, Red asked nervously, "What are you doing now?"

Nirim smiled. He could hardly blame the kobay; the last time he saw Nirim touch the iether drive power controls, it was a harrowing experience for all parties involved. "Don't worry, Red. We are just nearing our stop, that's all." Red breathed a sigh of relief and looked out the port as a large collection of ruined buildings came into view.

They slid smoothly onto a different rail that rapidly split away from the loop and headed east. Red asked, "What is this place?"

Nirim glanced away from the controls long enough to look grimly at the remains of the eastern trackkus exchange station. He explained as he busily began to adjust their speed and set the breaking mechanism for a long, slow, steady stop. "This place was once a center for the exchange of goods and passengers between the trackkus system and the isper riverways. Most of the buildings would be for temporary storage, and the large, central one to the right served as a place for people to wait for the next trackkus or riverboat."

Nirim changed rails several times as they continued to slow gently. They came to a smooth stop between two derelict walls. It was, at one time, one of a number of sideline houses for maintenance and short-term storage of trackkuses. All that remained of the current building were the walls of the sides, with both the roof and the end walls long gone. Nirim was not entirely sure where their next stop would be, but without further directions, he was planning on returning to the old imperial capital and looking for clues as to the cause of the blight in that area. The reality was that he had no idea what they were supposed to be doing once they assembled the four guardians. Beyond that, he was not even sure what level of urgency there was. Was there a dire situation that demanded their immediate attention, or was this a problem that was ten years away?

Animus appeared out of nowhere and excitedly said, "Finally we can get off this hurtling box of potential death! Now open the door, Nirim. I want to feel the solid ground beneath my tail."

Nirim rolled his eyes, but walked over to the door and obliged her. Animus did not hesitate at all. As soon as the door was lowered, she darted out onto the firm ground, letting out an exaggerated sigh of satisfaction. Nirim had to chuckle at her antics. "Don't you think you're being a little melodramatic here?"

She held her head up haughtily and answered, unable to hide her own smile. "Just because you like living in a stuffy metal box that might go careening off its rail at any moment and kill you, doesn't mean that I do."

Nirim shook his head and turned to Red. "Could you keep an eye on Animus? I will stay here until Hinna wakes up."

"I will gladly keep her out of trouble."

Animus taunted, "You? Red the pacifist? Keep me out of trouble? And how do you plan to do that? By lecturing me into submission?"

Red descended the stairs, saying, "Well, I initially thought I would appeal to your intellect, but I keep forgetting that you don't really have one."

Nirim quickly made his way toward the dining area in the iether bloom, both to obtain some semblance of breakfast, and to avoid becoming dragged into a conversation that could only end badly. It surprised him how Red seemed to be somewhat less tactful with Animus than he was with the rest of them. He wondered if that was because Red found her particularly provocative, or if he simply had trouble resisting the temptation to tease her.

***

Hinna blinked sleepily at the bunk above her, wishing that it had not been a dream. She sighed and got out of bed on slightly trembling limbs. She was a little surprised to see that this was Nirim's bunk rather than her own. The last thing she remembered was putting her head down for a moment while she was watching Nirim, concerned that he might have seriously injured himself by overextending his use of the red iether.

She entered the hallway and followed the low, rustling noises she heard, to find Nirim in the logistics room, plotting their trip into the isper lands. Nirim looked up and smiled ever so slightly. "Ah, good, you are awake. We've reached our stop, and we will be leaving in a short while, so be ready as soon as you can."

Hinna nodded. "Oh, okay." She quickly made her way to the iether bloom's door and exited, too self-conscious to speak further, and afraid she might blush just standing there in the doorway. Her dream had been so vivid that she was still coming to grips with reality.

As she ambled around the iether bloom, trying to put some mental distance between herself and the dream, she thought it strange that she could not remember ever having such a tangible dream before. She saw Red poking at a pile of rubble just beyond the foundation of the once-building where the iether bloom rested. She walked over to him, and, peering at the rubble with curiosity, asked, "Where is Animus?"

Red pointed in a particular direction. "I believe she is down by the river that way, freshening up." He studied her all too perceptively and inquired bluntly, "Hinna, what's wrong?"

Hinna hesitated. Could she possibly discuss this with him? Then again, Red would be the only person in their group she could ask about it. So she said, a little sheepishly, “Well, I had a very vivid dream, and I am not sure what to think about it.”

Red looked thoughtful. “Hmm, sometimes dreams can be portents of things to come, but most of the time, they are just caricature reflections of one's thoughts from the past day. Why? What did you dream about?” Hinna felt her face turning bright red and she stared hard at the ground, embarrassed to think that he knew she was thinking about it. Red’s calm voice broke through her mental chaos. “Oh, that. Well, you will have to ask Nirim if you would like to know anything more.”

Hinna recoiled sharply, her words growing shrill. “WHAT! I-I-I-I can’t ask him about that!”

“I suppose I could ask him for you.”

“NO!” She quickly reduced her tone to something a little more controlled. “Errr, no, thank you, Red. I think it was just a silly dream.” She turned from him, her face still burning as she hurried away, berating herself and wishing fervently that she had never asked Red about it to begin with.

***

Red watched her walk away quickly, wondering exactly how he should handle this particular situation. Animus materialized beside him. Catching a glimpse of Hinna, she asked, “What was that all about? I heard her yell something from halfway across the ruins.”

Red said simply, “Apparently she had an especially vivid dream.”

“A dream about what?”

“I can’t really say, as she didn’t tell me.”

Animus simply shrugged and began to make her way toward one of the other moldering buildings. “I am going to see if there is anything useful in this old place.

Are you coming?"

Red nodded. "Yes, in just a bit."

Animus waved her hand dismissively as she continued investigating the nearest dilapidated building. Red turned toward the iether bloom at the same moment that Nirim came down the ramp. Seeing Red, Nirim made his way over to the kobay.

"Nirim?"

Nirim stopped in front of him, distracted by their surroundings as he answered. "Yes?"

While being vague worked well for extracting information from Hinna, being direct was better suited for Nirim. "Did Hinna tell you about her dream?"

There was no missing the sudden discomfort and nervousness emanating from Nirim. "Uhhh, no. No, she did not."

"It seems that it involved you, and her, and some kind of intimate exchange?"

Red was uncertain what to make of the long, blank look Nirim gave him before he muttered sarcastically, "Yeah, I woke up before that part."

"But, Nirim, did you say you had a nightmare?"

Nirim turned and walked away, not even slowing his pace as he called back over his shoulder, "Don't worry about it, Red. I am sure it was just a strange dream, that's all."

Red found his statement to be of no help whatsoever, and decided that he would never understand humans, no matter how much he read about them.

***

They traveled to the river that ran along one side of the trackkus exchange station, and then east along its bank. It took most of a day's travel before they reached a small human settlement, where they purchased a simple, flat-bottomed boat. It was another day before they reached the isper lands, and when they did, it became obvious that Hinna was ecstatic about being in her homeland once more. Nirim tried valiantly to humor her, rather than be bitterly jealous because his homeland did not technically exist anymore. Repeatedly reminding himself that there might still be an opportunity for him to return to his own time by some means helped ease his internal emotional conflict.

The river essentially stopped at the edge of the isper lands, where the once-flying land mass had fused with what was at one time the northern coastline of the lands of the kobay. It was another day's journey along the highly maintained isper roads until they reached the great wall that surrounded much of their lands. Nirim looked up at the massive structure that ran as far as the eye could see along a north-west, south-east transect from where he stood. The wall had to be ten times his height, and he was led to believe that it was contiguous all the way around the isper lands. Nirim noticed the conspicuous absence of any kind of gate or passageway. The road just stopped at the wall.

He watched several isper travelers take to the air and fly over the wall with ease. He guessed that this made screening the people coming and going extremely easy. You were either an isper capable of flight, or you were not permitted beyond the wall. Where the road ended, there was also a large mechanical lift at the top of the wall for transferring heavy materials over it. The lift was mostly metal, with a tripod-like boom that allowed it to be swung out over either side.

While he stood there taking in the impressive construction, one of the numerous watchmen on the wall called out to him, "What is your business here, human?"

Nirim cleared his throat and returned his answer loudly so that it would carry clearly to the top of the wall. “I wish to travel beyond the wall.” Nirim was not sure if they had misheard him, or if he should be insulted, as about half of them doubled over in laughter, while the others appeared highly amused. Hinna responded by spreading out her wings and rising to the top of the wall in what amounted to a single bound.

Nirim had not seen her fly before, as the last time she had done so, he had been stuck inside a box. He watched, stupefied for a moment at how incredible she looked, enshrouded in brilliant yellow light, her crystalline, luminescent wings accenting her slender form, stretching against the blue sky like delicate, translucent, golden eagle’s wings. Red’s voice made his ears burn. “Don’t stare, Nirim. It’s not polite in any culture.”

As he forced his gaze to wander everywhere other than where Hinna stood on the wall, Nirim muttered back, “I was not staring, just lost in thought.” He expected Animus to chime in with some snide remark, but instead she merely looked contemplative.

Hinna hopped off the wall and glided to a soft landing next to them. Animus spoke first. “And are they going to let us in?”

“I am sure of it. I asked them to send to Prax of the Reigning for a formal summons, which should be sufficient to grant you passage beyond the wall, though only within the limits of the summons.”

Nirim knew that the isper’s form of governance centered on a large group of men known as the Reigning. Every town or village had at least one member of the Reigning. He did not understand how one became a member of the Reigning, but they were essentially the ruling class of the isper lands, and commanded a great deal of respect from their fellow isper. He wondered how Hinna had sufficient connections to simply ask one to write a summons for a bunch of non-isper strangers he had never met. It was rather surprising to him that anyone would know her well enough to trust her judgment that much, but then again, this could also be a return on some kind of favor.

Animus made it obvious that most of Nirim's private observations would not have occurred to her as she asked, "What's a Reigning?"

Red immediately began an overly lengthy and detailed explanation of the isper system that he had apparently learned from reading on the subject. Nirim listened for only a moment before he turned to Hinna and asked, "So what do you think we should do if this Prax does not give us a summons?"

Hinna put her hand to her chin thoughtfully. "Well, he will be angry at me, but I am sure he will grant you one."

"You're not getting yourself into some kind of trouble on our account, are you?"

Hinna met his gaze directly. "Probably." Then she smiled broadly and added, "But you are more than worth it."

Nirim decided that he would pretend she had intended that comment for all of them, even though she seemed to be speaking emphatically about him.

Chapter 25

After about half an hour, one of the guards flew down to them and read aloud from a formal-looking document. "Hinna, you and your traveling companions are formally summoned to the residence of Prax of the Reigning. You are to present yourselves immediately into his esteemed presence with utmost haste!" The guard signaled to the others on the wall as he folded the summons and handed it to Hinna, looking at the rest of them dubiously before gesturing to the lift. "This way, please."

The earthbound individuals boarded the lift while the isper ascended the wall by flight. Animus marveled out loud, "That didn't take long. Do the isper have an iether link ability like the seerrine?"

Red shook his head. "No, the isper messengers fly at high speeds with the aid of the gold iether, but only during the day, of course." Once the lift was at its apex, the boom swung them slowly over the wall, and then the lift began to descend. Hinna waited for them at the bottom.

Nirim glanced at the bustle and asked, "Aren't they going to escort us?"

Hinna shrugged. "Isper despise traveling as slowly as walking when there isn't something of value being transported, so they decided I was escort enough." Nirim could not tell if he found this comforting, as he was not getting treated like a prisoner, or disconcerting, as he was being treated like worthless refuse.

They traveled the rest of the day along one of the minor roads. Hinna excitedly pointed out all the landmarks that she knew, and chatted happily about her life as a records keeper. At one point while Hinna had stopped at a roadside store to buy them some food, Red turned to Nirim and said plainly, "Remember, Nirim, we need her help to complete this part of Miralla's song, so the least you can do is return her kindness by showing interest in what she says."

Nirim observed that Red was far more perceptive of people than he would have expected from a solitary kobay; his exact thought just a moment before had been how tired he was of listening to Hinna happily share more random information about the area. It was not that he did not enjoy Hinna's perspective on their surroundings, but rather that it was grating against his own sense of irreparable loss.

Nirim said nothing, but Red seemed satisfied with simply stating his opinion, as he turned back to his conversation with Animus about the isper way of life. Hinna returned and went into wearying detail about the local cuisine and her favorite dishes as she passed out the food she had purchased for them. In some ways, Nirim could see that this was the same Hinna who had been traveling with him since he awoke in the secret chamber in the imperial city's ruins. But the familiarity of her surroundings, and the strong sense of security within the walls of the isper, made her far bolder socially.

The change gave him no small sense of concern that she might directly confess her affection to him. This would most certainly result in her staying home, as he would have to politely inform her that he was not interested. However, the conundrum was that he did not really want her to stop traveling with them, which made him mentally challenge the truthfulness of his previous thought.

Nirim looked toward the center of the isper lands, trying to take his mind off the confusing whirl of emotions and ideas that thinking about his own situation brought him. The husk of the mountain-sized machine, the Supra-Machna, remained a most jarring part of the landscape. It was this enormous structure that the isper wanted to forget about.

The great empress and her companions had destroyed the machine that had long been the source of their livelihood—and their death. It had turned living sacrifices into pure gold iether that could then be used to power their way of life. With the destruction of the machine's quasi-sentient crystal core, their land had plummeted from the sky. It was only the intervention of the great empress that had spared their lives, but it forever changed isper society. Gone were the incredible machines that they had relied on for generations, and they had to relearn many basic skills. Because of this rather dark history, the isper were not terribly fond of humans.

***

As the sun was setting behind them, they arrived at a spacious villa that sat just outside of the small isper town of Filatai. The large building formed a rectangle around an inner open-air courtyard. It was a fairly ordinary isper construction, made of gleaming white marble, with its slightly frosted translucent roof offering a nearly unobstructed view of the sky. Nirim noted with some humor, remembering Hinna's comment about the dirty human cities, that the place was literally spotless, inside and out.

As they approached, the front double doors of the villa opened, and a regally dressed man emerged, followed by two finely dressed women and a handful of servants. The man looked less than happy to see them. Nirim stepped forward to introduce himself and his companions, but Hinna let out a cry of joy and flew past him, her arms open wide, giving the stern-looking isper a nearly overwhelming embrace. “Father, I have missed you so much!”

The man stood there awkwardly for a second before returning her embrace with substantially more reserve as he said, “Welcome home, Hinna.”

He turned to them while Hinna distributed hugs liberally to the two women, who, by deduction, must have been her mother and sister. The man nodded politely to Red and Animus. “I am Prax of the Reigning. It is a pleasure to have you as guests. Please feel welcome in my home.” He gestured toward Nirim dismissively. “Your slave will find fresh bedding and feed in the animal stalls behind that outbuilding.”

Nirim decided to show some restraint, as it was probably considered as rude to laugh in the face of one’s host in isper culture as it was in his own. Hinna rallied to his defense quickly. “Oh, Father! That’s Nirim. He has been our leader!”

Prax let out a long, exaggerated sigh. “I am not sure I can permit it in the house.”

Hinna’s sister leaned forward and said, “Come now, Father, you used to let my dog in the house.”

“Oh, very well, but it had better be housebroken.”

Nirim was fairly certain that if Prax was the fourth guardian, it would be less painful if he threw himself out of the iether bloom while it was moving at full speed.

Prax turned around and led the way back inside,

with Hinna close beside him, chatting endlessly about her adventures. He listened with what Nirim thought was a remarkable degree of patience. They walked inside the beautiful home and arrived at a large dining table spread with a great variety of enticing foods. Nirim did not make it that far, however, as he was at the end of the party, and stopped suddenly, staring through a delicate lattice wall into the enclosed garden courtyard in the center of the villa.

There, amid flowers and delicate marble colonnades, was the astral saber, the Light, that had been carried by his cousin Rim, the fourth guardian. It was thrust deep into a short stone pillar, but how it got there, or why it remained there, was lost to him.

His momentary absence was apparently distressing to at least one person, as he heard Hinna call out, "Nirim!"

It was hard for him to pretend like her voice did not sound as if she was calling the family pet to dinner. He walked swiftly down the hall and turned into the dining room, where the others were already seated and waiting for him. Hinna's sister spoke lightheartedly. "Don't tell me you got lost between the front door and the dining room?"

He took a seat and looked at them as they all watched him with intense interest. He calmly addressed their unspoken questions. "My apologies, but I noticed a sword stuck in a pillar in your courtyard."

Hinna's mother gave a gentle laugh. "That old thing! It's been in the family for a while, but I can't convince Prax to replace it with genuine garden art."

Prax watched Nirim with barely concealed disdain as he spoke. "It was a gift from a dear friend of the family some generations ago. We will not be replacing it."

Red studied Nirim curiously. "Is it important?"

"Probably."

Prax spoke up firmly, ending the conversation. "Enough prattle. Let us eat."

As they ate, Hinna chatted excitedly with her sister. They were talking about her sister's having been recently vowed to some fine gentlemen who was likely to be the next Reigning of their town. It was the isper form of engagement, only it was substantially more binding, and as long as the girl's father was living, he had full veto power over all marital situations.

Nirim wondered how the saber had come to be in this place. And for that matter, surely Miralla could not have predicted that they would end up here? Or maybe she did, but if that was the case, why would she have been so vague about the fourth guardian? He was mulling over the possibilities when he abruptly realized that he would not be able to avoid the conversation storm that was brewing but a few seats down from his.

He looked up in time to hear Hinna's sister ask her, "So how about you? Have you found a man to suggest to Father for your vowing?"

Hinna smiled sheepishly. "Well, not exactly."

She lifted her warm, affectionate eyes toward his stoic ones. Nirim wanted to hide under the table at the cold, calculating look that Prax gave him. "My daughter will live a long and lonely life before I permit any kind of union between her and a mere human."

Nirim felt the man's opinion was unnecessarily harsh, and that it was hardly appropriate for it to be expressed so publicly; however, it was rather the out he was looking for, or so he thought for the briefest moment. But when he saw the look on Hinna's face, he could not help wanting to comfort her. She looked genuinely heartbroken, as though any hope for joy was forever cast beyond her reach. Nirim felt a little guilty for not having been more direct with her, thus making way for this particular event.

Hinna simply got up, blinking hard, and left the room wordlessly. Her sister took in the whole scene with wide-eyed wonder, but surely she understood what had just happened. Hinna's mother watched her disappear and whispered, "Poor dear."

Nirim rose slowly from his seat. Animus and Red looked at him with some concern, but Prax said coldly, "Human, your room is by the front door."

Nirim bowed stiffly but spoke in a measured tone. "Thank you for your hospitality."

He turned and walked back toward the door. He found a small room, presumably the one Prax had intended, that was entirely empty, but he supposed it was better than sleeping outside. He sat down on the floor. He closed his eyes and focused his mind. He had to calm down, or their adventure could end abruptly, and before they discovered who the final guardian was. A soft and gentle voice spoke into the silence, like pleasant music. "Nirim, I do wonder why you are here of all places, but I suppose it doesn't matter."

Nirim whirled as he rose and stared face to face with his cousin Miralla. Nirim resisted his impulse to make sure there was not another ceremony and scarcely whispered, "Miralla?"

She turned toward the wall with a slightly pained expression on her face as she said, "Nirim, if you can hear me, please understand that I am projecting myself into the future from what is now your past, and I can neither see nor hear you." Nirim breathed out heavily. Of course he would never have the joy of embracing his cousin again.

Miralla looked rather haggard, and as she spoke, he felt her pain. "Nirim, I am so sorry. I never could have known how hard it must be to suddenly be cast out of home, beyond any family or friends." She sighed sadly before she continued. "But now I know, Nirim. Now that Ista is gone, the heads of the orders have decided that it would be best for the line of succession to be re-voted on, and everything is just a mess. The guardians have been disbanded, Spite and Friska have returned to their respective homelands, and I have carried Rim's saber here for safekeeping."

She turned back toward him, her eyes wet. "Nirim, I am afraid that everything we knew as children will be gone in a matter of a few years, and there is nothing I can do about it!" She shook her head and spoke with a sense of something important that was lost. "I remember thinking as a little girl that we had the best life imaginable, and that no matter what happened, we would always have one another. But now I feel so alone, and I know that the dream I had as a little girl was only wishful thinking. Your sudden absence is my fault, but Ista's . . . ."

She took a deep breath and composed herself before she continued. "Rim has become distant over the loss of his sister, and I fear he might run away." She shook her head and looked thoughtfully at the wall. "I am sorry, Nirim. You aren't here to hear me fill your ear with all the bad news. When I set you on this path, I had a clear focus and a good idea of what you needed to do. However, the more the Creator revealed to me, the less I understood, and I can't tell you who the fourth guardian is. What's more, I was wrong, Nirim."

She paused, as though she were looking for an easier way to say what she was thinking, before she resumed. "Nirim, there is another guardian. Yes, I know it seems impossible, as we know of only four astral weapons, but I am certain of it. I can't say I understand anything more than this. You will have to trust the Creator to lead you in this, as I have in that you are even hearing my message."

Miralla chuckled as she muttered, “I must look pretty bad, standing here talking to myself in conversational tones.” Her face became serious once more. “Nirim, I know you, so I feel that I must say this before I run out of time. I am not as powerful as our ancestor, which is to say that I cannot bring you back to our time. You are stuck there in the future, and you need to live like it, so don’t keep telling yourself that I will find a way to bring you back. It is simply beyond me.” She sighed and held up the long astral saber that glowed brightly in her hand. “Even with limitless iether I cannot bring you back.”

She cocked her head as though she heard a distant sound and looked toward the doorway, which was incidentally the direction he stood in. “Goodbye, Nirim. Goodbye.” In the blink of an eye, she vanished.

Nirim slumped to his knees as he felt the weight of Miralla’s words. It was bad enough that he was on some seemingly pointless mission, without having to deal with the knowledge that his friends and family did not live particularly long or happy lives. Or worse, that he would never be reunited with them or his home. The dark reality that he had desperately tried to avoid was now inescapable.

He pulled the astral blade staff, the Flame, from its carrying place on his back, and stared at the gleaming silver blade. It was a powerful weapon, but he fervently wished that he had some other, more practical skill. The Flame was completely worthless in his current circumstances. Rather akin to himself, actually.

Fortunately for everyone else, Nirim’s skill set did not change with this wish, as the state of things rapidly did.

Chapter 26

A bloodcurdling scream ripped through the villa. Nirim gripped the blade staff tightly. “Hinna!”

Nirim burst from his “room” with blade staff and blue iether rune glowing brightly. He instantly dropped to his knees onto the smooth marble floor and slid under what would have been a killing blow by a shade, as it swung at him with its long blade-like arms. With unerring precision, Nirim turned as he slid and pushed off the floor to a standing position and brought the gleaming blade of the Flame up in a clean arc that cut the shade in half. It evaporated in a puff of black steam. Down the hallway, Prax stared at Nirim, pale as a sheet.

Just beyond Prax, his wife screamed as a shade pounced on her. With no hesitation, both runes surging with iether, Nirim threw the blade staff with the accuracy of the rune of second sight, and the reduced friction of the rune of flux. The astral weapon shot like a blue streak over Prax’s shoulder, a finger’s width from his ear, to catch the shade midair and pin it to the wall. The creature was engulfed in blue iether flame and vaporized. Nirim darted out into the open courtyard. He was defenseless without an astral weapon, but it just so happened he knew where there was an extra one.

The courtyard was astir as Animus used the astral bow as a sort of bludgeon to hold the shades at bay, while Red stood behind her calling out enemies. Despite the seriousness of the situation, Nirim smiled slightly when he saw the astral rod gripped in the kobay's hands.

Nirim grasped the astral saber by its hilt. The blade erupted into brilliant gold light as it responded to Nirim's iether control. The sword came free as easily as though it had been stuck into water. While the Flame was a weapon of raw destructive power, the Light was one of incredible precision and speed. Its gold iether accelerated not only the blade but also its wielder. Nirim ran like the wind past Animus, striking down three shades as he moved swiftly around them, sliding on the marble floor as he re-entered the villa from the other side of the courtyard.

Two shades jumped at him from the walls where they were waiting to ambush someone, like horrible, monstrous frogs. Nirim accelerated forward, racing by them as the astral saber flashed through the air, reducing them to mere vapor. Finally, he thought in the passing, something he was actually trained for.

He burst into Hinna's room to see Hinna's sister cowering in the corner with three shades baring down on her with deadly intent. The astral saber was sheathed in brilliant gold radiance as he swung it in three sharp arcs, sending gold iether crescents cutting through the air and into the shades. In a fraction of a second, they were gone, and in a matter of minutes, the attack was ended.

Nirim had a bad feeling about this, as it was plainly obvious that Hinna's room was empty, though there was no sign of injury or exit. Hinna's sister was clearly not in a condition to communicate about what had happened. Nirim turned and walked back toward the courtyard, the shining saber held low as the rune of second sight informed him that no shades remained.

As he stepped into the courtyard, he stopped.

Every other member of the household, as well as his own companions, were staring at him as though he were more frightening than the shades. Red spoke a little nervously, "Good job, eh?"

Nirim shook his head as he said, "Dispatching a handful of shades is nothing, especially not when they seem to have been successful. Has anyone seen Hinna?"

Hinna's sister walked past him, shaken but passably composed. "They took her and simply vanished!"

Hinna's mother's face turned ashen. "Prax, it's just like all the others. Now we will never see her again!"

Prax did not take his eyes off Nirim as he said, "Now, Anna, we don't know that."

"But Father! None of the others have ever been found!"

Prax raised his hand to calm her and started walking slowly toward Nirim. "Lysile, they did not know anyone who could help them, but I see that is not our situation."

Prax walked up to Nirim and stopped directly in front of him, watching him seriously. His words were sober, almost stern. "We do not normally speak of it to outsiders, but our people have been plagued by kidnappings for nearly a year now. Though these crimes are rarely accompanied by murder, there are never any witnesses. The Reigning have begun to entertain the notion that the land itself is cursed, and some have suggested that we simply occupy the coastal lands of the humans."

Nirim thought darkly that the human territory was rapidly becoming prime real estate. Prax continued, his tone changed to something softer. "Nirim, forgive me for misjudging you. I see now that the blood of heroes runs in your veins."

Nirim wanted to dismiss his words as empty flattery, but realized that whether Prax knew it or not, it was true. Apparently Animus wanted everyone to understand the weight of the statement, as she announced to no one in particular, "Nirim is a direct descendant of the great empress herself!" Nirim remained calm but gave her a brief dour look before returning his attention to Prax.

Prax's tone and gaze did not change as he continued. "Though history is not kind to the memory of the humans, we cannot forget that it was that very human that saved the isper race from extinction." Prax put his hand on Nirim's shoulder as he said with great intensity, "Nirim, please rescue my daughter from these mysterious abductors."

Nirim nodded firmly. "It would be my pleasure."

He thought that Prax was about to walk away, but the isper stopped and turned his gaze back toward Nirim. "I would be honored to have you as a son-in-law. If you succeed, my daughter will be yours."

Nirim stood silent, unsure of how to respond, as Prax moved to join the rest of his family. He felt mildly cheated, as his honorable venture to save his friend was now marred by overtures of mercenary motives. He managed to mutter, "Thank you, sir."

Nirim turned toward his companions, who stood looking at him with silly grins on their faces. Nirim spoke only partly rebukingly as he snapped at them, "Would you stop that! Now let's go find Hinna." Nirim retrieved his blade staff from the wall, its perfect finish untouched by having been embedded into solid marble.

He returned to Hinna's empty room and examined it while Red and Animus peered around him. There was nothing out of the ordinary about the room, but, since it lacked any windows, Nirim wondered how the kidnappers had exited with Hinna. If they were just shades, it seemed possible that they could have passed through the walls, but last he checked, Hinna could not pass through walls. Nirim raised his left arm, his rune filling with blue iether. The room flooded with blue iether motes. Nirim watched as the iether floated back the direction they had come. He turned toward the doorway as he spoke. "Outside."

They followed the iether motes' slow but steady course as they drifted away from the villa and began to collect at the corner of a flat, square, metal thing set into the ground. Nirim looked to Red for his input. The kobay scratched his head and said with minimal certainty, "Uhhh, well, there isn't much written about the isper, but it appears to be an entrance to the old conduit passages of the Supra-Machna." Nirim shrugged and opened it. They could see a ladder leading down into a tunnel.

Nirim slid down the ladder effortlessly and held his arm up to provide a dim blue light in the passage. Red landed beside him silently. Nirim waited a moment, but Animus did not immediately follow, so he glanced up at the opening. She had not entered yet, and was looking down at them with a worried expression. "Seerrine weren't made for ladders. So maybe I should just wait here?"

Nirim called back, "Don't worry. Just jump. Red will catch you."

Red stared at Nirim in shock. "Say what?!"

Nirim had no time to answer, as Animus came crashing down on top of Red, with both of them screaming in surprise. Nirim glanced both ways down the long, sloping tunnel as he said, "Sure, that's close enough."

Animus yelled reprovingly at him as she got off of Red. "NIRIM!"

Red rose, dusting himself off, and added, "I need

time to prepare for something like that, Nirim! I could have been killed."

"And what is that supposed to mean?"

"Well, it, uh, err, it means that you are a substantial young lady of sufficient mass—errr—form to require my full attention. Yes, exactly that."

Animus narrowed her eyes at him as she said in a low voice, "Try saying that in plain language."

Nirim ignored them as he headed down the tunnel in the direction of the Supra-Machna. He thought he heard something. Something other than Animus and Red, that was. If their enemy was as aggressive as it seemed, his completely non-stealthy companions could bring them face to face with their adversary. Nirim stopped and passed the saber back behind him. "Here, Animus, hold on to this for me. You might be more successful with it than the bow."

She pulled it out of his hands, grumbling, "I am not that bad of a shot."

Red attempted to reassure her. "Do not worry, Animus. I am sure the hordes of darkness will be large enough to render accuracy irrelevant." She frowned angrily at him but managed not to say anything.

After they had traveled at a steady rate for about half an hour, the sloping tunnel led down to a large room. The room had several other tunnels that connected to it, but in one wall stood a black metal door that was twice as wide and tall as the others. It was closing with the sound of metal-on-metal clanking.

A robed female figure stood between them and the door. She glared at them angrily, as though some long-held vendetta burned within her heart. Her skin was an odd ash-gray tone, and her eyes and hair were coal black, fading to a pale gray at the tips. The most striking feature about her was the thin, jagged, black lines that ran along the sides of her face to wrap around her chin and continue down her neck. There were reminiscent of iether marks, but not of a kind Nirim had ever seen before.

She called out to them. "Fools! You will regret coming down here. No one can stand against the dark iether!"

She raised her hand sharply, palm up, and the black lines on her face emanated a dark vapor. Within seconds, a dozen shades rose out of the ground, shook themselves, and darted towards them. Red and Animus stepped back hesitantly, but Nirim lunged forward, freeing the blade staff from his back and swinging it in a wide, luminous blue arc. The iether edge of the weapon extended far beyond the astral one, and the shades slid in half in near unison and rapidly evaporated.

Their aggressor flinched sharply and put her hand to her midsection unconsciously, as though she were afraid that the same fate had already taken her. The door came to a full close with a metallic clang, followed by the finality of the clank of a locking mechanism. Her voice carried a strong sense of disbelief. "But how did you do that? That's impossible! You're a mere mortal! I will get you this time!"

She raised both hands sharply, and shades began to claw their way out of the ground in a terrifying number all around them. Red and Animus huddled behind Nirim, and Animus said, "So, you can fight the ones on that side, and I will fight the ones over here, and Red can—"

Nirim interrupted her as he spoke in a soft but grim tone. "Whatever you do, don't move." The purifying power of the Flame was unrivaled, but its blue iether flame made no distinction between friend and foe. Nirim had learned how to isolate individuals' areas to prevent them from being reduced to ash, but he had to pick such locations before he started. The rune of second sight informed him that there were over one thousand shades in the room, not that the quantity was relevant to what he was about to do.

He thrust the astral weapon into the ground in front of him and threw his arms wide as he focused. The room became flooded with dancing iether motes that streamed from everywhere, running rapidly toward the vertical handle of the blade staff until a floor-to-ceiling column of intensely bright blue iether stood before Nirim. The shades flinched away from its radiant light. Their opposition screamed at her minions as loud as she could. "KILL THEM!" The shades resumed their advance, at least for a few moments.

Nirim brought his hands together sharply, and there was the deafening sound of a thunderclap as the blue iether column exploded into a firewall that left the walls of the room smoking, and reduced the shades to nothing more than a memory. The woman looked around the room in dismay, but then she stopped and stared dumbfounded at the floor. There were only two places in the entire room that remained untouched. The first was around Nirim and his companions, but the second was around the woman. A perfect circle that was not charred by the flame.

She glared hard at Nirim as he drew his weapon out of the floor, then growled, "You will get yours, mortals." She whirled to face the door. She tried to take a step toward it, but the floor remained hot enough that she yanked her foot back quickly. She brought her arm out to the side in a dismissive manner and utterly vanished in a puff of dark vapor.

Animus sighed with relief, then asked, "What was that thing?" She looked at Nirim with suspicion as she added, "And why didn't you kill it?"

Nirim stared at the closed door thoughtfully. "I am not sure."

Red arched an eyebrow. "And to which of those questions does your answer belong?"

Nirim grunted and said sarcastically, "I just can't imagine." He then glanced around reflexively, as though he expected to need to clarify his statement, something Animus instantly recognized.

"You miss her already, don't you?"

"Just because I am now in the habit of watching my sarcasm does not mean I miss needing to explain the obvious."

Red interrupted with excitement. "Ah! I know! Nirim didn't kill her because he found her attractive!"

"Red, don't be such a moron. That can't possibly be the case because Nirim only has eyes for Hinna."

"Oh, right."

Nirim sighed as he walked toward the door, muttering, "Remind me again why I brought you two along?"

Red followed after him, while Animus tested the floor with her hand, not wanting to scorch her tail. By this time the floor had cooled appreciably, so she darted after them. As they reached the door, Nirim answered Animus's earlier question carefully. "I did not kill her because we need answers, and frankly she really wasn't that threatening."

"Are you crazy! She must have been filled with evil, what with that shade-summoning stuff. Has anyone ever heard of such a thing?"

Red stroked his chin thoughtfully. "Of course no one has seen such a thing, but I do appreciate how Nirim is tastefully following my example instead of yours."

Animus narrowed her eyes at him. "Shall I demonstrate my example on you now or later?"

Red took a step back from her menacing gaze. "Uh, uh, uh, so, Nirim, how do you intend to get through this door here?”

Nirim had his left hand raised and planted firmly on the surface of the door. “The door is metal-clad granite, and it is more than a hand’s length thick. The locking mechanism is rather complex, and the whole door appears to be operated by some kind of machine.”

Animus asked cautiously, “Can you open it?”

“No, it would take more power than I have.”

Red looked appropriately sad. “Well, I guess we will have to call off the wedding then.”

“I didn’t say anything about not getting through it, just not unlocking it. And would you stop bringing that up!”

Chapter 27

Nirim stepped back from the door and held the blade staff in front of him. The astral metal alone could pierce the door, but there would be a substantial amount of work on his part in cutting the door open. The iether-sheathed edge of the blade staff, on the other hand, could cleave the door in half in an instant. Nirim swung the blade staff swiftly in four successive cuts along the frame of the door.

The door remained in place, but Nirim reached out and poked it with his forefinger, and it fell inward. Nirim brought his right hand up sharply, and the door landed noiselessly on a cushion of air before he let it settle to the ground with a thunk. He glanced at his companions, whose jaws were hanging open. He thought they were going to have to get over their shock and awe every time he did something if they were to be of any use, but then he remembered ruefully whom it was he was thinking about.

They proceeded down a ramp and into another room where several metal platforms were suspended over a deep, narrow chasm. Nirim noticed that one of the platforms appeared to be missing. He stepped on to one and felt it sway slightly.

Red and Animus joined him cautiously, and Animus eyed it in suspicion. “Is it safe, and for that matter, what is it?”

Nirim took in the series of levers on a small pedestal in one corner of the platform. "A lift, I believe." He pushed a lever forward, and the lift began to descend slowly at first, but then with increasing acceleration. Red frowned grimly. "I hate to think what provides this lift with power."

Nirim nodded. The isper had previously used their own people as a power source, and seeing that this machine was far from any other known mechanisms of the other races, it seemed a foregone conclusion. However, the Supra-Machna had been destroyed, and the lift seemed to run far deeper than just the isper landmass.

Hinna's very life was in danger. If what Prax said was true, he wondered what was being done with all the energy, and why whoever was behind this had not been kidnapping people before. Nirim had the sickening feeling that he was going to find out very soon.

They traveled for a good ten minutes before the lift began to decelerate in preparation for stopping. As they stepped off the lift into another large room, Nirim braced for the worst. However, his initial concerns proved unwarranted. Nirim took several steps into the room. It was empty, with one sizable opening that lacked any kind of door.

Animus asked softly, "Now where did they go?"

Red gave her a look of disbelief. "Let's see. A bunch of lifts, and a single exit. Oh, I do wonder where they could have gone?" Animus glowered at him, but Nirim raised his hand for silence, and she complied. They continued to the doorway, and Nirim stopped as he stared at the incredible vista that lay before him.

The doorway opened at the top of a wide staircase that descended a fair distance to the floor of an enormous cavern, far larger than Nirim could ever have imagined of an underground space. It ran farther than the eye could see. In a normal cave, this was hardly a feat of any kind. However, at what seemed to be the far end of this massive space was a vertical column of solid, glowing material akin to fire. For it to be visible from their current distance, it had to be larger in diameter than a city at least. He was tempted to determine its true distance and size, but he feared giving himself away in the relatively dim space.

Red whispered as he pointed. "Down there."

Nirim could see the strange woman who had opposed them earlier, as well as a dozen others milling about outside of a metal building. Next to the building was a large tube-like chute that ran towards the column of fire. The walls of the tube were clear like glass, with wide metal bands occurring at regular intervals. Nirim watched as a vehicle flew down the tube from the direction of the fire column to disappear into the metal structure.

Animus muttered, "Ugh, I hate stairs. It's like they designed this place specifically to be a nightmare for seerrine."

Nirim decided not to point out to her that stairs had great utility for the rest of the races, and instead watched as the distant figures suddenly all turned toward the building and hastily made their way into it. "That's our cue."

They descended the stairs as quickly as possible, with Animus in tow. Nirim stopped as they approached the building. Red looked at him warily and asked, "What's the matter?"

Nirim turned to his side and stared at the empty cave wall for a moment before he shook his head. "It's . . . it's nothing. Let's go."

The interior of the large building was dark, and it was impossible to see what was beyond the large opening. Red cautioned, "This seems odd, Nirim. I feel we should find another entrance."

"I agree, but I don't think we have time to find another entrance."

Red looked at the doorway and nodded. "Probably so. Let us be careful."

Nirim held his blade staff at the ready as he entered the building. The moment Nirim stepped across the doorway into the building, he knew he had made a mistake. The door behind him slammed shut, separating him from his companions.

The darkness cleared away, and a tall, lean man with a long black cape, dressed in rather antiquated clothing, stood at the other end of the large, sparsely furnished room. A quick glance around him revealed more than thirty of the strange women like the one they faced back in the abandoned Supra-Machna conduit room.

The man spoke tauntingly. "Well, well, what rat have we captured today?" He bowed with a sweeping, exaggerated gesture and said, "Meager human, I am Woteril, the Progenitor. Welcome to the heart of the world."

Nirim said nothing, trying to decide if his conscience would bother him if he killed this Progenitor where he stood before he finished yapping.

The man laughed. "What's this, human? Are you too shocked to speak? Let me tell you that I have waited a long time to crush one of your kind like a bug, but I am very busy working on the climax to the end of your miserable little race, so I have no time to play with you."

Nirim would deal with the end of the world next, but he had something else on his mind for the moment. Keeping his tone level and calm, he asked pointedly, "Where is Hinna?"

Woteril pulled back slightly, looking unsure. "Hinna?" He glanced around the room as though looking for her. "I suspect she is around here somewhere." The rune of second sight gleamed brightly on Nirim's arm, but try as he might, he could not sense Hinna.

The Progenitor looked at him suspiciously and exclaimed in a fake delighted tone, "What a marvelously and completely useless rune! The Creator must really hate you!" The Progenitor jerked a finger into the air, as though he had just remembered something. "Right! This Hinna must be one from that last lot we captured."

He snapped his fingers twice. Two of the women disappeared and simultaneously reappeared on either side of a door at the far end of the room. They opened the door, and more of their kind filed out in single file, and the two closed the door again. Nirim knew only confusion; there was some import to what had just happened, but he did not understand what it was.

Seeing Nirim's uncertainty, the man shook his head. "You poor, poor human." He clapped his hands sharply. "Take the new recruits to the station and wait for me there." He pointed to the same woman that Nirim had fought with. "Kyne, you stay here." As the creatures from the door came by Woteril, he grabbed one of them by the arm and pulled her out of the line. "You stay here, too." She obeyed without protest.

As the last of them exited out the door, he turned to Nirim with a sly smile. "You seem slower than I would have expected, even for a human. You see, I designed the Supra-Machna many, many years ago, and I was the first to be subjected to it in a glorious self-sacrifice for my once great people. It seems that only I understood that the complete depletion of an isper's gold iether does not kill them, but rather leaves a void in them that is easily filled with the marvelous power of the dark iether.

"So I created a secret underground laboratory, and a gate, where I could collect both the gold iether, and the empty husks that were once isper. And I must say, it has been quite successful. The dark iether gives immortality, near limitless power, the ability to move instantly between two points in space, and then there is that whole forfeiture of free will to the darkness. The darkness has made its own race that makes those of the Creator look shabby by comparison. Behold! The dark isper."

Woteril brought the dark isper in front of him, as though presenting her for Nirim's approval. Nirim gasped in horror as he realized that it was Hinna who stood before him, silent, emotionless, staring. Woteril squealed with scarcely concealed fiendish delight. "Ah! So I am getting through that thick head of yours. She is much better this way, don't you think?"

Nirim had trouble taking his eyes off her. Her once beautiful, multihued hair was now coal black, fading slightly to gray near its ends. Her skin was ash gray, and the color of her eyes was so dark that they appeared black, set against the whites of her eyes. She bore several parallel black marks that ran from her cheeks, down the sides of her chin and onto her neck.

Shifting his gaze off the eerie visage of his friend, Nirim gripped his weapon and spoke gravely. "I think we should test this immortality theory of yours." The blade staff gave off a fierce glow as it became ensheathed in iether.

Woteril held out his hand in surprise. "What's this? You are one of the gifted, are you? Well, I can only guess then that you don't belong in this time." Nirim hesitated; how could the man know that? The fullness of Woteril's eyes seemed to cloud with darkness as he spoke. "We believed that we had exterminated the three gifted ones from the human lands, but perhaps we missed one. Hmmph. Regardless, if you desire I can send you back to your own time, and who knows? You might even be able to save your precious family from our efforts."

Nirim felt frozen, not sure how to respond. Woteril's power was obviously different in nature than Miralla's had been, and he seemed remarkably genuine. Nirim let his eyes return to the creature that had so recently been Hinna, and who was now a dark isper, barely recognizable. His hesitation lasted only for a moment. Miralla would not have sent him to this time if it were not at the Creator's bidding, and the Creator could not err. Even if Woteril could send him back, he would not go, and he knew that he had been a fool for thinking that it would be something he wanted.

Nirim spoke with conviction. "I will not go back. My life is here now."

Woteril sighed, as if exasperated, as he shook his head. "Another worthless fool, grasping at worthless ideals. Very well, human, show me your martial prowess." Woteril drew a long, black dagger from his belt and handed it to Hinna. Pointing at Nirim, he ordered, "Hinna, kill him."

Hinna nodded solemnly and darted at Nirim, blade out. Nirim deftly reflected her first blow and stepped aside from the next one as he shouted, "Hinna! You have to snap out of it." She swung at him relentlessly, and it took all of his skills to evade and parry without receiving any injury or delivering one. Desperately he endeavored to reach the real Hinna as he spoke between dodges. "Hinna, it's me, Nirim. Remember I rescued you from slavery in the human capital? Hinna, you have to remember Animus, and Red?"

Woteril interjected tauntingly. "There is nothing wrong with her memory, silly human. She has simply accepted her new self. If she had been trained on how to use her new power, you would be dead by now."

Nirim racked his brain for what he could do. He

leapt back from an incredibly precise swing and deflected a sharp thrust at his throat. Hinna had never said anything about knowing how to handle a blade. Reminding Hinna of their times together was not working at all, and he feared that she was a lost cause. Yet even so, he knew he could never bring himself to strike her. It was like a terrible nightmare, where everything familiar was warped into a horrible caricature of itself.

Nightmare. That gave him an idea.

He brought his right arm up sharply, and Hinna became stuck fast in the air around her as he spoke quickly, knowing he had little time. "Hinna, the dream was real!" Nirim leapt back as a precaution and dropped his arm before he could begin to feel the effects of the red iether.

Hinna stood motionless, even though the air around her had returned to normal. She spoke softly and, Nirim thought, refreshingly like Hinna as she said, "Nirim, did Red tell you about my dream?"

Nirim was certain that he was standing on thin ice here. "Yes, yes, he did."

She looked intently into his eyes, and for the briefest time, he thought he saw a flicker of light. "And what about you, Nirim? Did you dream about me?"

Nirim glanced at his audience. Woteril looked mildly bemused by what was occurring; Kyne, who stood well behind Woteril, looked oddly remorseful. Returning his attention to Hinna, he whispered, "Yes, Hinna, I also dreamt about you that day."

She smiled, a soft, sad smile. "Father would never allow it."

"Actually, he seems to have changed his mind after I fought off the attackers in your home."

She looked up slowly to meet his gaze. Nirim could not read her expression, and after a moment's silence, Woteril interrupted with some frustration. "Oh, please just kill him already!"

Hinna's eyes hardened, and her face took on a grim determination. Nirim braced himself, but it turned out that he was not the one who needed to.

Chapter 28

In a single, smooth motion, Hinna whirled and threw the black dagger at Woteril. He looked rather surprised, but he was not to be underestimated, as he caught it smoothly out of the air. Flipping it end to end, he then returned it with deadly precision. Hinna screamed and collapsed to the floor. Woteril snarled, "What a perfectly good waste! It is regrettable that you had to fill her head with such nonsense that she turned on me, but no matter."

Woteril pivoted and walked toward the station, and in the passing, he said, "I have calamity to bring, and no more time to mess with the likes of you. Good luck with the elevators, if you make it that far." He looked at Kyne and said briskly, "Do clean the rats out of this place for me, Kyne."

She swept into a bow. "Yes, Progenitor!" Woteril vanished in a cloud of black mist, and the sounds of the tram echoed as it departed from the building.

Nirim scarcely heard any of this as he raced to Hinna. He removed the dark blade that ran cleanly through her lower right side. She gasped for breath. "Nirim, I am so sorry for everything. Please, will you forgive me?"

"Shhhh, don't spend your strength, Hinna. But yes, I forgive you." Nirim ripped a long strip of cloth from his clothes and began to wrap Hinna's wound. Nirim felt cold, and his hands trembled. There was a lot of blood, and while he was no healer, he knew that Hinna did not have long.

Nirim heard the sound of a mechanism driving the door, and he glanced over to see Red and Animus rushing in. Animus looked down at Nirim and winced at the growing blood stain on the makeshift bandage that suggested the severity of the injury. "Nirim, whose is that?"

Red spoke grimly. "It was Hinna's."

Nirim corrected him as he lifted Hinna gently into his arms. "It is Hinna's." He felt his body shaking slightly, but his voice stayed calm. "We have to get to the surface."

He looked over at Kyne, who had made no move toward them, but stood rigidly by the door, hands clasped behind her back, staring hard at the floor. Nirim walked towards her and asked, "Kyne, is there a rapid way out of here other than the elevators?" Red and Animus exchanged equally uncertain looks.

Kyne jerked her head up, a strange sort of self-frustration written on her face. Her eyes were red, and she spoke harshly. "WHY!"

"Why what?"

"Why didn't you kill me back in the tunnel? Why didn't you kill the isper who clearly betrayed your confidence? I have seen your power. You could have stopped the Progenitor!"

Nirim sighed as he looked down at Hinna's pale face. She returned his gaze weakly, but with one that told him he would hate himself for a lifetime if they did not get out of there fast. "Because I am first and foremost a guardian. I stand against the night for the sake of the living, for the sake of the Creator. My enemy is secondary to those living entrusted to my care. I did not kill you because I needed to find my friend, and I did not kill you because I knew that you were not my enemy."

Nirim turned slightly and nodded toward Red and Animus. "This is Red. He won't hurt you because he is a pacifist, and this is Animus, who is too inept of a bowman to hurt you."

Animus's face twitched. "Nirim, was that really necessary information?"

Nirim turned his full attention back to Kyne. "Now, an exit?"

Kyne did not look entirely satisfied with Nirim's answer, but after glancing at Hinna's still form, she focused on the tram station. "They have cut the power to this part of the cave, so neither the elevators nor the tram will function. The surface is much too far for me to transport even myself there, let alone your bunch." Her face was grave. "It's a three-day walk to the next substation."

Nirim considered this, then walked toward the door. Kyne shook her head as she said in a low voice, "You're insane, aren't you?"

Nirim smiled weakly as he passed her. "I have been accused of that before."

Red spoke off to one side of him as they walked. "Nirim, I, uh, don't want to be the bearer of bad news, but I am thinking we don't have three days, if you know what I mean?" Nirim did not answer as he walked back toward the cavern wall.

Kyne, falling in beside Animus, asked in a halfhearted tone, "What is he doing?"

Animus shrugged. "Who knows? He often does idiotic things." Kyne looked a little taken back at the seerrine's bluntness.

As they traveled, Nirim asked Kyne, "What is Woteril planning?"

"He intends to erupt an artificially created volcano in the center of the human lands. He siphoned the lava from the magma beds under the western lands, and he drained the water to create the necessary pressure from the southern lands. It should be ready any day now that we, or should I say, he, has the sufficient power to activate it. All that remains is to prepare the ruins above."

Animus groaned. "Oh, great, so he is the reason my people are faced with migration."

Red commented, "Mine, too, it would seem."

Kyne nodded. "Yes, the goal was to drive all the races together for their mutual annihilation."

Animus shook her head in disbelief. "But why?"

"Woteril claimed that it would prepare the surface for our arrival, and allow us to take over without the need for open warfare. However, I have never been convinced that this story was the real one."

Nirim spoke gravely. "Woteril is possessed by the darkness, and its only motive is to erase every memory of the Creator from the world. Back when the human race was the sole bastion of belief in the Creator, it sought our annihilation on several occasions, but now that the knowledge of the Creator has returned to the other races, the darkness is bent on destroying them also."

Nirim stopped at the blank cave wall he had noticed before and said, "We are here."

Red looked around curiously. "Wherever 'here' is."

Nirim re-positioned his arms around Hinna so that he could place his palm flat against the cave wall.

Animus blurted out, "Just what are you doing, Nirim!"

His blue iether rune flared brightly. "The ancients before us left behind many secrets, and though I don't understand it, I can feel them when they are close by."

The blue iether from his hand raced through long-hidden iether tracks, and a section of the wall came alive with intricate, vaguely floral patterns. It glowed for but a moment, and faded away. As it did so, a doorway became visible as a perfectly rectangular portion of rock disappeared. Kyne blinked in shock. "How could something like this be under our noses for so long?" Nirim entered the passageway, and his companions followed him.

At first, the walls were made of rough-hewn stone, but as they progressed down the passageway, the stone became glassy smooth, as though it had been fired in a furnace. They entered a large, perfectly spherical chamber. A staircase ran down to a platform in the center of the space. An iether-powered lamp of some sort hung from the ceiling, granting a measure of visibility.

Nirim descended the staircase. Animus watched him inquisitively. "Nirim, why are we here?"

Nirim scanned the space as he said, "There is something here. I can feel it." Red just shrugged, and the rest of them started looking around.

The place had only a scattering of odd stone furniture and a seemingly random collection of storage containers. Nirim sat down on a blocky seat, and Hinna whispered, "Nirim?"

He looked down at her, trying with a measure of success to smile instead of grimace. "Yes, Hinna?"

"Are you going to save your people?"

"Yes, right after I save you."

Hinna winced, but then her face softened into a small smile. "Nirim? I want you to do something for me. Will you promise?"

Their circumstances made it difficult for him to

even begin to guess what her request might be. However, he refused to be stubborn with his dying friend. "Sure, Hinna, I will promise to do what I can. What do you want?"

Hinna coughed weakly, and then said, "Nirim, your priorities are off. I want you to stop Woteril first, and save me next."

Nirim's voice grew thick with emotion. "But Hinna, you will—"

He broke off, having difficulty saying what they all knew was the only possible outcome of Hinna's situation.

She closed her eyes, a content, peaceful look on her face. "It's okay, Nirim. I have lost what makes me isper, so I am nothing now. I don't want to remain a tainted minion of the darkness, so I think this is probably best."

Nirim spoke reflexively as he squeezed his eyes shut to prevent any tears from escaping. "Hinna, don't say that . . . ."

Nirim let the words drop as he realized that telling Hinna why she should stay could rob her of the peace she seemed to have concerning her fate. He held her close, and she nestled her head against his chest.

Nirim looked around the room again as his friends rifled through work benches and bins of scrap metal. In the center of the room was a stone box filled with water. The place had obviously been a forge room designed for a special purpose. Nirim spoke calmly, but loud enough for the others to hear. "Check in the water."

Kyne stood closest to it, and walking to it, reached into the water and lifted out a long dagger. Its metal gleamed in the dim illumination of the chamber. The blade was finely engraved with intricate patterns, which, to Kyne's surprise, nearly instantly filled with a gray-silver light. Silence reigned momentarily before

Red asked, "What's that?"

Animus turned to Nirim. "What's going on here?"

Nirim stood up and walked toward Kyne, who narrowed her eyes at him and repeated Red's question. "So what is this?"

Nirim looked at it with a strange smile as he said slowly, "It's the weapon of the fifth guardian."

Animus raised her hand as though she were a student in a classroom. "Wait. I thought you said there were only four guardians?"

Nirim nodded. "Yes, that was then, but this is now, and now there are five."

Kyne was unconvinced. "And where is this fifth individual you speak of?"

Nirim broke into a full smile. "She stands before me." She looked at him incredulously, as did Red and Animus.

Nirim had no intention of talking her into her new position right now. Instead, he queried, "Can you transport us to a destination that I choose?"

Kyne answered with high sarcasm. "Sure, just focus your mind on the location. Oh, and provide me with limitless quantities of power."

Nirim merely said, "Done," and closed his eyes to focus.

Kyne gave the others a frustrated look, but Red and Animus simply shrugged. Kyne rolled her eyes as she returned her gaze to Nirim and muttered, "Fine, waste my time." She put her hand on Nirim's arm and shifted to the destination Nirim had in mind. There was a swell of iether from the dagger, and in a completely disorienting whirl of gray light, they vanished.

Nirim opened his eyes to see that they were all standing in the ruined trackkus exchange yard. It was late in the night, but Nirim could not tell exactly when. It was only adrenaline that prevented him from feeling the effects of having been up so long. He carried Hinna toward the iether bloom. As they entered the decrepit building where the iether bloom sat on the rail, Kyne asked with some trepidation, “What is that ugly thing?”

Animus shuddered. “I know. It’s pretty terrible, really.”

Nirim ignored them as he unlocked the iether bloom and lowered the ramp. He moved into the control room and set Hinna down gently in a sitting position on the room’s small bench. The others joined him as he fired up the iether drive. Red asked, “So, where are we going on such a beautiful night?”

Nirim smirked at him wryly before turning his attention back to the controls and replying, “My dear friends, we are headed to the imperial capital to stop Woteril before he completely ruins the world.”

Red cleared his throat and glanced at Hinna, who sat very quietly on the bench, eyes closed, and whispered, “Hinna?”

Nirim sighed and blinked, his shoulders slumping, his hands still as he stared at the control panel and muttered, “It was her final request.”

Red’s expression grew sad. “I see.”

Kyne interrupted only partially tactfully as she said, “Does this thing even move?”

Snapping back to the urgency of the moment, Nirim looked knowingly at the others. Red grabbed the nearest handrail, and Animus braced both herself and Hinna. Nirim threw the booster lever, and the iether bloom leapt forward, causing Kyne to stagger backwards and nearly fall. She scowled at Nirim. “Was that really necessary?” Nirim smirked slightly as he returned his attention to the controls.

He navigated at low speed out of the exchange yard and onto a rail that would take him straight to the imperial capital. Nirim turned the iether drive dial as high as it would go, and they shot toward the capital at an incredible speed. Animus threw her arms around Red, who tried to pull away from her. "What are you doing!"

Animus's grip was unyielding as she muttered without looking at him, "I am scared, so hold me, you dummy." Red looked down at her in surprise, but hesitantly complied with her request.

Kyne glanced at Hinna, who remained conscious, but unlikely to be very aware of her surroundings. "So how long is this going to take?"

Nirim raised his left hand, and his iether rune filled with blue light. A second later, he answered, "At this speed, a matter of minutes."

Nirim felt something else out there at the capital city. The dark isper had erected some kind of barrier to prevent anyone from interfering with their plans. The barrier was made out of dark iether, generated by the thousands of them, condensed into a thick physical shell. The iether bloom would probably crash into it, rather than punch through it. Nirim stepped over to the other control panel and placed his palm on the console. His own iether flowed through specialized runes cut into the device that served to make it inaccessible to all but a few individuals. The console came alive, and Nirim pulled a centrally located lever. There was a repeated clanking noise. Animus looked up from where she stood tightly gripping Red, and asked, "What was that?" He smiled grimly but did not reply.

Metal leaflets that enclosed the back half of the iether bloom unfolded and slid out of the way. Two large metal corkscrews turned slowly, elevating a platform to a level parallel to the roof of the iether bloom's front half. On top of the platform, a sword-shaped object extended, easily spanning half of the iether bloom's total length. The blade-like object was mounted into an enormous turret base that occupied two-thirds of the platform's space.

Nirim's hand hovered over a small nondescript lever. The limit to the iether bloom was that it only had enough energy for a single shot, and once the weapon was charging, there would be no turning back.

Red watched his every move. "So I guess this isn't just a luxury mode of transportation?"

"No. It is a weapon developed by the old guardians for the purpose of dealing with threats of the darkness that exceeded what any individual guardian could address. It is the last answer to our nemesis. The arc-reach cannon."

Kyne looked at him, her face a mixture of concern and curiosity. "So why then do you hesitate?"

"It has never been fired before, so I can't say if it will fire, or explode."

Kyne grunted. "You humans are more bloodthirsty than I thought."

"It was designed after the primary weapons on the isper capital ship from the time of the great empress."

Red whispered in awe, "The *Solaria*!"

Kyne looked sheepishly at the wall as she reluctantly admitted, "Oh, uh, I guess there was that old thing, I suppose."

Chapter 29

Hinna sat silently on the short bench against one side of the iether bloom's control room. She felt cold; the dull, burning pain ebbed and flowed with every breath. She was tired from the long, exhausting trek, and likely from her injury. Her strength was slowly but certainly flowing away, and she knew it was only a matter of time.

It really had been a terrible day. Her father had made it clear: the very thing she had hoped for most, that she had dared to dream might be possible, he in a single instant had crushed to the ground. It was remarkable, how the person who had begun as a means to an end, had become the end itself. Then she had been kidnapped and knocked unconscious, only to awake as something else, a kind of monster. Everything was different, it seemed. She felt different, looked different, and even sounds were different. Perhaps the worst part was the initial compulsion to do as the man Woteril had bid her. She wanted to obey him, she felt powerless to resist his influence, and she had willingly attacked the man she had come to care so much about.

Nirim was as odd as ever, in his rampant refusal to harm her. Yet when he mentioned the dream, the one that she felt had been cast into the pit where all the things she held precious seemed to go, something inside her mind seemed to bloom, and with little effort, she threw aside the compulsory force. She wondered if Nirim could love her as she was now, the visage of the darkness. He had said that her father had changed his mind, but how comprehensive was the change?

Even so, it would not matter now. She just hoped that she would not be in the way too much. It seemed no small irony that she was now what Nirim had always been since she had known him. She was of a people who did not exist in this world, of a race of legend that the world despised, or, at least, she presumed, would despise. It brought on a nearly unbearable sense of loneliness and isolation. She opened her eyes to watch Nirim's calm control in a frightening situation and pondered how strong he must be to function every day of this strange journey with complete selflessness, and devoid of complaint or malice.

***

Nirim finally decided that there was no reason not to try, and pulled the lever that would flood the arc-reach cannon's pre-discharge coils with vast amounts of blue iether. They crested the hill overlooking the capital city, which lay in the center of the valley. Nirim looked gravely at the black dome that surrounded the city's ruins. He raised his left hand as his right hand flew across the numerous controls that comprised the arc-reach's targeting system.

It was no exaggeration to say that there was not another person living who could intentionally succeed at what Nirim was about to do. The arc-reach cannon was meant to be fired from a stationary position at a large, distant target, not at short range while moving. Nirim flipped the priming switch, and the long cannon separated in the middle, and, true to its name, blue iether arced with a hissing sound across the gap. The back of the iether bloom began to emit a luminescence that flooded the surrounding valley with blue light as iether poured into the gap between the two halves of the cannon. A small rune dot started to gleam on the control panel.

Animus was muttering over and over, “Please, please, please don’t explode,” as she squeezed Red tightly.

Red coughed. “Animus, please yourself. I am trying to breathe here.”

Nirim placed his hand back on the panel. The luminous dot flickered out, and there was an unearthly booming sound that caused the iether bloom to rattle violently.

A singular burst of blue iether shot like lightning from the arc-reach cannon and streaked through the air, resembling a blue comet. It was very much the size of the trackkus that had fired it, and it slammed into the black shell that surrounded the city. The dome absorbed the shot entirely, and for a paralyzing second, it looked like there was no effect. Then, the whole barrier simply flickered and vanished.

Nirim cranked the iether drive power all the way down. “Hold on tight!”

Red looked at Nirim with trepidation. “Don’t tell her that!”

Kyne was not interested in being bowled over again and grabbed a handrail with one hand and steadied Hinna with the other. Nirim engaged the emergency brake, and the rail clamps snapped closed onto the rail, with the water tank dumping profuse amounts of water onto the rail to reduce the intense heat of the friction. The iether bloom jerked sharply backwards as it decelerated, rapidly approaching the ruins. Nirim hoped it would slow to a safe speed before they hit the part of the track that was buried in rubble.

A sudden, sharp tremor shook the iether bloom, and to everyone's horror, it slipped off the rail and slid upright across the ground like a huge metal sled. It might have slowed a little faster, but it still reached the edge of the ruined city with enough force to punch through several crumbling buildings before it came to a stop.

Breathing hard, Nirim spoke, trying to sound positive. "Well, we didn't explode."

Animus frowned at him disapprovingly. The iether bloom lurched, and Kyne spoke with urgency. "We have to get out of this thing."

Nirim stepped over to get Hinna as the others quickly filed out of the iether bloom. He stopped and looked at her sadly. Her eyes were closed, and she appeared motionless. He sighed mournfully, but reached for her just before she whispered, "Please don't leave me here, Nirim."

He smiled with some relief. "I won't leave you, Hinna." He scooped her up in his arms and made his way out of the iether bloom and to a clear space where the others waited.

The ground suddenly heaved under him, and he staggered. Nirim turned to see the center of the city buckle and rise. The once-flat street became increasingly inclined, and rubble slid down it towards them. Kyne stepped in front of them, and the marks on her face seemed to glow as she held out both of her hands while clasping the astral dagger, and a gray dome of smoky-looking material surrounded their small group. Rubble and rocks smashed into it and slid off to one side. Nirim fell to his knees as the ground trembled again, to prevent dropping Hinna.

It felt like hours, but in only a few minutes, the center of the ruined city had become a respectable low-altitude volcanic mountain, complete with a lake-sized magma pool. Most of the buildings had slid down the now sloping sides and formed a ring of rubble at the base. Nirim noted that they were far closer to the center than he had realized, as he could see Woteril standing with his back to the lake of magma. In the dim light before dawn, there appeared to be thousands of dark isper standing before him as he gave a speech about their upcoming victory.

Kyne dropped her hands, and the shell protecting them vanished. She turned slowly to look at them as she said with resignation, "It's too late. We cannot stop him now."

Red looked at the distracted dark isper that were barely a stone's throw away. "I suppose they would fight us if we tried?"

"Yes, they would fight to the last to kill you if you interfered."

Nirim did not particularly care for the notion of fighting off thousands of shade-summoning, bloodthirsty dark isper.

Hinna's voice reached him in the faintest of whispers. "Nirim?"

He looked down at her, and she spoke slowly, as though it were difficult to talk. "Thank you for all you have done. I can't begin to say how much you mean to me, but I don't want to cause you any more pain than I already have."

Nirim shook his head as he murmured, "Oh, Hinna, you could never . . . ."

With great effort, she lifted one hand and placed it on the side of his face. "Goodbye, Nirim."

She sighed and closed her eyes, her fingers slipping away. Nirim felt her body completely relax, and she was gone. The first person he had seen in this strange world, the isper who had been his most faithful traveling companion, and a reliable friend, was gone. Nirim did not prevent the tears that ran down his face to fall on her black hair. "Goodbye, Hinna."

He remembered that it was her last wish, and his standing promise, to save their world from Woteril. He had not been able to save Hinna, but perhaps he could still keep his promise. Nirim set Hinna's body gently on the ground, and rose with a resolute expression on his face. There would be time to mourn later, but only if they could prevent Woteril from getting any further.

Nirim walked toward the rest of them, and stopped. Nobody's eyes looked dry, and Animus said hesitantly, "Nirim, I . . . I am sorry." Red nodded silently, and Kyne seemed unable to meet his gaze.

"It wasn't your fault, Kyne, so don't subsume a guilt for crimes you did not commit." She muttered some sort of gratitude, but Nirim could not hear what it was.

He pulled the blade staff from his back and thrust it into the ground in front of him, and then held out his hand towards Animus. She looked at him with confusion, so he clarified, "The saber. It is the only way I can get close enough to stop Woteril."

Red stepped forward, his face set. "We will help you."

Nirim shook his head. "I cannot allow you to violate your oath, and I cannot ask Kyne to slay her own, nor do I trust Animus to actually hit what she is aiming at."

Wordlessly Animus held out the saber, and wordlessly Nirim took it as he turned and began to walk toward the dark isper and their inspiring leader. In the pre-dawn light, Nirim became enveloped in brilliant gold iether as the saber filled with power. Nirim went from a walk, to a run, to something much faster, as the gold iether accelerated him beyond mortal speed. Like the light itself, he shot past dozens of startled dark isper to the spot where Woteril stood.

Nirim thought that if Woteril had blinked at the

wrong moment, he would have been cut in two. Regrettably, he turned into black mist an instant before the saber cut through the place he had been. He rematerialized about a hundred paces away and stared at him, shaking his head. "You are a resourceful one, aren't you? Well, no matter, I will just have to deal with you myself." A black blade flew at Nirim, but in a flash of the saber, it flew off to one side harmlessly. Nirim lunged at him, but he relocated instantly.

The Progenitor smiled coldly. "It seems that you cannot hit me, and I cannot hit you. Shall we dance until your mortal body collapses from exhaustion, or shall we try something a little different?"

Nirim's voice was icy. "Let's try something different." He darted forward, his red iether rune aglow as he attempted to hold Woteril in place by condensing the air around him. The dark isper rolled his eyes tauntingly and vanished again as Nirim swung at him.

Woteril laughed at him. "My turn." He summoned half a dozen shades that shot toward him, swinging their bladelike arms. Nirim bolted past them, and they fell prey to the gold saber as he headed toward Woteril and swung at him again.

Woteril reappeared further away and tried to reason with Nirim. "Come now, human. You can't hit me, and all I have to do is flood the right chamber with water, and this whole place will erupt. By the time the ash cloud clears, there won't be a person left alive, and we who are accustomed to living where there is no light will emerge and rule this land! Now, join us! It would be so much easier for you."

Nirim felt not even remotely tempted to join the ranks of the dark isper. He swung the saber in several short arcs and sent gold iether crescents flying at Woteril, who promptly moved to a safer spot. The man tried a different tack. "You may have noticed that I am the only male dark isper. If you joined us, think of all the options you would have to choose from! And who says you need to have just one anyway?"

Nirim's astral blade cut through the large flagstone Woteril was standing on as he vanished a second before Nirim swung at him. Woteril shook his head, looking mildly annoyed. "You humans have such a freakish persistence in pointless tasks that I truly feel that your extinction is warranted."

Woteril relocated again as Nirim's saber cut through his previous position. Nirim panted under his breath, "Just hold still for a second."

"Well, you can't say I didn't offer you something better than the alternative you so fervently want." Woteril snapped his fingers loudly. "So here are your new choices. Continue swinging at me like a fool until you drop dead from exhaustion, delaying the end of your crummy race by maybe an hour, or saving the lives of your worthless companions just in time for you all to experience the most climatic end to your puny existences imaginable."

Nirim glanced quickly behind him. His friends stood surrounded by hundreds of dark isper. Woteril drummed his fingers impatiently. "Well, pick one! I haven't got all morning, you know."

Nirim wondered how long the others could hold out against the horde, and for that matter, he wondered how long he could hold out against Woteril. Having gone almost a whole, turbulent day without sleep or much food, he was exhausted both physically and emotionally. He suspected that the others felt similarly, except perhaps Kyne.

He hated the false decision that was being thrust upon him, and he desperately wished for an alternative option. But he could think of nothing, and Woteril's assessment of the situation seemed to be infallible. Even the rune of second sight did not provide him with any suggestion that might resolve their current dilemma. Doom was inevitable.

But at that exact moment, the sun peaked over the edge of the horizon as morning dawned anew, and the Creator's intricate plan came together flawlessly.

Chapter 30

At first Nirim did not notice anything, struggling as he was with the dilemma presented to him. But when Woteril opened his mouth to mock Nirim's indecisiveness, and no words came out as his expression changed to utter shock, Nirim became aware that something worth his attention was occurring.

Woteril stared at him as though he had transformed into a hideous monster. Nirim looked down at himself to see gold iether wisping off of his clothing in the sunlight. Actually, wisping was not a strong enough word. It was billowing, and it was starting to form a gold iether cloud around him. Woteril's ashen face grew paler as he turned his gaze slowly from Nirim to Nirim's companions. He scarcely whispered, "Geniluminos . . . it must not be . . . not now!"

Nirim's thoughts raced to understand what he saw. As the sun rose, and the shadows shifted, and the light fell on Hinna's body, gold iether began to radiate from her. The encompassing dark isper flinched and backed away. Confusion pulsed through his mind. Had not Hinna's gold iether been taken from her? And for that matter, she was most certainly dead.

There was a momentary flicker of bright light from Hinna, like the twinkling of a star, and then it came. Gold iether erupted from her still form in an unbelievable torrent, and swept outward in all directions.

It was a tsunami of yellow, reaching incredibly high into the lightening sky, and moving faster than a rider at gallop.

Woteril flinched visibly and began backing up, holding his hands in front of him as he shouted, "No . . . no . . . NO!"

In spite of himself, Nirim raised his hand in warning. But Woteril was too distracted to notice, and one more step sent him over the precipice and into the magma lake. Nirim stepped quickly to the edge, barely in time to see Woteril hit the magma with a sickening sizzling noise, and hear his momentary scream, before the charred ashes of his remains spread out on top of the simmering surface. Nirim grimaced as he turned back to face the roaring wall of gold iether as it slammed into him. Or, rather, it washed over him. He was grateful that it did not behave like the blue iether, which would have burned him to a crisp. Instead, it felt like the warm embrace of a friend.

Nirim walked a dozen paces toward his companions before he stopped again. The gold iether was slow to dissipate, and its thick, warm, brilliant fog surrounded him. Actually, all he could see, other than the ground in front of him, was luminescent gold light everywhere. It was surreal, and slightly terrifying at the same time. For a strange moment, he wondered if this was real, or if he had merely died at some point and he just could not remember.

He took a couple more careful steps, but halted when he heard a voice. Stunned, he muttered out loud, "Was that . . . ?" And then he heard it more clearly.

"Nirim!"

Nirim hesitated before he called back, "H-Hinna?" He heard someone stumbling through the gold iether fog towards him, and he began to see an indistinct form of someone become clearer as they approached. At first, he thought that the gold iether must be distorting the approaching individual's figure, as it seemed highly regular, almost as though they were . . . .

Nirim realized with a quickening sense of awkwardness that the gold iether was not distorting anything, but rather, that this particular individual was devoid of any kind of garments. He immediately stared at the ground and shielded his face with his hand.

Hinna's voice sounded relieved and happy. "Nirim! There you are. Here I was worried you might have been hurt or—wait, are you okay?"

Nirim tried to sound as calm as he could. "Hinna, I am so glad you're all right. But, uh, um, w-where are your clothes?"

There was a long, awkward silence before Hinna answered, a little timidly, "Is . . . is that a joke?"

Nirim wondered how it was she could not know she was naked, but that aside, he smiled. If she could not tell if he was joking, there was no doubt the person that stood but a handful of paces away from him was truly Hinna. Nirim restrained the humor that crept into his voice. "No, Hinna, unless it's your joke."

He heard her gasp, and her next words were panicked. "Nirim! Don't look." There was a moment's pause before she stuttered out nervously, "Y-you didn't see me, did you?" Nirim chose silence as his hiding place, and held out his traveling cloak toward her. She snatched it hurriedly from his hand and wrapped it around herself.

Nirim changed the subject. "Hinna, what happened to you? I thought you . . . you were . . . ." He could not finish his statement; he had no desire to relive the pain that went along with that memory.

"I don't know what happened either, Nirim. The last thing I remember was being in your arms, and then blacking out."

Finally looking up again, Nirim confirmed his suspicions that Hinna was entirely Hinna once more. Her beautiful multihued hair flowed over her shoulders and framed her face perfectly. The black marks were gone from her face, which was filled with the warm, gentle expression that he had grown fond of.

As the gold iether fog faded around them, his other companions seemed to emerge from it as they joined him and Hinna. A voice asked forcefully, “Would someone please explain what just happened?”

They all stared at her for a moment, and then Nirim asked tentatively, “Kyne?”

“What, are you going blind, human? Yes, it is I.”

Nirim simply shook his head slowly. Kyne’s appearance was so different that he scarcely recognized her, as though the gold iether had burned away the darkness of her features, lining them in a flawless metallic silver. Her hair was a dark silver at the roots and ran through a gradient to a pure white at its tips. Her skin retained the faintest gray tint, but looked otherwise normal. The marks on her face remained, but they were fainter, a silvery gray color. Her eyes were also a gray blue, instead of the dark color they had been. Nirim decided that it might be easier if she figured this change out on her own.

Kyne glanced at Hinna. “Hinna, what happened to your clothes?”

Hinna merely shrugged, and Nirim quickly veered the conversation in another direction. “So does anyone know what Geniluminos is?”

Animus shook her head, and Kyne looked confused again, but Red said simply, “Yes.”

They all turned toward him, and he rubbed the back of his neck, looking a little embarrassed. “I once read about a legend that the isper were also granted a gift by the Creator, like the kobay and the seerrine with their respective ware-souls and Ankenkind. Geniluminos, the ones with the power of resurgence, the ability to return unharmed from a fatal wound. Essentially, such a person cannot be slain, and they are born anew with the dawning of the day, as the sunlight is the isper's source of iether." Red exclaimed with delight, as though it had taken him this whole time to draw the connection to Hinna. "Oh! Hinna, you must be Geniluminos! So that explains your clothes. As you would not be born naturally with any clothes, neither would your rebirth include such amenities."

Nirim winced and muttered to himself, "Could we possibly talk about something else?"

Surprisingly, Hinna saved him by saying, "So what are we going to do about all those new silver isper?"

It was then that Nirim noticed that Kyne was not the only one affected by the gold iether. Several thousand silvery-haired young isper women ambled about, confused by their appearances and their newfound freewill. He sighed. "This is going to be the longest walk of my life." He looked over at Kyne, who had grabbed a length of her hair and was staring at it with a sense of wonder.

Animus brought him back to the immediate context. "What next, fearless leader?"

"Well, we need to see if we can resettle these isper in their homeland. Kyne, can you assemble these people so that we can leave as an ordered group for the isper lands?"

Kyne nodded briskly. "Yes, I can assemble my people."

Nirim smiled at the way that she was already taking responsibility for the new isper. He mused over all they had learned in the past hours. "Can we return the water and magma to their respective owners?"

Kyne shook her head. “No. Not unless you can repermeabilize the soil in the kobay lands and run a small ocean’s worth of water uphill for hundreds of miles. A similar problem exists for the western lands.”

“So I guess we either need to work really hard at our diplomatic skills and make room for far more people in far fewer spaces, or we need to find another way to fix the problems.”

Nirim began to walk down the slope of the newly minted volcano, and Red asked him, “So what are you going to do right now?”

“Sleep.”

The iether bloom was unlikely to be in good condition, but if it had not gotten buried, it did offer a sheltered place to rest. Nirim had no idea how they could fix the mess left behind by Woteril. For this moment, however, it did not matter, and he felt confident that they would figure out something. He was slightly more concerned about what would happen when he returned Hinna to her father. She was truly a precious treasure, but he thought that now might not be the time to form such a bond when they had so much work to do.

The iether bloom was still upright and still accessible, even if it looked beat up. Nirim entered and made his way to his bunk. His last thoughts as he drifted off to sleep were for his cousins, whom the Progenitor had claimed had been “exterminated.” Yet the Progenitor, or rather the darkness that he served, had been wrong about him. Could it be wrong about any of the others?

Thank you for reading our book!
We hope you enjoyed it.

If you would like to contact us, or to find out more about our other books and latest news, visit us at dartkaymckinney.com.

Milton Keynes UK
Ingram Content Group UK Ltd.
UKHW030938301124
451950UK00008B/109